GREENGAGE PLOTS

EMMA STERNER-RADLEY

Heartsome Publishing

SIGN UP

Firstly, thank you for purchasing Greengage Plots.

I frequently hold flash sales, competitions, giveaways and lots more.

To find out more about these great deals you will need to sign up to my mailing list by clicking on the link below:

http://tiny.cc/greengage

I sincerely hope you will enjoy reading Greengage Plots.

If you did, I would greatly appreciate a short review on your favourite book website.

Reviews are crucial for any author, and even just a line or two can make a huge difference.

For Amanda, without whom I never would've moved here and wouldn't know the first thing about Brits.

Other than that they stick cucumber on sandwiches.

ACKNOWLEDGMENTS

The first THANK YOU goes to my wife Amanda for beta-reading and promising me that I am indeed funny when I was panicking that no one would get my weird sense of humour. (And for making sure I treat myself to that expensive coffee in Tesco. I still think five quid for a bag of ground coffee is daylight robbery, though.)

Huge wheelbarrows full of thanks to my editor Jessica Hatch and my proofreader Cheri Fuller. You are both unbelievably excellent at your jobs and a true joy to work with. I'm so glad that this book made you both laugh as you worked on it.

Thanks as always to my family for their patience and support. And to all the friends I neglect when I bury my head in a new book. You're the best for being there when I come back up for air!

Finally, I think you would've really liked this one, Malin.

In memory of
Malin Sterner
1973-2011
Jag saknar dig.

Chapter One

WELCOME TO GREENGAGE

Standing on top of the grassy Greengage Hill, Katherine "Kit" Sorel peered at a beetle with pity. Not only was it big and ugly, it was also about to have a terrible time. It had decided to crawl up Kit's friend's boot, clearly not aware that Aimee hated bugs. And any animal not on a leash, in a zoo, or cooked in butter.

While wondering how to save the creature, Kit mused, *This is your island, and we're the outsiders stomping around and bothering you. Well, if I'm to become a native, I'll have to learn to stick up for fellow Greengagers.*

Kit bent down, pretending she was wiping dirt off Aimee's boot but was actually launching a bug rescue attempt. Aimee caught her, spotted the beetle, and screamed to high heaven before flailing about until the poor beetle flew across the field.

Aimee pointed to Kit. "Aha! I knew going for a walk was a crappy idea. Is this island of yours crawling with bugs as well as Neanderthals?"

"It's not my island. And I never said they were Neanderthals. Just that they were old-fashioned and a bit... eccentric."

"What you're saying is that they're all mad as a bag of ferrets?"

Kit rolled her eyes, used to Aimee's bluntness. "No, not that bad. More like quirky."

Aimee was wiping her clothes free of imaginary beetles. "Still. I don't see how a city lover, not to mention a lesbian, can decide to move to a remote island where people are 'old-fashioned.' They'll stone you when they realise you chase skirt."

"I do not 'chase skirt.' And several of them know I'm gay and have been fine with it. There were some pensioners who were confused between *lesbian* and *Lebanese*, but when they found out I was from England and not Lebanon, the homosexual thing became clear."

"The short hair should have been a clue." Aimee patted Kit's hair. "I like this new haircut. What do you call that? Boy cut?"

Kit shrugged. "Pixie cut, I think. Anyway, we're veering off topic. What I'm trying to say is that they're not completely cut off from the outside world."

"No, but the ferry ride over here made me realise why they might not make the trip often. I'm still nauseous."

"I'm trying to say that they're nice people, Aimee. Greengage is a great place. Beautiful and quiet but not desolate. I've enjoyed the past three months here."

"Also, it had a library job. Something which is scarce now that everyone buys books online, right?" Aimee didn't wait for a reply but simply sniffed the flowery air before adding, "If they even read, that is. Most of us spend our commute playing on our phones and our evenings watching TV."

Kit kicked at a twig. "Thanks for the depressing reminder, mate. But yeah, the fact that there was a library job was the main pull. You know, this island has a surprisingly big library for a place with only about six thousand residents."

They both looked over at a man shouting at his dog on the other side of the hill.

"How are they eccentric, anyway?" Aimee asked.

"As I said, they can be old-fashioned. And they fixate on weird stuff. Like superstition and... oh!" Kit snapped her fingers as the memory of what she had wanted to tell Aimee popped up. "Family feuds! Did I tell you about the Stevensons and the Howards?"

Aimee tilted her head. "Hm, no."

"After I'd lived here for about a month I was told about the fight between the island's two longest residing families."

"The Stevensons and the Howards?" Aimee supplied.

"Exactly. There is a huge orchard, or fruit farm or whatever they call it, here called Gage Farm. Amongst other things, they grow the greengages that the island is named after and make jams, juices, and booze of them."

"Ooooh. Wine or cider? Or something stronger?"

"All kinds, I think. Stop interrupting! You're a mum, you have to stop habits like that."

Aimee waved that away. "George is a toddler, he's not going to pick up on my interrupting yet. But sure, I'm sorry. I guess I'm still edgy after that beetle incident. Go on."

"The first settlers on this island were a bloke with the surname Stevenson and another with the surname Howard. A third guy arrived, a Frenchman."

"Makes sense considering France is right over there

somewhere." Aimee stopped walking and squinted over the hill in the direction they'd come from.

"Aimee!"

"Right… no interrupting. Carry on."

"The French guy brought greengages with him and decided that this island would be great for growing them."

Aimee held her hand up high in the air.

Kit stared at her. "Why have you got your hand up? This isn't school."

"I didn't want to interrupt!"

"Fine. What?"

"What the hell are greengages?"

Kit zipped up her jacket. It had been an unusually warm spring, but the clouds had just come out, threatening rain. Typical English April weather. "They're a sort of… green plum."

"Okay, cool. Carry on, the Frenchie arrived with the plums."

"Yep, and he decided to start growing them here. Howard and Stevenson helped out and the gages grew like weeds. For some reason, the Frenchman had to go back to France. Dead mother or something."

"That's family for you, always spoiling stuff."

"Shut up, Aimee. Anyway, he left the farm to one of the lads who'd helped him. And now, both the Howards and the Stevensons are convinced that he left it to *their* ancestor and that the other one is lying."

"Don't they have some sort of legal papers?"

"Nah, this was ages and ages ago. Paperwork was optional, if existing at all. Somehow, the Howards run it now and have made good money selling under the name of Gage Farm. Biggest exporter on the island."

Aimee whistled low. "And the Stevensons?"

"At some point, they brought out their own products under the brand South Gage Farm. Apparently, their lands are right next to the Howards, and they both claim that they have the actual land which was the original Gage Farm."

"Wow. Still?"

"Yep. They don't let things go on Greengage."

"I can tell. Are you going to get involved?"

Kit adjusted her glasses. "What are you on about?"

"Well, you know what you're like. Always mediating between couples if they fight or finding missing socks. You know, meddling in other people's business."

"Helping, you mean."

Aimee sniggered. "Sure, let's call it that."

"Shut up. Anyway, no, I don't think I'd be invited to help as an outsider. Nor am I qualified to solve something that's been going on for so many generations. Too rich for my blood."

"Fair enough." Aimee looked around. "Still, weird residents or not, you're right when you say it's beautiful. It's all so green and leafy. And the sea is gorgeous." She pointed down as she added, "All those cute chocolate-box cottages down there and all this birdsong which sounds so pretty it seems fake. Is this... *it*, though? Is there more to the island?"

"What? Like other towns? Nope." Kit scratched her neck, pondering how to briefly sum up how Greengage was laid out. "Okay, so, the middle of the island is like a city centre, with a tiny cinema, shops, and a school and all of that. Some rundown terraced houses and a few apartments, too. Then around that is a ring of small villas and cosy cottages and this hill. In the circle surrounding all of that are a few farms and their fields."

Aimee appeared unimpressed. "Then what?"

"Water, Aimee. That's what usually comes at the end of an island. There's water all the way to a few other tiny islands, then there's the Isle of Wight and then good old mainland Britain. In the other direction is more water and then France."

"Okay." Aimee surveyed Kit's face. "And you're totally sure that isn't too quiet for you?"

Kit pushed her glasses up her nose. "You know I like to stay in. Read, watch movies, and be online."

"Sure. However, you also really like Thai food and West End plays."

"True. But I can make my own Thai food, and I couldn't afford going to many West End plays after Samara and I broke up anyway."

Aimee scowled. "Samara. Yeah. At least here you are far away from her. Have you heard from her?"

"Why would I have heard from her?"

"Well, you were together for, like, ten years."

Kit did the math in her head. "Six years. We met when I was twenty-three, and I'm twenty-nine now."

"Still a bloody long time. We all thought you'd end up married with kids by now, like the rest of us. Well, divorced with kids in my case, but still… I can't believe that cow dumped you."

"Don't call her that. It's not her fault. We just wanted different things in life. I wanted to settle down and focus on work while she wanted parties and travels. The love wasn't strong enough for all the compromises we'd need to make it work."

"Also, she hated books."

Kit chuckled. "Yes, that was a problem."

"For a librarian and book addict? Yep, I'd say so. So, not heard from her then?"

Kit looked down at her worn, blue Converse shoes. "Nope. You and Dad are the only ones I've heard from during the time I've been here. I guess everyone else wrote me off when I moved."

Aimee draped an arm around her shoulders. "Well, that just means you have more time to socialise with the quirky islanders. Found any lovely women to secretly pine for in true Kit Sorel style?"

"I don't secretly pine!"

Aimee snorted. "You constantly did before Samara scooped you up. You never hit on anyone in your life."

"You don't know that."

"I've known you since you were six. Unless you were chatting up all the girls at the tender age of five, I *do* know that."

Kit shoved her hands in her pockets. "Fine. I may be a little reticent to make the first move or to notice when someone likes me. There, guilty as charged. Anyway, I doubt I'll do any dating here. I think I might be the only gay on the island."

"Well, then you either import other sapphic ladies or look closer to see if the straight women on the island are as hetero as they seem."

Kit glared at her. "Uh-huh."

Aimee was inspecting the view of the town and distractedly said, "Make them watch tennis or pick out home decorations or whatever it is you gay ladies do. Then see if anything stirs."

"First of all, careful with the clichés there. Secondly, I want them to fall for me. Not the idea of playing tennis and decorating a house."

"Oh, they'll fall for you." Aimee pursed her lips into a kissy mouth and Kit knew what was coming. The dreaded cooing baby voice that Aimee used to torment her with. "They'll go *cwazy* for the incredibly *pwetty* Kit with her fit figure, ebony hair, *libwarian* glasses, cornflower *bwue* eyes, and *wosy* cheeks."

"Shut up," Kit said, putting her hands to her cheeks. "They're not always rosy."

"Love, most days you look like you've just run a marathon in Antarctica. They're unnaturally pink."

"Can we change the topic?"

"We can, but I don't want to."

"Aimee, you're aware that there are more bugs on this island, and I can find them and stick them down your cardigan, right?"

"Fine. Changing topic."

"Thank you."

"Can we go somewhere that isn't... outside?"

Kit laughed and linked arms with Aimee. "Sure, this way. We'll go back to my place. Well, as 'mine' as it can be when I'm renting a room from my boss."

"I can't believe you agreed to rent from some bloke who interviewed you and now bosses you around all day."

"Rajesh is a sweetheart. Well, he's a grumpy old man built like a barn with a beer belly. But he's funny and was happy to help me. I think he sees me as something between a disciple and a charity project."

"How so?"

Kit peered down at the view while thinking of an example. "You know how the library is closed on Fridays?"

"Like today, yes. You said. Weird! Aren't libraries usually closed on Wednesdays and Sundays?"

"Not ours. We close on Fridays and Sundays.

Annoying and inexplicable. Typical Greengage, or so I've been told. Anyway, last Friday morning we went out for breakfast, and he tried to set me up with the woman at the bakery."

Aimee giggled. "How did that go?"

"Great," Kit said with a grimace. "Her husband thought it was hilarious and gave us free Bakewell tarts."

"You hate Bakewell tarts."

"Yeah," Kit muttered. "All in all, it wasn't a great day."

"This living arrangement isn't permanent, right?"

"No, I'll get a flat somewhere when I have time to go looking for a place. I have enough for a deposit and rents aren't that high here."

"Not compared to London, I bet."

"Exactly. But I'm in no hurry. His maisonette has a nice spare room and is right next to the library, so there's no commute. Besides, it's nice to share a place right now. Less lonely and scary."

"You always did like living with others, huh? After all, you *loved* living with me in our first apartment."

"Love is a strong word, Aimee."

"Oh, come on! I had to force you to move out when you needed to be closer to your job."

Kit sighed. "I can't help it. I like having someone around all the time. Someone to make hot drinks for and have midnight picnics on the kitchen floor with."

"So exactly like when we lived together then," Aimee said with a chuckle.

"Yes, but with my current roommate, there's less parties and me making bad coffee for any stray person you brought home. Instead there's Bollywood movies, discussions about Dickens, and me making excellent tea for just him and me."

"Sounds more like your thing."

Kit laughed. "Good point. I'd say you could meet him, but he's spending the night at a lady friend's house. As usual."

"Good for him, but a shame I won't meet him. Well, I can at least see the house and hear all the gossip."

"And meet his dog."

Aimee scowled. "Oh, right. I forgot about the dog. Hm. Priscilla, was it?"

Kit stifled a laugh. "Phyllis. She's a huge bulldog mix who loves cuddles."

"Please tell me the mutt doesn't smell?"

"Frequently! You'll hate Phyllis as much as I love her." Kit spotted dark clouds above. "Come on, it looks like it might rain, and I'm not getting drenched on my day off."

Chapter Two

BACON-ARSE FACE AND THE KITTEN RACES

It was Saturday, and the library would open in thirteen minutes. Kit rushed in, late because she'd overslept. She blamed Phyllis. The dog should've warned her against going back to bed after walking Aimee to the ferry this morning.

So much for man's best friend, she thought in a huff.

Rajesh was switching on the last of the library's computers. He'd clearly been working for hours. For an old man with a weak heart, he sure didn't take things easy.

Now he strode towards her, holding up a hand in greeting. "Aha. There you are. Morning, Katherine."

She smiled at his stubborn refusal to use her nickname. "Good morning."

Rajesh stepped behind the library counter. "Did you make sure Phyllis' box of toys wasn't wedged under the sofa again before you left?"

"Yep. Stop fretting. She has food, her toys, and, like all old dogs, she is busy sleeping and snoring loud enough to wake, if not the dead, at least those in a coma."

His scowling, wrinkled face softened. "Phyllis is a good girl. Did I tell you I rescued her?"

Kit hung up her leather jacket. "No. I don't think you did. Is that why she has a weird name for a dog? Crazy previous owner?"

"No. I named her that."

Kit winced. "Right… sorry. It's, um, a cute name for a dog. Anyway, you said you rescued her?"

"Yes, three years ago. It'll tell you all you need to know about the local lads when you find out that a group of bored teenagers bought her as a fighting dog." He slammed volume eight of *British Birds* down on the counter in anger. "Not realising that she was a three-quarters bulldog and one-quarter pug mutt, *not* a pit bull or other kind of fighting dog. Nor that it's illegal to fight dogs or that it's an arsehole thing to do." He slammed volume nine on top of its predecessor. "Or even that you have to wait until they're grown up to fight them. They simply stood around staring at this wrinkly little puppy, arguing about what to do next."

Kit shook her head as she put on the lanyard holding her library ID card. "Bloody idiots. What did you do?"

"Told their parents. Told the police. Took the puppy home."

"And named her Phyllis?"

"Well, they'd named her Bacon-Arse Face. Which is not what you call a lady. Or anyone for that matter. Phyllis seemed to fit her."

"Okay," Kit said.

She was picturing the slobbering, wrinkly bulldog mix with a wonky tooth sticking out on one side and one ear bigger than the other. That dog didn't remind Kit of a Phyllis at all. Still, she was a sweet dog and Rajesh was a sweet old man. They could call each other whatever they wanted.

Rajesh put change in the till and then leaned back. "There, we're all ready for opening. Anyway, how was your day off yesterday?"

"It was good! I had a visit from my friend Aimee."

"Oh, yes, you mentioned. She's from London, too, isn't she?"

"*Greater London*, but yeah. We grew up together out in Raynes Park."

"Hope you told her all the good things about Greengage. We need more off-islanders coming here to tourist and spend their money."

Kit laughed. "Of course I did. I told her all the brilliant things about the island and the people here."

"The people here," he muttered with a frown. "Don't we all seem cracked and inbred? Well, everyone but me of course."

Kit nodded. He had told her how his parents had come here from India in the sixties. He'd been four years old and remembered nothing of his old country. Except that it smelled better than Greengage. He was always very persistent about that.

"No, you're not all crazy. Nor inbred. You're kind and interesting. Everyone on Greengage has been welcoming. Just look at Laura Howard, Marjorie Jones, and that bloke who owns the newsagent's, what's his name?"

"Steve Hallard."

"Yes, that's right. Those three brought me a welcoming basket with products from the island on my first night here. I mean, that only happens in books and movies, right?"

"And on Greengage," Rajesh said with a chuckle.

"Yeah. This place is pretty different. I was actually telling Aimee about that. Greengage hasn't really adapted to the rest of the world, has it?"

"No. We don't get all that influenced by the rest of the world. Few people move here, and we have very little tourism. That's why I wanted you to talk up the place to your London friends."

Kit smoothed down her hair, realising she hadn't combed it in her hurry this morning. "You know, I haven't seen more than a handful of tourists in my months here. Why is that?"

"The surrounding islands. As they're smaller and closer to the mainland, they don't have their own industries and such. Meaning that they've focused on being tourist destinations." He paused to give a wheezy old man cough. "They all have cute little gardens, picnic spots, and quaint, old-fashioned tea rooms. One of them has a pretty lighthouse and another has a yarn museum – all to attract visitors. We don't have all that gubbins."

Kit pointed a finger at him. "Aha, I get it. Since those islands are closer to Britain, the ferry ride is shorter, too, meaning the tourists don't need to venture all the way out to Greengage."

"Exactly. Bad for business, but it does allow our island to be different. A lot happens here which doesn't happen elsewhere," Rajesh said. "Like kitten races."

"Like *what*?"

"Kitten races. Every Easter we race kittens on the common. I'm part of the group that make a papier-mâché track for them to run on. Or, as the case usually is, to sit down and wash on. Or play-fight on. This year we are thinking about doing a mock-up of the Swiss Alps."

"I… okay… I have questions."

"And I have a chocolate biscuit waiting for me. And a cup of tea which is cooling. So, walk and talk or watch me walk out on you."

Kit raised an eyebrow. "Well, I mean, that's rude. But to be expected from a grumpy old codger, I suppose. Let's go."

Rajesh mumbled about not being "that old" as they ambled into the library's kitchen corner. It was made up of a sink and a single countertop, which held a lime-scaled kettle, an old mayonnaise jar filled with sugar which had dried together in lumps, and two chipped mugs. Lastly, there was a biscuit tin containing two spoons, a bottle opener, and a scratched-up CD from a collection of Engelbert Humperdinck's greatest hits.

When Kit had asked if they shouldn't have a fridge, so they could have milk in their tea, Rajesh had stared at her and asked if she wanted the moon and the stars as well. She had stopped asking for stuff after that.

Rajesh stretched, making his back pop almightily. "I'm glad they gave you a welcoming basket," he picked up their earlier thread of conversation. "Good trio to meet, too. Laura's lovely. 'Greengage's favourite daughter,' some call her. Shame she's a bit of a doormat. Steve is a good lad, despite being a Tottenham supporter. And Marjorie is… Well, did you get a look at those legs?"

Kit gaped at him. "No. I didn't. Marjorie is like eighty years old."

"She's seventy-eight. Those legs of hers, however, belong on a twenty-five-year-old. Not a varicose vein in sight! She asked me to check once, that led to one of the best nights of the decade."

Kit rubbed her forehead. "I utterly and totally didn't need to know that. But she's nice, so are Steve and Laura. I haven't spoken much to Steve other than when I'm in his shop, but I've had lunch with Laura loads. In fact, I'm meeting her at our usual place on Monday."

"I remember you saying. I do listen, you know!" Rajesh grumbled. "You mentioned that she's been explaining the Stevenson vs. Howard feud, right? Silly buggers."

"Yeah. We mainly chitchat about books, TV, and stuff like that, but for the last couple of weeks she's been filling me in on the island's history and gossip. She talked about a fight between the Derricks and the Smiths, too?"

Rajesh scoffed. "Sure, but that's only about Judith Derrick giving Timothy Smith crabs in the eighties. Not such a big feud. More like a quibble over where the crabs came from originally. My bet is on Timothy's cousin Alfie."

"What? They're still fighting over... you know what? Forget I asked."

He sat down with his tea and biscuit. "Ahhh, that's more like it."

"I'll go make myself some tea, shall I?"

"Sure. There's no water in the kettle."

Kit put her hands on her hips and tried not to smile at him. "Why? Because you couldn't guess I'd want tea? Like I *always* do?"

"No. Didn't cross my mind."

"Course not," Kit muttered. "Why did you call her a doormat?"

He slurped his tea. "Who?"

"Laura Howard. You said she was lovely but a doormat."

"Ah, yes. Little Laura Howard. Sweet, smart, and friendly. I called her a doormat because she lets that silly aunt of hers rule her life. All to maintain the family peace and to keep her job."

"Keep her job?" Kit asked while filling the kettle.

"Mm, she's next in line to run the family business. Gage Farm. The orchards, the business, and the big house they live in. They all come as a package. One which Laura will receive if she plays by her aunt's rules."

"What about Laura's parents?"

Rajesh frowned. "Dead, I'm afraid. Car crash when she was a teenager."

"Whoa," Kit exhaled, sympathy stabbing at her heart. "Both parents? Ouch. Poor Laura. No wonder she clings to the family business; it's bound to mean a lot to her since she lost her parents. Maybe that explains why she puts up with the shitty aunt, too. Any family she has left must be important. Is there anyone else? Does the aunt have kids?"

"Sybil? No, she's got another brother, though. Laura's uncle, Maximillian. He's got children, but they're all barmy and have secluded themselves on a small coastal farm on the other side of the island. Laura has a little brother, however. Tom. He's Sybil's favourite relation, meaning that if Laura doesn't please Sybil, Gage Farm goes to Tom."

"What's he like?" Kit asked while fetching a mug.

"Utter moron. Races through town in a sports car and tries to chat up all the lasses. Even the ones who don't like him. Which is most of 'em. If he got Gage Farm he'd probably up and sell it to the highest bidder and move to Ibiza."

"Then surely the aunt won't leave it to him?"

"Sybil wouldn't if she knew what he was like. But the little bugger has enough brains to get on her good side and pretend to care about the family business. He's a pretty boy who knows how to play vulnerable and flatter. Nothing turns an older woman's mind like one of them."

Kit hummed and got on with making tea, pondering what she'd been told.

So strange that everyone on this island knows everything about each other. Strange in general. Maybe Aimee's right... Maybe I'll never fit in on Greengage.

After a few minutes of pensive silence, Kit gave up and asked the question which had to be answered.

"Now. We have almost five minutes until I have to go unlock the doors to let everyone in. So," she fixed Rajesh with a stare, "tell me about these kitten races."

Chapter Three

LAURA HOWARD

The following Saturday, Rajesh told Kit to head home while he locked up. Kit picked up her rucksack filled with newly borrowed books and hurried out to get some fresh air. Barrelling through the door, she almost bumped into Laura Howard.

She was about to cheerily say hello when she noticed Laura's appearance. Her full, freckled cheeks were even paler than usual, and her eyes were brimming with tears. She was letting her big auburn curls fall down by her face, masking her distress from passing cars but not from someone standing right in front of her.

"Laura? Are you okay?"

"Oh. Hello, Kit. I was on my way to my car after having coffee with my aunt. I'm fine... I merely... I'm..."

"Not fine at all?"

Laura's shoulders sagged. "Exactly."

"Has something happened?"

"Yes. Or rather, something isn't being allowed to happen. Which is sort of ruining my life. Not to be overly dramatic."

While trying to decide on the appropriate action, Kit searched the face of the teary woman who was now wrapping her arms around herself.

"I'm so sorry to hear that. Um, if you want to talk, I've been told I'm a good listener."

Laura watched her for a moment. "I… think I'd like that. If it's not a bother or inappropriate? I mean, we don't know each other very well."

Kit shrugged. "Sometimes it's easier to talk to someone who's not too close to you."

"All right. Thank you. But not here perhaps?" Laura indicated the pavement.

"No, of course not. Want to go to a coffee shop or something? Our usual lunch place maybe?"

Laura blinked away her tears and sniffed. "They're all so busy on a Saturday. I don't want anyone seeing me like this. I try to project an image of being normal, perhaps even something of a role model, not a weeping mess. How about going back to my place? Have you ever visited Howard Hall?"

"Nope, can't say I have."

"Would you like to?"

"Sure! As long as I won't be put on the Stevensons' kill list. As a librarian, I have to serve all the community. Can't take sides."

Laura laughed. "We'll keep your visit secret."

Kit's heart changed rhythm as she watched Laura's beautiful but tear-filled eyes light up when she laughed. When it was back to normal beating, she heard herself mumble, "What do you call it when eyes are a mix between green and brown? There's a precise word for that."

Laura tucked a few locks behind her ear, seeming self-conscious. "Hazel. If you're referring to the sort of green-brown that my eyes are."

Shit. That wasn't a normal thing to say. What the hell? Comfort her, don't babble about her eyes.

"Right, yeah. Hazel. Sorry, I'm a bit of a word geek. I hate using several words for something when there's an exact word which means that. Like defenestration."

Still babbling. Stop!

A line formed between Laura's auburn eyebrows. "What does that word mean?"

"Throwing someone out a window."

Laura laughed again. "Okay. Use that one often?"

"More often than you'd think."

"I see, I'll be careful around you and windows then."

Unsure of what to say and certain she was blushing, Kit simply smiled and shoved her hands in her pockets.

"Are you ready to go and have that chat?" Laura asked sheepishly. "My car is right over there. You don't drive, do you?"

"No. Between the Tube, buses, and trains – not to mention that driving in the city can be a nightmare – I didn't need to in London. So, no, it's your car, taxi, bus, or we walk."

"My car, then," Laura said and began strolling towards a red Volkswagen Beetle. Despite not being one of the vintage ones, it was still a fittingly quirky car for a quirky family on a quirky island, Kit mused as she got in on the passenger side.

&

After a short drive filled with small talk about the weather, a large building appeared in front of them. Kit had seen it before while traveling around the island. It was an Edwardian manor house in faded sandstone. Small compared to some of the mansions one saw on the mainland, but big for Greengage. Kit had presumed it was some old aristocrat's residence which had now been turned into a museum by the National Trust.

"*This* is Gage Farm?" she half-squealed.

"Well, it is the grounds where the products of Gage Farm are made. This is Howard Hall. Built in 1905 on the spot where the Howard family's large farmhouse used to be. It's still a working fruit farm." She paused to honk at a bunch of pigeons in their way. "We sold off a lot of land, tore down the stables, and closed up several small buildings when the economy took a downturn, but we kept all the orchards. Greengages, plums, apples, and cherries mostly. Oh, and we turned the gamekeeper's cottage into offices. It's a quick drive away west from here."

"Wait. Are you a lady or a baroness or something?"

Smiling, Laura shook her head, making her curls dance. "No one on the island has any titles. Which is good. If the Stevensons or the Howards had a title, they'd – pardon the pun – lord it over the other family for the rest of time."

"Yeah, I suppose they would. Still, you must have overfilled piggybanks."

"What? Oh no, we're not rich. My ancestors who built Howard Hall were well off. However, due to decades of cheaper jams and juices being imported from abroad, and people preferring chocolate spread and cola these days, well, we're barely able to maintain this place. I keep saying that we should try to rent it out for weddings and events to generate income, but my aunt refuses to let strangers near the place."

"Shame, people would love to rent this place. It's quite the building."

Laura hummed in agreement. "It is. I've always loved it. Some days I still can't believe I get to live here. Then Aunt Sybil makes my life a living hell, and I remember that my favourite house and my dream job come with a big negative."

"Your aunt?"

"Precisely."

"You've mentioned her at our lunches, but I haven't quite figured out what her deal is."

Laura parked up and muttered, "You'll see."

Kit sat forward on her chair and slathered more greengage jam on her scone. She hadn't gotten the clotted-cream-to-jam ratio right, and that always annoyed her.

Laura wasn't eating. She was staring at the large hallway stairs, which could be seen from their seats in the lavish drawing room.

"Waiting for your aunt to come down?"

"Dreading is a better word. She's in a foul mood."

Kit took a bite and then tried to hide it in her cheek to ask, "Why?"

"I've displeased her."

"By doing what?"

A crease appeared between Laura's eyebrows. "That's what I was crying about in town. Incredibly embarrassing, by the way. Please don't tell anyone I did that."

"Your secret's safe with me." Kit sought Laura's eyes and added, "Anything you say or do will stay between us. Promise."

"Thank you." Laura smiled, but it soon died on her lips. "What I did was fall in love. With the wrong person."

"Huh. Well, as a lesbian with a conservative mum, I know how that goes."

"Sorry to hear that. I mean that your mother didn't take it well; I'm glad you're gay. Like I said the first time we met, we need more diversity on the island." She put her cup of tea down. "Oh! That reminds me, I want to introduce you to the people who run Pub 42. They're two homosexual couples. One female couple and one male. All best friends. So lovely and so important for the island's increased range of people."

Kit wiped scone crumbs from her lips to hide her disappointment.

She's definitely not gay. Bollocks.

Throughout their acquaintance, Kit had been holding out hope for Laura being if not gay then maybe bi or pansexual. Now she examined Laura's long auburn curls, upturned nose, and plump cheeks and lips with a sense of loss.

She's sweet, smart, cultured, and bloody pretty. Of course she'll be off limits. Straight and apparently taken, too.

She shook her thoughts away, set her affection meter to platonic, and focused on Laura's problem. "Anyway, you were telling me about how being in love with the wrong person ticked your aunt off?"

"Yes. Dylan. Have you met him?"

Kit ran through the citizens of Greengage she had been introduced to. "Don't think I've run into a Dylan here."

"Makes sense. He doesn't go to the library, and he certainly didn't want to be part of my little welcoming committee on your first night here. He says baskets are for hot-air balloons. Not sure what he meant by that."

Kit only chuckled in response.

Smiling, Laura carried on. "Dylan is a Stevenson. In fact, he's next in line to run South Gage Farm."

"Ah, the competition."

"Competition is putting it mildly. More like deadly nemesis," Laura said while rolling her eyes.

"Now I get why your aunt doesn't like you falling for him."

"Mm. That's why we've kept our relationship and recent engagement secret. Both our families would disown us and never speak to us again."

"Very Romeo and Juliet," Kit said before helping herself to another scone.

"Yes. Well, minus any suicidal teenagers. Both Dylan and I are prepared to leave our families behind to be together. But I..." She trailed off, looking at her hands.

Kit put down the clotted cream. "But you what?"

"I truly love Gage Farm. At the moment I am basically running it, with Aunt Sybil's advice keeping me on the right course. I love the fruit we grow, I love the products we make them into, and I even love the marketing side of it. I enjoy having people working for me who both like and respect me. I've put everything into Gage Farm and I can't imagine doing anything else."

"But if you marry Romeo—sorry, Dylan—you can't run Gage Farm."

Laura slumped in her seat. "Precisely. In fact, I'd probably even be banned from buying Gage Farm products for the rest of my life."

"And Dylan would be thrown out of South Gage Farm?"

"Oh, he doesn't mind. He doesn't want to run a company. He wants to be a painter," Laura said proudly. "He's been secretly painting and studying through online courses."

"Cool. Is he any good?"

Laura hesitated with a frown.

"What?" Kit burst out. "Don't tell me that one of the sweetest people I've ever met isn't going to say that her beloved man is talented beyond belief?"

Laura wrung her hands. "He *is* good. He has a great way with colour. He's merely... I mean, he's... I suppose you could say that his paintings tend to be somewhat simplistic and similar to each other." She squeezed one hand with the other so tight that her knuckles whitened. "I feel awful now for not singing his praises. I know he could evolve as an artist if he got a chance to study with a teacher and not hide his dream away! He's not stupid or anything. Just..."

"Has bad luck when he thinks?"

"Kit!"

Kit stifled a laugh. "Sorry, I really thought that was along the lines of what you were going for."

Laura bit her lip again, looking pained. "Well, some might say it was. But I was thinking more along the lines of his strengths lying more in the field of drive and confidence. Which are also important for an artist! He'll get the other parts if he gets to practice more. After all, there's more to a person than intellect and creativity!"

Kit held up her hands in a placating gesture. "Sure. I didn't mean to insult him or question his talent. Okay. So, you want to marry this painter from the enemy clan and still be allowed to run the family company?"

"Yes."

"And your aunt is having none of that, huh?"

"Well, I haven't told her that he's a painter. Or that we're engaged. Word of us holding hands had reached her, and she mentioned it at breakfast."

Kit sucked in air between her teeth.

"Mm. When I didn't deny it, she threw a teaspoon at a bust of Isambard Kingdom Brunel. Then, when I met her in town before you ran into me, she was even more venomous. She started shouting about betrayal and mating with warthogs loud enough for the whole island to hear."

"She called Dylan a warthog?"

Laura shifted in her seat. "The Stevensons tend to be strong. You know, big built. And quite hairy. Aunt Sybil says they all look like warthogs."

"And do they?"

Laura shoved Kit's arm, nearly making her drop the scone. "No! Everyone says Dylan looks like a muscular god, with long, flowing hair. Like one of those heroes you see on the covers of romance novels."

"Great." Kit took a big bite of her scone, hiding her scowl.

"Anyway. Aunt Sybil said that I had to break it off with him right away or she'd leave the company to my brother Tom. Her darling angel Thomas who can do no wrong."

"Ah, yeah, I've heard about him."

"Then you know that Tom couldn't be in charge of a piggybank without spending all the profits on expensive watches and cocktails for any woman who put up with him."

"That's the impression Rajesh gave me."

"Then I'm sure he also mentioned that Aunt Sybil dotes on Tom. She much prefers the company of men to women. Especially young, manly men. That's why this is so silly. She'd adore Dylan if she got to know him. In fact, she'd probably try to adopt him if he wasn't a Stevenson."

Kit pondered that while Laura took her cup and topped it up.

"Cheers. You make brilliant tea," Kit said distractedly.

Laura beamed. "Really? Thank you."

Whoa. She's so starved for compliments that something like that makes her happy?

"Sure. The jam's great, too. I see why the island prides itself on its greengages and the products that Gage Farm makes."

Laura regarded the jam jar. "Nice, isn't it? Last season was great for the gages. The blossoms were astounding. You can tell by the fullness of flavour in the fruit. You could even tell by the island's honey."

Kit searched her brain for its scarce flora and fauna knowledge. "Honey? What does honey have to do with jam?"

Laura's eyes gleamed, still fixed on the jar. "Nothing, really. I only meant that the bees lived off the gage flowers last year, and I think you could taste it in their honey." She rubbed the tips of her slender index finger and thumb against each other, as if searching for the right words. "Running through the normal honey flavour was that... tell-tale taste of intense, fresh sweetness spiked with a tart bite which only greengages have."

She raked her teeth across her lower lip and continued, her voice steeped with smouldering reverence. "They always look so sharp and acerbic in their greens and yellows, but they're so much sweeter than other plums. So much more flavourful." Laura looked up at Kit, eyes still gleaming with an intensity which stunned her guest. "You know what I mean? It's like nothing else, natural or manmade. That warming, sweet taste… it's almost seductive in your mouth, like it seeks out and French-kisses every taste bud individually. And when its gone, your mouth misses it, wants it back. Wants *more*."

Kit realised that she was staring open-mouthed at the woman in front of her who spoke passionately of this fruit as if it was something… what? Sacred? Haunting? Sexual?

Laura frowned. "Gosh, listen to me. Ugh. Going on about something which no one who isn't obsessed with fruit can relate to. I'm sorry. That wasn't a normal thing to say. I must sound crazy or… something worse."

"Not at all! You sound like you're passionate about something you work with. And that you've grown up with. It sure as hell made me want more jam and greengages."

Laura still frowned, embarrassment emanating off her like steam.

Kit reached out to touch Laura, to reassure her, but something stopped her. She pulled her hand back, exactly as she decided to pull the conversation back.

"Anyway. Getting back to your problem. Just a thought here: you said that Sybil would like Dylan if she got to know him. Maybe that's the obvious key, then? If you're sure she'd like him if she gave him a chance?"

Laura tucked hair behind her ear. "Certainly, but he's a Stevenson. If he comes anywhere near her, she'll throw a teaspoon at him instead of at the bust of Brunel."

"Well, Dylan doesn't want to run South Gage Farm, right? So why doesn't he renounce his family? Publicly tell them to stick the Stevenson name where the sun doesn't shine? Your aunt should be impressed with that."

"Mm. True. But he'd lose his family for life. Also, I don't think that would be enough for Aunt Sybil."

Kit swallowed a mouthful of tea. "Okay. What if he asks her to come work here?"

"Pardon?"

"What if he comes to your aunt, grovelling like mad, saying that he can't stand his family and their company. That he wants to work at the *real* Gage Farm and keeps laying it on thick about how much better your products are?"

"Hm." Laura stared into space. "That might work. I mean, if we can get her to listen to him."

"Yeah, that would be the crux. But we're two clever women, we can work something out."

Laura beamed again. "You're turning out to be quite the hero, Londoner."

"Well, I mean I don't have big muscles and long, flowing hair so I won't be on any romance covers."

Laura smirked. "Oh, I think that depends on what the audience for the romance novel is."

While Kit was busy being smacked over the head by that sexy smirk, it vanished only to be replaced by a sappy expression and the words, "I must explain your little plot to darling Dylan. He'll be thrilled that there's a chance for us to be together. He's such a romantic. I'm so lucky."

"Uh-huh," Kit said, drinking more tea.

Don't be a bitch. He's probably a great guy.

"Anyway," Laura said. "I'll tell him and then I'll come back to you regarding plans for how exactly we're going to do this. If that is okay with you?"

"Sure. You're a really nice person, Laura, you deserve to be happy. Besides, I enjoy plotting and planning to help people. Fixing sticky situations."

"Aha. Are you going to be the island's amateur detective? Or the matchmaker, perhaps?"

Kit snorted. "Considering how many old people who like to meddle Greengage seems to have, I'm sure those roles are already filled."

"True," Laura admitted between laughs. "Nevertheless, thank you for helping me. And for coming here and listening to me whinge."

"Not a problem. I'm sort of disappointed I didn't get to meet this Sybil, though."

"Oh, she'll be on the grounds, no doubt. I'll introduce the two of you. You need to get a feel for the foe we're facing."

Kit ate the last bite of her scone and stood up. "Lead the way."

As Laura walked out of the room—without clearing the table, Kit noticed—she said, "Speaking of meeting people, remind me to take you to Pub 42 later. Like I said, you have to meet Rachel and Shannon. Oh, and if they're back from their holiday, Josh and Matt."

"Will do. It's good that I've gotten to know someone who can direct me to the other gays on the island."

Laura tried to tuck her big curls behind her ear, but they pinged back. "Well, they're the ones who are currently in same-sex relationships, at least. There are others on the island who might… well, I mean the reason I know them is that Rachel was my first crush. Or rather, first relationship, I suppose. If you count two nineteen-year-olds being together for a few months as a relation-ship." A blush was creeping into Laura's full cheeks.

So… experimented with women when younger. She's still not available, but at least my gaydar isn't quite as broken as I thought.

"Right. Well, I'd like to meet them all. And it sounds like a good excuse to have a pint."

"Yes! They have a large range of drinks and a nice little menu. It's only pub food like hamburgers and chips, but it is the only place on the island where you can get quesadillas. It's not a gay bar per se, but anyone who goes in there knows it's owned by queer people and consequently belongs to the open and modern crowd."

"Unlike some of the old man pubs around the island?"

As she held the front door open, Laura winced. "I didn't want to say that... but yes."

Kit walked past her while pulling her leather jacket on. "I get it. Thanks for the heads-up."

"Not that anyone would be rude or unpleasant. They might, however, well, treat you like a strange, new animal at the zoo."

"Double thanks for the heads-up."

They smiled at each other.

Laura locked the door and then turned to survey Kit. "You know, you're really easy to talk to."

"Told you I was a good listener. It's how I've gotten most of my girlfriends and friends. Even some job offers."

"I'm certain there's more to it than that. Who wouldn't want to employ you? Who wouldn't want to be your friend or your..." Laura moved her gaze to the path. "Anyway, Aunt Sybil is probably down by the cherry trees. She talked about checking in on them this morning."

They walked on, the gravel crunching under their shoes and the birds chirping as if trying to make the most of the day's last rays of sun. When they got away from the house and further into the grounds, Kit saw lanes of trees with tiny flecks of white amongst the leaves.

"Wow. They're really pretty."

Laura's eyes lit up. "I know! The blossoms are just opening. Give it a week or two and the trees will be awash with pinkish-white flowers. Like a sea of bright, fragrant blossoms. It takes my breath away every year. You'll have to come see it."

"I'd like that."

Kit swallowed and tried not to dwell on how stunning Laura was when talking about cherry blossoms. Nor that Kit seemed to have stepped in something unfortunate which she, with every step, tried to scrape off her shoe.

She failed on both accounts.

Chapter Four

SYBIL AND THE KINGS AND STUFF

K it and Laura reached the orchards right as the sunshine gave in to twilight. The colours mottling the sky made the long rows of trees look mysterious in their silent beauty.

Kit, still trying to clean her shoe on every bit of grass she saw, startled when a shrill and nasal voice rang out and shattered the calm atmosphere.

"No, you peabrained mammoths! I said to meet me at the cherry trees. Have you really been spending the last thirty minutes waiting for me by the plum trees? *Cherry* and *plum* sound nothing alike, you hulking idiots!"

Kit squinted and saw a short, stocky woman screaming at two giant men. Getting closer to the group revealed that the men looked like boys being told off by a teacher. The short woman's face was turning purple as she kept shouting about how they'd wasted her time by making her wait. And how much more important her time was than theirs.

So that's Sybil Howard. Yeah. Charming.

She noticed Laura stiffening next to her. "Auntie?

Pardon the intrusion, I wanted to introduce you to the newest resident on the island. This is Kit Sorel."

Sybil took her eyes off the shamed men with a look of anticipation. Then it faded. "Oh, you're a woman. I thought Kit was a man's name."

Kit took her hands out of her jacket pockets. "It's gender neutral. In my case, it's short for Katherine." She extended a hand, with some hesitance, Sybil took it.

"Katherine," Sybil drawled like she was tasting the name. "Quite dull, I see why you would need a nickname. So, what brings you to our island?"

Laura, looking embarrassed enough to explode, interjected. "Firstly, don't be rude. Katherine is a *beautiful* name. Secondly, Kit took Alma's old job at the library."

"Ah. Good. She was useless."

"Aunt Sybil! Alma passed away. Show some respect," Laura whispered while glancing around in horror.

Sybil shrugged. "Dead or alive. Useless either way." After that she focused back on the closest tree, running her hand over its bark with a scowl.

Laura shifted her weight from foot to foot. "Anyhow. As I said, I wanted to introduce you to Kit. You might not remember this, but I've told you before that I've been having lunch with her quite a bit so…" She trailed off, her gaze flitting from her aunt to her shoes.

First time I've seen her look frightened, Kit thought. *I guess this is where Rajesh's comment about being a doormat comes from.*

Sybil was now scraping at the bark with a long nail. "What? Speak up, girl!"

Laura stood up straighter. "So she might come by for lunch or dinner sometime."

Sybil waved her hand dismissively without turning. "Fine. As long as she doesn't chew with her mouth open."

Kit adjusted her glasses. "Since I'm right here, I can take the opportunity to promise you that I don't. I do tend to stick peas up my nostrils, though. Broccoli, too, if the pieces are small enough to fit."

Finally, Sybil turned away from the tree and back to Laura and Kit. "What? What was that?"

"Nothing," Laura squeaked. She put a hand at the small of Kit's back and began ushering her towards the gravel path. "We'll take our leave now. I'll see you at dinner, Auntie."

"Mm," Sybil said before returning to the cherry tree's bark.

"Sorry, I couldn't resist messing with her," Kit whispered when they were a few steps away.

"I noticed," Laura said. She clicked her tongue. "You can be very bad."

"I'll take that as a compliment. Besides, that trait will come in handy when we plot a way for you to get your man."

Laura smiled. "I'm sure it will. Now, let me drive you back to town."

❦

The following Monday, Kit heard the pounding of high heels breaking the library's silence. Looking up from the trolley of books she was weeding out, she spotted Laura rushing towards her with a huge grin.

"Kit! Guess what?"

"There's a sale on painfully loud high-heeled boots?"

"No, silly. Although that would be great." Laura

looked wistful but then collected herself. "No, I told Dylan about your plan and he's on board. He wants to meet as soon as possible to discuss how he can wheedle his way into Aunt Sybil's heart." She paused to grimace. "Assuming she has one, of course. I have wondered at times."

"Okay. Um, since none of us have our own place…" Kit had to laugh. "Nice bunch of thirtysomethings we are, huh? Anyway, since we all live with someone, I suppose it'll come down to who can get their house empty for an evening of plotting."

Laura hummed and tapped her fingers against the book trolley. "I think I've got a solution. There's an old games room in the basement of Howard Hall. Neither Sybil nor Tom go down there because it's messy and cold. It has a door to the garage, I can sneak Dylan through that and Aunt Sybil will never know. You can come in through the front door, obviously. I think she quite liked you."

Kit pushed her glasses up her nose. "That was her *liking me*?"

"Well, yes. That's as warm as she gets, I'm afraid."

"Living with her must be a barrel of laughs."

Laura raised her eyebrows. "It's a challenge. But I do love her. She has her good side, too."

"I'm sure she does. So, you were saying about sneaking Dylan into the games room?"

"Oh, right. What about if the three of us meet there tomorrow night? I'd pick tonight, but Dylan's grandmother has a birthday bash so he'll be tied up."

"On a Monday?"

"Well, it's not like she has to get up early for work tomorrow. She's eighty-two."

"And being a haughty Stevenson, she doesn't care that

others might have work to consider? I know the type. Anyway, tomorrow works for me. I can come over after I've left the library and grabbed something to eat."

"Brilliant. Don't be too full, I'll provide drinks and snacks."

"Sustenance always helps with scheming," Kit said and adjusted her glasses. She was aware of always doing when she was nervous or excited but had never able to stop it.

Wonder if that qualifies as a tic?

In the momentary silence, Laura was applying lip gloss, creating a tremendously distracting sheen on those plump lips of hers.

Kit kept her hand from going to her glasses again. "So, um, I guess you won't be going to Grandmother Stevenson's party then?"

"No, they'd probably stone me on sight. Silly, I know, but that's Greengage for you. I actually don't know what I'm going to do tonight. Read the latest Emma Donoghue book and try not to brood about my future in-laws hating me, I suppose."

"While I don't want to rob you of a good reading session, the brooding sounds crappy. If you want distraction, I'm going for a run tonight. Just around the town, not venturing out into all the muddy fields and such. Fancy tagging along?"

Laura scrunched up her nose. "I'm not really a runner. Unless there's ice cream to run towards or wasps to run from."

"Running isn't really my thing either, but as Greengage doesn't have a gym, it's my only way of working out. At least if I want some cardio."

"Huh." Laura knitted her brow. "I'd never considered that we don't have a gym. Well, there's the one at the school and the one that the Greengage wrestling team uses."

"Yeah, but I'm not sure I'm allowed in either?" Kit said. "So, I bought some weights to keep in my room, and I'm trying to get used to running a few times a week to get the cardio in, too. I can switch to a long walk tonight instead, though. If that's more your cup of tea?"

Laura beamed. Kit had never met anyone who embodied that expression more than Laura did when she was happy or excited.

"Much better! I'm in, thanks."

"Don't mention it, I'm happy for the company," Kit said truthfully. "Meet you at the square after dinner?"

Laura's always slightly upturned nose scrunched up even further.

"Uh, want to meet somewhere else?" Kit asked.

"No, no. It's not that. I was merely remembering that we're having halibut for dinner tonight, Aunt Sybil's choice. I hate halibut."

Kit grinned. "I guess asking her to pick food that everyone likes isn't an option?" Laura gave her a pained look, making Kit laugh and answer her own question. "Nah, of course not. Your aunt clearly forgot to pick up the considerate trait at birth."

"She didn't forget. She simply declined it." Staring into space, Laura slowly added, "I suppose I might get out of it by saying that I'm meeting you for dinner. Do you like pizza?"

"Who doesn't?"

"Marvellous. There's a good pizza place by the square. Maybe we could eat there and then go for a walk and try to get rid of at least a third of the pizza calories?"

"Sounds like it'll be a long walk to achieve that. It's a deal," Kit said with a wink.

Laura thrust her hand up at about head height. After a second's deliberation on what the posh woman wanted, Kit realised it was a high five and slapped the raised hand.

"Sorry. Was that awkward?" Laura asked with a self-deprecating chuckle.

Kit shrugged. "Everything seems more or less awkward to me these days. I'm still trying to fit in on Greengage and find the right tone of communication with you islanders."

"You're managing nicely. Anyway, we can dig deeper into that over pizza tonight."

"And during the walk."

"Yes, yes." Laura rolled her eyes. "I haven't forgotten about the exercise." She checked her elegant gold watch. "I should be getting back to the office before everything falls apart. Take care and I'll see you at six by the town square? Next to the statue of the huge greengage?"

Kit slapped the side of the book trolley. "Aha! That's what that thing is! I thought it was some sort of weird artsy thing symbolising birth or something. Sure, see you there."

Laura waved goodbye and left. Kit couldn't stop herself from watching her go. Her high-heeled boots were annoyingly noisy, but they made her taller than Kit and certainly gave her body a nice sway when she moved. Kit closed her eyes to not look at any swaying parts she shouldn't.

Her eyelids popped open at the words, "Where's the books on, like, kings and stuff?" which came from a slumped teenage boy next to her.

Kit cleared her throat. "I'll take you to the Kings and Stuff shelf. We keep it by the Queens and Crap shelf."

"Huh?"

She shook her head. "Never mind. Come with me and I'll show you."

Kit marched off, focusing on the teenager and certainly not on the warm, charming Laura Howard. Or those full lips of hers. Or those soft-looking curls. Or how those generous curves swayed when leaving a library on a Monday afternoon.

Chapter Five

WHO WILL RAISE THE PIZZA ROLLS?

That night, Kit and Laura were seated in what was clearly a rip-off of a famous chain of pizza restaurants, considering its name was Pizza *Tent*.

They'd just ordered and were sitting comfortably sipping their drinks.

Laura peered at Kit's glass. "I don't think I've ever met anyone who picks Diet Pepsi when there's other options. Don't you want one of the non-sugared colas which taste more like the original?"

Kit looked at her glass, too. "Huh. No one's ever asked me that. Uh, no. This is less sweet, yeah, but I like that about it. I don't have sugar in my tea either."

Laura shook her head. "You clearly don't have my sweet tooth. Except for my gin and tonics," she held up her clear drink, "I always pick the sweetest option."

"That explains why you picked a pizza with pineapple on it. Fruit doesn't belong on pizza."

"I run a fruit farm, Kit. In my world, fruit belongs everywhere."

"Fair enough. So, having booze before taking a long walk, huh?"

Laura shrugged. "Well, it's bound to make it more fun."

Kit opened her mouth but then closed it with a snap.

Laura raised an eyebrow and matched it with an amused smirk. "What? Time for a lecture?"

"Sort of. I was considering whether to warn you about drinking before any kind of cardio." She pointed to her own chest. "I read that it's dangerous for the heart."

Laura took a demonstrative gulp of the G&T. "Good thing I'm only going for a leisurely walk then."

"True," Kit said with a laugh. "Ignore me, I tend to stick my nose where it doesn't belong."

"You did mention liking to plot and solve problems, but my impression was that it came from a wish to help others, not that you like to 'stick your nose where it doesn't belong.' I think you're being too hard on yourself."

"I don't know," Kit murmured. "I've always been the person people turn to for advice and to fix sticky situations. From when I was a kid and my dad would ask me how to make his indiscretions up to Mum, all the way to helping my ex patch things up with her estranged brother a year ago."

"Why do you think that is? Could it have started with helping your dad as a child?"

Kit cleaned her glasses with the bottom of her jumper. Not because they needed cleaning, but because it got her out of eye contact. "Maybe. He was always so happy and so grateful after I helped him patch up the relationship for another couple of months. Mum ran out of patience in the end of course." She forced her trembling hands to stop making her glasses shake. "Mum got tired of him sleeping around, tired of the apologies, and even tired of me helping him charm her back. She left Dad and she cut down contact with me to a minimum."

"Oh, Kit. I'm so sorry."

Kit squirmed under Laura's overwhelming sympathy. This was why she didn't talk much about herself. Putting things into words left you so exposed.

She replaced her glasses. "It's okay. Her choice, I guess. It taught me that there's often a cost for getting involved. I'm more careful now."

"Ensuring that your help doesn't hurt others along the way?"

"Something like that, yeah." Kit drank deep from her glass, almost regretting that she didn't have alcohol, too. "Anyway, that's enough about me. What about you? It can't have been easy growing up being a Howard. Everyone on the island must know who you are and about your family's epic feud."

Laura blew out a long breath. "Yes. People are well aware of who I am and everything that happens in my life. I suppose I'm... ah, I can't believe I'm saying this... some sort of Greengage celebrity."

Kit laughed and lifted her glass to toast the comment. "Wow! How posh."

"No. My home is posh. I suppose my accent is posh. My designer clothes are certainly posh, they have to be to impress. The celebrity status, however, is merely a pain in the—" Laura interrupted herself with a self-deprecating smile and finished with the word "neck. That was one of the things that drew me to Dylan, actually."

Kit put her glass down. "Really? How's that?"

"We were at school together. He's two years older than me but, on an island where there's only one school, you see everyone around even if they're not in your class. I'd notice him walking away from the others. They'd claim he thought he was better than them, but I knew differently. There's pressure on being a Howard or a Stevenson. Everyone was always watching us, expecting us to duel in the school assembly hall."

"Christ. Really?"

"Yes, really," Laura said wearily. "Everyone looked at you as if they knew you. As if they could stare at you and gossip about you as much as they wanted. And of course, there was the envy and bitterness. We're the two wealthiest families on an island which is certainly not affluent."

"Right, of course."

Laura regarded her hands which were clasped on the table. "I know, I know, poor little rich girl. I've been lucky to be born into a privileged family and such a safe place. I've no right to complain, but it was like being under a microscope, and during your teenage years that gets particularly hard."

She looked up and smiled, but it looked about as real as the plastic flowers on the table. Her gaze returned to her hands which were fidgeting now. "And, of course, both the Stevenson and Howard clans expected their offspring to be the best students at school. Which stressed me so much I got skin rashes. Still, I managed. I never had a problem with picking up new skills or sacrificing sleep and parties for more studying. Dylan didn't fare so well. He struggled more each year. The worse his grades were, the more his family punished him. It was torture to watch."

Laura cleared her throat. "I started trying to help him. At first, he pushed me away, even shouted at me. Then, after a while, he saw how I could help and he let me. I've adored him from that moment on. Caring for him, loving him, is second nature to me after all these years."

"And you've done that in secret ever since?" Kit asked quietly.

"Mm. Many islanders suspect something, of course. But both our families keep themselves apart and don't care for gossip, so we've been able to get away with it. As long as we don't flaunt it, never meet in public, and keep up the appearance of the feud, we seem to be okay." She looked up at Kit. "However, I'm tired of hiding. This is not the 1880s, for heaven's sake, we shouldn't have to hide our romance because of who our families are."

Kit shook her head.

Laura took a gulp of her G&T. "So, a couple of weeks ago, I started taking him along to events. To hold his hand in public. And, of course, that got back to Aunt Sybil. The rest you know."

Kit nodded, then ticked it off on her fingers. "The teaspoon thrown at Isambard Kingdom Brunel's bust in the morning, then coffee in town where she told you to stay away from the Junior Warthog Stevenson. Then you end up outside the library crying under your curls."

Laura glared at her for a second but then cracked a smile. "That about sums it up, yes." Her smile faded. "During coffee Aunt Sybil said in no uncertain terms that if I was seen with him in public again, I'd lose Gage Farm, my chance to live at Howard Hall, and even the right to use the name Howard."

"What? How was she going to enforce that? She can't legally change your name."

Laura scoffed. "Oh, I wouldn't put it past her. Sybil Howard is a force of nature, and she runs half of the island. All the councillors answer to her. The mayor is her godson, for Pete's sake."

She peered around, and Kit followed her gaze. The other tables were either full or filling up with Greengage residents who were all sneaking glimpses at them. Or rather, they were glancing at Laura.

Laura kept her eyes down, avoiding their gaze. "Either way, Aunt Sybil can turn my remaining family, not to mention half of the island, against me. I don't want to lose anyone or let anyone down. I know that probably makes me weak. But I can't help it." Her voice cracked. "Most of all, I don't want to lose Gage Farm. It meant the world to my parents when they were alive, and it means the world to me now. It's all I have left of them. And it's a *good company*! It's struggling because of the dwindling market, but it's financially viable and it still has a strong beating heart."

Laura's voice was raising, and the people around them were glancing over more frequently.

Kit put her hand over hers on the table. "Shh. It's okay. I promise you that I'll help you keep Gage Farm. And Howard Hall. Hell, even the approval of your relatives. Although, no offence, if your family treat you like that – they don't deserve you. Screw them."

Laura examined her with knitted brows. "True. Tom and Aunt Sybil are awful. Uncle Maximilian and my cousins abhor people and choose to live on benefits they haven't earned in a derelict, faraway farm. Nevertheless, I still love all of them." She tilted her head, seeming to survey Kit. "I see what you meant by your statement, but —and forgive me for bringing this up—but if your mother shuns you because you, as a child, helped your father cover up his sins, or because she's conservative and you're gay, she doesn't deserve you. That doesn't matter in the end, does it? You still miss her? We cannot help loving the people who matter to us," she whispered while taking Kit's hand and squeezing it.

Kit pondered that, chewing her lower lip. "No, but we can try to limit how much power they have to hurt us, right?"

Laura squeezed her hand again and then slowly let it go. "I suppose so." She sat up straighter before adding, "And if they stand in our way, we can ask a brilliantly clever friend to help us work around them."

"That's the spirit! We'll get your aunt to love Dylan like he's family."

Laura lifted her glass. "Cheers to that!"

Kit clinked their glasses together and took a sip before scanning the restaurant. "Shouldn't our pizzas have been here by now? We ordered when we got in and that's got to be fifteen to twenty minutes ago."

Laura called over to a squat woman in the corner. "Hi there, Leslie. Sorry to bother you, but do you know if our pizzas are on the way?"

The woman smiled. "I'll go check, Ms Howard."

As she walked off, Laura blushed and said, "I've told her to call me Laura. Sadly, few people seem comfortable doing that."

"Hey, you could be *Lady Howard* and they'd all be calling you 'your ladyship' or 'your nibs.' That'd be worse, right?"

"Ugh! Very true." Laura sat back and giggled. "You know, I do have a nickname which many Greengagers call me, including Rajesh. I'm sure you've heard it."

"Bob?"

Laura burst out laughing. "No, you plum! It's 'Little Laura Howard,' which makes me feel about five years old."

"Rajesh calls me Katherine. I told him to call me Kit, even my parents call me that. But he checked my ID during the job interview and saw my name was Katherine. Since then he sticks to that."

"He's a lovely but very stubborn man. Aunt Sybil says that's why he won't settle down. He was in serious relationships with quite a few women when he was younger, even engaged once, I think. But he always broke it off when they wanted him to change in any way."

"That tracks. In general, he seems like someone who's happier being on his own. Sticking to friends-with-benefits relationships, you know? Sex without romance."

"There's a name for that now, isn't there?" Laura said hesitantly.

"Um." Kit racked her brain. "Do you mean aromantic?"

Laura pursed her lips. "Sounds familiar. But that also sounds like *aromatic* and that's not a word I'd use to describe him."

"Well, he's pretty fragrant when he puts on too much Old Spice before his dates. Or when he makes his terrible curries."

"Yes, he never could cook," Laura whispered, as if afraid he could hear them. "Anyway, we should stay out of his affairs. He's happy, that's what matters."

Kit crossed her arms over her chest. "I'm trying to stay out of his Casanova ways, but it's hard when you live under his roof. He says he likes my company but grumbles when he wants to bring a date home."

"What about when you want to bring a date home?"

Kit pushed her glasses up her nose. "Hasn't happened.

I'm not exactly looking to get lucky. I'm still busy settling into the job and life here on Greengage."

"Fair enough."

The squat woman came over to them again. Kit scrambled to remember what Laura had called her. Tessie?

"Your pizzas are coming now, Ms Howard. There was some confusion in the kitchen."

"Okay, thank you so much, Leslie," Laura said with such warmth that it made both Kit and Leslie smile.

"Hungry?" Kit asked.

"Famished!"

Leslie went to another table and left Kit and Laura to gaze towards the kitchen in hopes of spotting their food. Kit realised they must look like parents waiting to see their new-born baby for the first time.

Soon a gawky bloke struggled through the doors. He was probably a grown man but looked about sixteen, with arms and legs too long for him to control. In his hands were plates of the biggest pizzas Kit had ever seen. He snail-paced his way along as to not drop the plates or bump into anything.

Kit got up to help, but Laura grabbed her arm and whispered, "I wouldn't. That's Jason Smith, his mother is our cook at Howard Hall. Jason struggles with socialising and has a real chip on his shoulder about managing on his own." She lowered her voice even further. "Probably because he's been bullied for being a mummy's boy all his life. He won't want any assistance. Just act casual and let him get on with it."

Kit sat back down. "Okay. But those pizzas are way too big for those plates, he should be happy for some help."

Jason kept trudging towards them. So slowly that Kit wasn't sure he was actually moving.

The seconds ticked by. The awkward wait was grating on her. She pushed her impatience and second-hand embarrassment away and smiled at Laura who was sipping her G&T.

A female customer patted Jason's leg as he passed, making him turn towards her. The motion made Kit's pizza slide an inch off the plate. Some pepperoni and a splodge of cheese slopped onto the floor.

The customer said, "Hello there, our Jase. Could'ya get me a refill, please?" The annoying woman held out her empty glass to him.

Kit clenched her jaw, sending Jason a message with her thoughts. *Tell her you'll come back for it. Or get Leslie to do it. Whatever as long as you bring us the pizzas before they both slide off their plates.*

"Are you sure I can't go help him?" she whispered.

Laura shook her head. "Afraid not. Not unless you want him to start shouting and stomp out of here."

Jason surveyed his two big plates and then the customer's glass.

Don't do it. Don't you do it, Jason.

"All right," he mumbled.

Kit squeezed her eyes closed but opened them again, she couldn't help but watch.

He put one plate, Laura's one with the inappropriate pineapple, on his forearm. It balanced, but only barely. At the very same moment, Leslie had spotted the disaster clearly about to occur and came rushing over. So fast that she startled Jason who turned whiplash-fast towards her, making them bump into each other. His arm lowered, and

Laura's pizza slid off its plate and on top of Kit's pizza, laying itself perfectly flat on it.

Kit gaped at Laura. Laura was busy laughing but stopped when she saw Kit's expression. Then she held up her glass in a toast and said, "Well, *you* might not be getting lucky on Greengage, but I think your pizza just did."

Kit took embarrassingly long to get it, but when she did she couldn't help but laugh as well. "Well, if your pizza gets mine pregnant, I'm not raising the little pizza rolls."

She picked up her glass and clinked it against Laura's.

Chapter Six

NEVER BUY A WHEELBARROW

L ater that night Kit sat at the small kitchen table. She'd slumped down there as she came off the adrenaline boost of the dinner with Laura and their long walk. Now she was drawing little stars on a notepad, listening to her iPhone beeping. She was trying to get through to Aimee to no avail.

Beep. Beep. Beep. Beep.

A click and then a voice croaked, "Mm. Who? I mean, uh, hello?"

Kit stooped doodling. "Aimee? Were you asleep?' She checked her watch. "It's only a quarter to ten and you're usually a night owl."

"What? Sleeping? I... What? No. Of course not."

"Uh-huh. You were asleep."

"Okay, maybe I was inspecting the insides of my eyelids a bit. George has a cold again and kept me up the last two nights. He's sleeping on my chest right now. I bet I'll get his cold, I keep catching every damn virus."

"You've been stressed lately, especially since the

divorce. Maybe that's taken a toll on your immune system?"

Aimee sighed. "Sure, I'm stressed. I wouldn't say it's due to the divorce so much as buggered-up finances and my parents giving me a hard time. On top of that, I started my new part-time job today and there was a hell of a lot to take in."

"Sounds awful."

Aimee's only reply was a grunt.

"Anyway, I hope I didn't wake George when I called? Should I let you guys get back to snoozing?"

"No. He's sound asleep and I want to chat. I miss you. What's on your mind?"

"I miss you, too." Kit went back to doodling. She drew another star and then a heart inside it. "I wanted to tell you that I now officially have a real friend on the island and… I have gossip."

"Congrats on both! Wait, is the real friend funnier than me? And why is it a 'real' friend? As opposed to all your imaginary friends? Have you been talking to unicorns and gargoyles again? Also, what's this about gossip?"

"One thing at a time!" Kit said. "No, she's not funnier than you. Neither as in *funny ha-ha* or as in *funny weird*."

"Good. So, is it someone I've heard of?"

"It's Laura Howard. And by 'real friend' I meant that she's gone from lunch-buddy-acquaintance to close friend tonight."

"Good stuff. And the gossip? Don't hold out on me!"

"The gossip is that she has a soap-opera-mixed-with-Jane-Austen dilemma going on. She's heartbroken because her awful ice-queen aunt won't let her marry the man she loves."

"Hang on. Howard? Why does that sound familiar?

I've got it, the feud that started with the French guy with the plums! Gage Farm, right? Let me guess... her lover boy is a Stevenson?"

Kit drew another star and a plum next to it. "Green-gages, not plums. But yes, he's a Stevenson. In fact, he's the heir to South Gage Farm – the rival fruit farm and fruit products company. Although, unlike Laura, he doesn't want to inherit the company."

"Oooh, juicy!"

"Was that a pun?"

Aimee yawned. "Of course it was. I'm the funny friend, remember?"

"Sure, Aimee." Kit rolled her eyes at Phyllis who was watching her from her tatty old dog bed. "Anyway, Laura's clearly able to plan and to make hard decisions when running Gage Farm. But now she seems to be at a loss for what to do. If she marries him, she loses her dream job and the home she wants to stay in. *And* becomes a social pariah who feels like she let her deceased parents down. So, I thought up a scheme for her."

"Please tell me you're not plotting to bribe the aunt? Or kidnap her or something else criminal?"

"Aimee! No. Why would I do that? My schemes aren't usually illegal."

"No, suppose not. They do sometimes bend laws and rules, though."

"Yeah, but not to the point of bloody kidnapping!"

"Okay, okay... sorry. Tired remember? Spill the plan."

While still doodling, Kit explained Laura, Dylan, Tom, and Sybil's situation and the plan of how Sybil was supposed to get to know and approve of Laura's beloved Dylan. She went slowly, not omitting any details. When she was done she saw Phyllis yawn.

Wow, I'm that dull? Thanks, you rude mutt.

Aimee clicked her tongue. "Not bad. What *is* bad is how you're trying to pretend that nothing's wrong."

Kit stopped in the middle of drawing a star. "Huh?"

"Usually when you figure out a plot to help people, you sound as excited as a kid. And you started this call sounding like that, then you began sounded like you were hard-core sulking."

"I'm not!"

At Kit's exclamation, Phyllis grunted in her sleep. Probably only a snore, but it sounded like disbelief.

Kit ignored the disrespectful animal but lowered her voice. "I'm not sulking, just... reflecting. Laura is wonderful, inside and out. I suppose she's reminded me of everything I'd like to find in a woman."

"Which makes it weird when you're setting her up with someone else?" Aimee suggested.

"Yeah. Someone else who doesn't seem to give her the attention and support she deserves? I don't know. Maybe I'm jealous. She'd be exactly my type if she was available. And into women." Kit reconsidered her words. "Well, she might be since she dated a girl when she was nineteen. Never mind, none of that matters now, she's engaged to Dylan."

"Aha! There it is."

Kit took off her glasses to rub the bridge of her nose. "There what is?"

Aimee sniggered. "The Kit Sorel secret pining."

"It's only a little crush. She's a great person – smart, sweet, funny, sexy – who I happen to be attracted to. Not a big deal." Kit paused to catch her breath. "You'll get a kick out of where she's taking me, though."

"Ooooh. What is it? Bingo? Burning off-islanders as a tribute to the wicker god?"

"You know what, I'm not going to tell you now."

"Ah, come on, Kit. I'm sorry. Seriously, where is she taking you?"

"Pub 42. It's exactly what it sounds like, a small place to get drinks and some food, located on 42 High Street, Greengage."

"Okay," Aimee said uncertainly. "Why would I get a kick out of that?"

"It's where the island's *other gays* are. Apparently two queer couples banded together and opened this place. The four of them run it."

Aimee gasped. "She's taking you to your people! How sweet. Are at least two of them women?"

"Yep. One couple is two women and the other is two men."

"Yeah, yeah. No one cares about the blokes. I certainly don't, not since my good-for-nothing ex-husband refused to look after George today. Ugh! Tell me more about the other lady-loving ladies on the island. You pondering a three-way?"

"What?" Kit startled. "You can't say that with George on your chest!"

She yawned again. "He's asleep. And only two years old. So, yes, I can."

"Well, I'm not thinking about having a three-way with them or anyone else. Just because the word *sex* is in homosexual doesn't mean all we do is shag. Come on, Aimee, you of all people know better than to fall for bigoted clichés."

"Sure, having Korean parents makes me a minority too, but not an expert on *your* minority. Not even hanging around with you since school makes me an expert on you lovely rainbow people and the confusing things you do."

"What are you on about? *We* do confusing things? Have you met your fellow heterosexuals? You're all confusing as hell. Actually, all humans are."

There was a groan on the line. "Of course. God, listen to me. Sorry, Kit! I'm still half-asleep and letting my mouth run on by itself."

"Yeah, I figured. Look, are you sure I shouldn't let you get back to sleep? You sound like you're half comatose and half depressed."

"No. I'm fine. Please stay on the line. I want to talk to you. I miss you. It's not the same here without you. I'm trying to juggle work and looking after George with an absent ex and parents who say I 'need to learn to look after myself' and consequently won't help me or even listen to me vent. You're all I've got."

"Oh, Aimee, I'm so sorry to hear that. Haven't you made new friends? Ones that have kids, too, and can relate? Maybe even help out?"

"A few. But they're more acquaintances. I don't have the energy to socialise."

"I can't believe John won't help you with George."

Aimee sighed. "He says that paying child support is all the help I can ask of him since he didn't want to have kids in the first place. Which we both know isn't true."

"God, he's a bloody nightmare. He never deserved you."

"Hm. You're a sweetheart. Speaking of men you feel don't deserve your friends... have you met this Dylan?"

"Nope," Kit said. "Not yet. I'm meeting him tomorrow, though. At Howard Hall, in something called the games room."

"Ah. I think that's where the murder took place. It was Mrs Peacock in the games room with the candlestick."

"Aimee!"

"Sorry! It's not my fault your life sounds like a game of Cluedo these days."

"Shut up."

"With the risk of sounding like a fourteen-year-old… *you* shut up."

"I told you to shut up first, Aimee."

At that moment, Rajesh walked by and pointed to Kit's phone. "You should both shut up, because you promised me you'd help me ten minutes ago."

Kit gasped. "Bloody hell, I did, didn't I? Oops. Aimee, I'm going to have to go."

There was a stifled yawn on the line. "Sure. I'll try to get myself and this disease-carrying child of mine off the sofa and into our beds. Call me if there's more gossip."

"I will. Thanks for listening. I hope you get some sleep and that you don't get as overwhelmed at work tomorrow. Oh, and if the finance situation gets out of hand, I can always lend you a few quid."

"I'll keep that in mind. Thank you. Bye, love."

Kit said goodbye and hung up. Rajesh was scratching Phyllis behind the ears, pointedly facing away.

"Raj. Sorry about that. I forgot you wanted help."

He still looked hard-done by. "Rajesh. Not *Raj*, remember?" He grunted. "I only need you to bring the slow cooker down for tomorrow's dinner, so I can use it first thing in the morning. You know how that heavy thing wreaks havoc on my old back. Oh, and peel the carrots and potatoes to go in it with the beef joint. Because that's too dull for me."

"Wow. You do know how to make a lodger feel right

at home." Kit grinned at him and got him to smile back. "Anyway, I'll happily do those jobs. I have a podcast I wanted to catch up on anyway, so I can do the peeling while I listen to the last couple of episodes."

"A pod person?"

"No, a podcast. It's a... you know what? Never mind. I'll go get the slow cooker down first." She began walking towards the kitchen.

"Katherine."

She turned. "Yes?"

There was a low scraping noise as Rajesh rubbed his unshaven chin. "Be careful when getting involved in this Howard-Stevenson affair. It might seem silly, but there's real emotion at the bottom of this. If you upset the wrong people, they could make life on this island pretty rubbish for you."

She took this in before asking, "Is that what you do? Make sure to never pick sides?"

"Yes. People here bicker and hold grudges over the daftest things. It's like a small town but even more isolated, meaning everyone knows what everyone else does. Add in that far too many people are bored and want to stir up trouble and you have a powder keg. You and I are counted as outsiders. We should keep our heads down and stay neutral."

"Look," Kit took a deep breath, "I don't want to step on any toes here. But Laura's a sweet person who only wants to keep her job, family, and home while loving who she wants. As someone whose love life would've been illegal and seen as a sickness a few decades ago, this matters to me. If I end up being gossiped about, ostracised, or used for target practise by mini-golf players, so be it."

He hummed, rubbing his chin again. "I suppose you have a point. I've seen my fair share of injustice in matters of the heart. People here weren't exactly happy back when a young Rajesh Singh started dating their white daughters. Obviously, you should help. Do what's right, and all that."

Kit took in his solemn face and nodded. She started towards the kitchen again but was stopped by him adding, "Make sure to be clever about it, poppet. Don't ruffle too many feathers. Look at what happened to Charlie Baxter."

Kit stopped, stifling a smile. "Okay. I'll bite. What happened to Charlie Baxter, Rajesh?"

He visibly perked up. "Remember the Derrick-Smith feud I told you about?"

"The one about who gave someone an STD?"

"In a nutshell, yes. You see, in the early nineties, Charlie Baxter decided to help mediate and—" Rajesh stopped to burp loud enough to wake Phyllis.

Kit rolled her eyes. "Excuse you. Anyway, Charlie mediated."

"No, he didn't. He tried, but he never got that far," Rajesh said dramatically.

"What? You're not trying to tell me they ran him off the island or something?"

"No. They stopped him by the use of his own wheelbarrow."

Kit placed her hand on her furrowed brow. "They… what?"

"Both the Derricks and the Smiths would agree to meet up and let him mediate. But every time he left his house to go to the meeting place, there it was. The wheelbarrow. His own wheelbarrow."

"Uh. I'm going to need more information."

Rajesh looked at her as if she was dense. "They kept

placing it outside his door, you see. Often blocking the door so he couldn't get out. Usually it was filled with things. Like the contents of his desk at his office. Or stones with little faces on them. Or pictures taken of him at a local rugby match. Well, that last one only happened once but still…"

"It was vaguely and weirdly menacing. Yes, I get it. Did he report it to the police?"

"No, not much they could do. The Derricks and the Smiths would all blame each other. And I'm not even sure that it was either of those families. That's my point, there are people on this island who get involved with spats simply because it's fun or passes the time."

"Question. Why didn't he get rid of the wheelbarrow?"

"He did. Took it to the dump once. The miscreants recovered it and left it by his door again. This time with bags of rubbish taken from the dump."

"Well, that's icky. Next question. Why the wheelbarrow?"

Rajesh held out his hands. "Who can say? Although, why not the wheelbarrow?"

"Right. Okay. Sure. Man, this island takes the prize for most random stuff." Kit ran her hand through her hair. "Fine, I'll be careful. Also, I'll never buy a wheelbarrow."

"Good thinking."

"I'll go get the slow cooker down now, shall I?"

"Absolutely," he said with a smile.

As Kit walked away she wondered how much of Rajesh's stories were true. And if she really wanted to know. These stories were more fun when you believed they actually happened on a daily basis on Greengage.

I suppose one day I'll find out, if I keep living here. Maybe that'll be the day I figure this place out.

Chapter Seven

DARLING, DASHING, DIM DYLAN

Tuesday night came around. There's no stopping Tuesday when it gets going.

It had been a warm night, so Kit was carrying her leather jacket under her arm when she rang the doorbell at Howard Hall. The second Laura opened the door, she reached out and grabbed the jacket. Then she gave Kit a quick hug and air kisses.

"Hello, you! I'll hang this up and then we better hurry downstairs. Aunt Sybil's on the warpath. Our cook, Mrs Smith, made a pasta dish tonight and it was served al dente. Aunt Sybil hates chewy pasta."

"I'm gonna go out on a limb here and say Sybil hates everything."

Laura linked their arms and led the way. "Not true. She loves Gage Farm. Isambard Kingdom Brunel. Watercolours of Provence. Oh, and scaring people."

There was a crash from upstairs, sounding like shattering china or possibly glass.

They both looked up and then Laura sighed. "Ignore it. Dylan's waiting down in the games room."

She guided Kit down the fancy hallway and through a creaking door. Wooden stairs led into a dimly lit room with a sofa, a coffee table, a couple of cabinets, and various sport and games equipment. Kit spotted croquet mallets and tennis rackets mounted on the wall ahead. As they descended the stairs, Kit could smell leather, wood, and a faint hint of damp. She shivered, wondering if she should've kept her jacket on.

A sizeable man drifted over, extended his hand, and said, "You must be Kitty."

"No, Dylan. *Kit*," Laura corrected. She smiled at him, almost maternally. Then she started back up the stairs, saying, "Excuse me for a moment. I'm going to fetch the snacks. You two get acquainted."

Kit shook Dylan's hand. He had a firm handshake but a slightly far-away expression. Kit took in the muscular build, the long, honey-coloured hair, a square jaw, perfectly even, white teeth, and soulful brown eyes. She tried not to be annoyed by how pretty he was. Dashing, that was the word they used for guys like this, right?

Dylan studied her. For a moment he looked as if he was about to say something deep and poignant. Instead what came out was, "How do your glasses stay together?"

Kit flinched. "Excuse me?"

"Your glasses. They have no… frames."

"Um. They're rimless. They're still attached to the metal bit that goes over my nose and the bits that go behind my ears, though."

"Yes, I understand how they stay on. But how do the glass parts keep from disintegrating without something containing them?"

Kit stared at him. What the hell? Was he joking? Was this some sort of philosophical Zen thing, like what one hand clapping sounds like? She wondered if she should explain that glass wasn't air or gas. Or if she should reassure him that the glasses they were probably going to have drinks from were unlikely to lose their shape and float out into space. Rajesh had mentioned that the Howards and the Stevensons sent their kids away for higher education in some of the best schools on the mainland. And Dylan used words like "disintegrating." How could he not get how glass didn't break apart without metal keeping it together?

"What are we talking about?" Laura asked as she came back down.

Kit sighed with relief at not having to explain. "My glasses."

Laura smiled. "Ah. They're cute. Subtle but with that librarian chic to them. They suit your face. Although, with that face, what wouldn't suit?" She said casually. As if she had only pointed out that the sky was blue and not given Kit a compliment which made her tingle all over. "Anyway, drinks, anyone? There's a cabinet down here which serves as a makeshift bar, and I brought ice and snacks."

"Yes please," Kit said, trying to sound unaffected. "I'll have anything with vodka in it."

"Brandy for me, babe. As usual," Dylan said, putting his hands in his pockets.

Laura looked up from the bags of crisps and peanuts she was placing on the table. "I was rather hoping you'd play bartender as I'm setting up the snacks, dear. Please?"

He looked at her as if she had said that the earth was flat. "What? Oh. Ah. Yes. I suppose I can. Where are the drinks?"

"That top cabinet over there." She nodded to the right. "By the snooker table."

He sauntered off, hands in pockets and eyes fixed on a framed black-and-white picture of what looked like an old cricket team. Kit would've guessed that it was from the early 1900s from the players' appearances. Dylan was squinting at it as if it were telling him a riddle, meaning he passed the drinks cabinet. He doubled back and opened the cabinet door. Inside Kit could see four big bottles, two of white alcohol and two with brown. Next to them were a couple of small tonic bottles which looked dusty and a stack of glasses.

"Cute little booze collection," she said to Laura. She couldn't help putting on her best posh accent to add, "Was that for when your dearest grandmama got too parched from playing croquet and lemonade simply wouldn't do?"

"Oh, ha ha," Laura droned. "Actually, my father used to play darts with his friends down here. The drinks were partly for them, but mainly for my mother, who came with them but usually got bored and settled down on that sofa over there, with a double gin and a good book. She always said she had to stay to keep score as they were all terrible at math and too busy gabbing to remember who was winning."

Kit chuckled. "Your mum sounds like my kind of woman."

Pensively, Laura picked up the bag of peanuts. "Mother was everyone's kind of woman. Capable and smart but always kind. I try my best to emulate her." She sighed. "Sometimes that makes the loss more bearable, sometimes it makes it worse." Laura began struggling with the bag. "Blasted thing. I've always been rubbish at opening these."

Kit held out a hand. "Here, let me."

"Thank you. Take your time. Darling Dylan seems to

have been distracted by that photo of the cricketers again. He's got such a dreamy disposition. A real *artist* in temperament."

Kit handed back the opened bag. "Mm. Meanwhile, as a real *librarian* in temperament, I'd like some booze."

Laura laughed. "I like your mean streak."

"Mean is such an ugly word," Kit said. "Let's call it playful."

Laura raised her eyebrows but didn't have time to answer as Dylan bellowed, "Look! I found the drinks. Do I bring them all over?"

Without even a hint of sarcasm or irritation, Laura replied, "Don't shout, darling. Aunt Sybil might come down here. And, no, thank you. Take three glasses. Fill one with about two fingers of vodka, one with one finger of gin and the third with however much brandy you want. Oh, and a bottle of tonic for my gin, please."

He looked at her. "Wait. Too much information. Say again but slower. Also, what do you mean by fingers? How do you measure anything with fingers? Is that like feet?"

Kit couldn't stand anymore of this. "Hang on, mate, I'll come help you."

As Kit set off towards him, she saw Laura mouth "thank you" to her.

Fifteen minutes and one vodka later, Kit swallowed her mouthful of crisps and said, "Everyone ready to start planning?"

Laura put down her drink and sat forward on the sofa. "Yes. Go for it."

Dylan was busy reading the back of the peanuts bag

with his lips moving. Slowly, and without turning her gaze away from Kit, Laura took the bag out of his hand and repeated, "Go for it."

"Okay. As we discussed before, Laura, we want Sybil to believe that Dylan has left the Stevenson clan behind and that he wants to work and live here."

Finally, Dylan paid attention. "Exactly! I'm going to sacrifice everything for love, like a true hero and English gentleman. Don't let them say romance is dead while Dylan Stevenson still draws breath."

Kit was taken aback by his sudden fervour. He emptied his glass and sat back with his arms along the back of the sofa, looking like he had solved a tricky problem.

"Yeah. Great," Kit said slowly. "Anyhow, I have a suggestion on how to go about that. I talked to Rajesh about this and he keeps saying that Sybil likes flashy young men who compliment her. We'll stay on that theme and keep it simple. Dylan, you need to win Sybil over by charming her. Try to look as dashing and manly as you can when you come for the chat. Then play on her vanity and total belief that the Howards are superior to the Stevensons. When you come in here and—"

Dylan pointed to the floor. "What, here?"

"She meant Howard Hall in general, dear. Let her finish," Laura said.

Kit took a deep breath. "As I was saying, you need to come here and ask to speak with Sybil. Tell her that you've had a major quarrel with your family. Say that you told them that you wanted to be with Laura and be part of the Howard family, which you've realised is much better than the Stevenson one. That you can't wait to be on the winning team. Then—"

Dylan held up a hand and then stood. "Wait, I'm going to go fetch the brandy bottle. I need to stiffen the spine and enrich the blood for my future heroics."

They waited. Kit caught Laura glancing at her, and they smiled at each other.

When Dylan returned, Kit picked up where she had left off. "So, yes. Lay it on thick. It might seem unlikely to us, but as Sybil's so stubborn, proud, and buried in this ancient feud, she'll probably buy it."

He creased his forehead. "Hang on."

Duly waiting, Kit fished out an ice cube from her drink and popped it into her mouth.

"This is rather convoluted," Dylan mumbled. "I feel like I should have been writing this down. Laura, should I have been writing this down?"

"No, dear." Laura stroked his knee. "I'll remember. Plus, you and I will practice it all before you talk to her."

His brow creased further. "Huh? Surely you can't remember all that."

She patted his knee again. "I can. Don't worry. Let Kit finish."

Kit chomped through the ice cube to take out her frustration on how slow going this was. "Yeah, so, you need to compliment the Howards and Gage Farm. Pushing on how great things have been since Sybil's been in charge. Tell her that it'd be an honour for you to start at the bottom of her company and perhaps one day be worthy enough to be part of her family. If you hit the right nerve and keep piling it on, that should work."

Laura bit her lip in her adorable, pensive way. "Yes, it probably will. Aunt Sybil is simply dying for people to dislike the Stevensons and praise the Howards. If you make it seem realistic, she'll eat it up!"

"Hopefully, yes," Kit agreed. "Then I bet she'll give you menial tasks to do, Dylan. Do them as well as you can and keep sucking up to her. Prove your loyalty to Gage Farm. Try to continuously look young and masculine since she has a weakness for that. And, you know, impress her in any way you can."

He nodded while pouring himself another brandy. "I can do the looking young and masculine. No one ever believes I'm over thirty, and I know how to look like a real man. The menial tasks might be harder, but I'll do my best. Anything to be with my ladylove."

Kit almost choked on what was left of the ice cube. "Mm. Great. So that's where we'll start." She turned to Laura. "I suggest you lay low with the relationship angle. Ensure that Sybil starts to appreciate Dylan first and let her bring up your romance. That way she'll feel like it was her idea and she'll be more likely to back it. Then you agree with her, thank her, and start talking about making the Stevenson heir a Howard. Stealing their golden boy and such."

"She'll love that! You're not only a good listener, but a good judge of character, too," Laura said with a grateful smile. "Thank you."

Kit hoped those rosy cheeks of hers weren't getting pinker. "Don't mention it. I said I'd help, so I will. The world can be really unfair, so I like it when I can help right something that's wrong."

Laura seemed to hesitate. "I hate to bring this up, but what if something goes wrong? If Aunt Sybil refuses to listen to Dylan or doesn't believe him if she does let him speak?"

Kit hummed. "I thought about that. There's always the risk that she might think he's a spy. Or that it's a double bluff and that when she's given your relationship her approval, you'll both go off to live with the Stevensons and run South Gage Farm."

Laura sat back and gulped her gin and tonic, looking at Kit as if someone had stolen her kitten.

Kit reached out to put a hand on her arm. "I'm sure that won't happen. Remember, Sybil *wants* to think that everyone would want to leave the Stevensons to become a Howard. Plus, she'll be blinded by an attractive young man ramping up the charm to full volume."

Laura put the glass down, smiling again. "You're right. Of course."

Kit withdrew her hand, unsure of how touchy-feely Laura was with friends. "Anyway, I'll be there with a new plan if this doesn't work. And if you keep me in the loop, we can keep tweaking this one as we go."

"Smashing!" Dylan bellowed before pouring himself a third large brandy.

I'd almost forgotten he was here, Kit thought. *Considering how she jumped, so had Laura.*

He downed his brandy and mumbled, "I'll come by to charm the old biddy tomorrow night."

"And after he's done that I'll contact you to let you know how it went," Laura said to Kit.

"Great. Okay, I think I'll call a taxi and head back to Rajesh's then."

Laura edged forward. "If you want some fresh air and company, we could all take a walk. Or we could dig up some of the old bicycles from the garage? Either way, we'd sober up for work tomorrow and make sure you get home safely in one go."

Dylan hiccupped, eyeing the bottle as if he was considering another drink.

Kit gazed from his pale, drunken face to Laura. "Nah, that's okay. I'm pretty tired so I'll take a taxi this time. We'll save the moonlit bike ride."

Preferably for a night when Darling, Dashing Dylan isn't here.

"All right," Laura said. "I'll ring for a taxi. You have to let me pay for it, though."

Before Kit had time to argue, Laura had stood to the side and was tapping on her iPhone.

Dylan leaned over to Kit. "So. Are you going to come clean?"

Kit stiffened. *Crap! Has he noticed my attraction to Laura?*

Maybe Dull Dylan wasn't so dim after all. Her pulse picked up. She looked over at Laura who was now talking to the taxi company and luckily not paying attention to them.

Kit focused back on Dylan. "What do you mean?"

"You know, about how your glasses stay together?"

The tension drained, and Kit rubbed her forehead. "Uh. Laura will explain it to you when I've gone home, mate."

He stared into space. "Mm. She'll have to be quick about it. I feel inspiration coming on." He hiccupped again. "I must paint tonight!"

That's not inspiration, that's a bunch of brandies in quick succession.

"Great. Good luck with that," Kit said.

Laura came back to the sofa. "The taxi should be here any moment. They said it was a quiet night."

"Good," Kit said on an exhale.

She really didn't want to be here when Laura had to explain the glasses thing.

Chapter Eight

GONE IN A FLURRY OF AUBURN

The sun did its usual trick of setting and rising repeatedly, meaning it was now a few days later. Kit was busy locking up the library and saying goodbye to Rajesh when a knock on the window interrupted them.

Rajesh peered through it. "Ah, it's Little Laura Howard. Go ahead and let her in while you lock up. You can use the company, and she needs someone to make her stand up to her aunt."

Kit immediately began to primp her hair. "Laura's here?" She squeezed her lips together to make them redder. "She's early. We were meant to meet outside after closing and head straight for the pub." She paused to give Rajesh a recriminating look. "And Laura's not little. She's my age."

He nodded. "Twelve."

"Late twenties or early thirties!"

She made a mental note to ask Laura about her exact age.

"Whatever you say, Katherine." His grumpy exterior briefly slipped into a smile as he put his coat on. "Well, I'm off, then. I'm going to read *Bleak House* to Phyllis."

"Sure, we all know dogs love Dickens. Have fun. I might be home late."

He waved his hand at her as he left. "Don't be home at all. Charm some lady somewhere. Get lucky."

With that he walked out the door while holding it open for Laura, who stared after him. "Did he just say…"

Kit winced. "Yep. He also thinks we're twelve. I had to tell him our actual age. Well, mine at least. I'm thirty this year. I guessed you were about my age? Maybe a little younger?"

Laura clapped her hands. "Woohoo! I'm not the only one turning thirty this year then. We should have a joint thirtieth birthday party. You invite all your Londoners over and I'll get the whole island to attend."

Kit tensed and punched the computer's off buttons. "Yeah, um, that doesn't sound like my kind of thing. Also, I really can't afford it."

"All right, that's fine. You can come to my party and I'll make a special toast in your honour. And have an extra cake with books on it. When's your birthday?"

"May."

"Mine's in June, so there you go!"

"Cool," Kit said distractedly.

Counted up the till. Put the money in the safe. The computers are off. There's no people hiding behind the shelves to be locked in the library overnight. What's left to do? The lights, the locks, and set the alarm.

"Are you okay, Kit?"

"Huh? Sorry, I was going through the list of closing-up procedures to make sure I've done everything."

"Don't apologise. You take your job seriously. I admire that in a person. I appreciate the dedication you seem to put into everything you do, whether it's work or helping people."

"Thanks," Kit said while trying to hide her puzzlement. Did this woman always compliment people so profusely or was it only with her that Laura was this full of praise?

As Kit saw to the final parts of locking up, Laura followed her around, talking about what had happened on Gage Farm that day.

"Aunt Sybil doesn't think the colours for the new label design work, but I'll convince her. We need a change. Sure, an old British fruit farm needs to have that homemade, old-fashioned feel. But we need it to look vintage, not shabby. The hipsters need to think it looks cool."

"I think you're right. You'll convince her in the end if you stick to your guns," Kit said while switching off the lights.

They stepped outside, and as Kit fiddled with the locks and the alarm system, Laura kept talking.

She does that a lot. Natters on without a reply. Doesn't matter, I could listen to her for days on end.

Laura had a soft, warm voice with the slightest hint of an accent, which reminded Kit that she wasn't in London anymore. Very pleasant to listen to. Perhaps a little too pleasant, Kit realised as she was closing her eyes to listen closer.

"Oh, I almost forgot the most important thing!" Laura exclaimed. "Dylan came over this morning to tell Aunt Sybil he's leaving the Stevensons and South Gage Farm. I was there. She seemed unsure and asked him to come back after lunch. He said he'd ring me tonight for an update." She checked her wristwatch. "Sometimes he forgets, but surely he'll call soon. He wouldn't forget something that important even if he's painting or anything—" She stopped mid-step and mid-sentence. "Gosh, listen to me babbling on. You haven't gotten a word in edgewise for yonks!"

"Hey, don't worry about it," Kit said softly. "I want to hear what's on your mind. Besides, I like your voice."

Laura surveyed her. "And I like how honest you are. You simply say what's on your mind. Well, at least if it's something nice."

Aha! Here's your chance to dig further into what Laura's compliments mean.

Kit put the library keys in her bags and mumbled, "Yeah, it sometimes gets me in trouble with straight women who worry I'm hitting on them. It can be tricky to know what is merely being complimentary and what is flirting, I guess?" She glanced at Laura, trying to spot a reaction. Laura only chuckled as if it had all been a funny anecdote.

No luck. I'll have to drop it for now.

Kit stepped away from the door. "Anyway, you were saying that Dylan is trying out the plan today?"

"Yes. As I said, I was there for his breakfast performance but not the lunch one. He did quite well this morning. My coaching seems to have helped. He remembered what to say and managed to put some real emotion in it. He perhaps... went a little overboard with the dramatic flair and flowery language."

Kit put her rucksack on. "Mm. He seemed to do that a bit when I met him. The 'stiffen the spine and enrich the blood' and 'true hero and British gentleman' stuff sort of caught me off guard."

Laura rubbed the back of her neck. "I suppose it's his artistic personality. He's very into tales of chivalry and love conquering against all odds. Not at all like other men around here. Which I think was one of the draws for me."

"Oh, was that what the draw was?"

"Partly that. It's all about the romance with him, not just sex and all that. Also, I suppose knowing him since childhood makes him the epitome of safety. Although, perhaps the forbidden nature of the relationship makes it a bit exciting, too. I wonder if that's why it survived being secret for so long." She looked up at the sky. "I don't know. Tom says my affection for Dylan is simply my way of rebelling against Aunt Sybil, but that's silly."

"Hm. Well, either way. I'm glad you're happy with him."

"I will be happy when I can have it all. Gage Farm, Howard Hall, and Dylan."

"Sure."

They strolled on, listening to a dog barking in the distance.

Out of the blue, Laura adjusted the shoulder strap of Kit's bag. "I like your rucksack."

"Thanks. My best friend Aimee says it makes me look like a student."

"Really? I think it makes you look like you are well prepared."

"I am. This thing," Kit reached back to pat her rucksack, "is full of books, pens, dried fruit mixes, medicines, tissues, a water bottle, hand cream, and my emergency perfume."

Laura steered their walk towards the town centre. "Your bag contains an emergency perfume?"

Kit kept the pace, happy that they were both quite short so they had the same step length. "Yep. I used to commute a lot and there's always that moment when you're not as fresh as you'd like or someone in your train carriage smells like cigarettes."

"I see. What's the perfume?"

Kit looked down at her shoes and scuffed one against the pavement. "It's, um, a bit of a strange choice for someone who's never had much cash. But, as I don't wear a lot of perfume or jewellery or stuff like that, I splurge on this *one* thing."

Laura eyed her. "Well, that settles it. Whatever the fragrance is, I'm buying you a big bottle for your birthday. What is it?"

"Voyage d'Hermès."

"Hermès?" Laura whistled. "You're right, certainly not a budget brand. I've never tried that one."

"It's unisex and smells of gin and… cardamom, I think it was. Either way, I love it," Kit said while fishing the perfume out of her bag. "Here." She handed Laura the bottle.

Laura flipped the silver top and sniffed it. "Can't really smell it. Hang on." She sprayed a little on Kit's neck, making her squeak in surprise.

"Hey! Spray yourself!"

"Can't," Laura said. "I'm wearing another perfume. Now stand still for a second so I can smell it."

She grabbed Kit's arm and gently tugged her closer so she could sniff her neck.

Kit's breath halted in her chest. She hoped Laura couldn't see how the little hairs on her neck were standing up. Or the goosebumps.

Laura let go and said, "I like it. I think you're right about the cardamom. Warm, spicy, sweet smell."

Kit was suddenly tongue-tied. As always when attractive women touched her.

Well, no, not always.

Only when she didn't know where she stood with the woman in question.

Or when the woman in question held Kit's libido in a gentle but firm grip.

She glanced over at Laura who had returned to sauntering along. A man on the other side of the street called her name, and she turned to wave at him, all smiles. The air was damp, promising rain, and it had made Laura's curls take on a life of their own. Kit could see strands frizz up and leave the clearly hair-sprayed shape they had been in a few moments ago. She resisted the urge to try to smooth them down.

Laura turned back to her. "Only two more streets until we're at Pub 42. Have you thought about what you fancy for dinner?"

Kit pushed her glasses up. "I'm not fussy. The quesadillas you mentioned sound good."

"Splendid. If you don't see anything you like on their limited menu, there's a tiny Indian place right opposite. And as you've surely noticed, three fish-and-chip shops dotted around the town centre."

Kit held up a hand. "No to the chippy's. I've had way too much fish and chips since I moved here."

"I see your point. I've had too much of it lately, too. Darling Dylan's guilty pleasure is battered plaice."

"It's always *Darling* Dylan," Kit noted. "You seem absolutely batty about him."

Laura smiled. "How could I not be crazy about him? He's my partner." She ran her hand over her frizzing curls. "And he's so unique. I can't fathom what he sees in someone like me."

"What do you mean?"

Laura wrapped her arms around herself. "Well, you know. I'm a workaholic with a need to please everyone, and I have freakishly big frizzy hair, pudgy cheeks, and… there's the weight thing."

Kit stopped so fast she nearly lost balance with her heavy rucksack. "Whoa. There's so much I want to argue about there, but I have to start with the last point. What *weight thing*?"

"Oh, you know…" Laura stopped, too, but wouldn't face Kit. "Dylan is this muscular, Greek god with zero-percent body fat who works out at least once a day and I'm… like this."

"What? A bit curvy?"

Laura frowned. "Chubby on the way to overweight."

"You. Are. Not. You're a healthy weight with smashing curves. Possibly, at a stretch, you have a little extra to get you through a cold winter. Which is certainly not a bad thing. Take it from someone who also has little body fat and works out a lot – you're perfect. Most fit women would kill for your softness and curves, please don't wish them away."

Laura surveyed her while brushing curls away from her face. "Crikey. You really *are* good with the compliments."

"And you're adorable for saying 'crikey,'" Kit said, giving Laura a friendly shove with her shoulder.

"Shush, you. I'm posh and from an island stuck in time. Of course I say crikey. I say blimey, too."

Kit pointed to her. "And 'gosh.' Don't forget that one, it's my favourite."

Laura looked down, almost hiding a smile. "Then you'll be happy to hear that I sometimes go all the way and say 'golly gosh.' Completely without irony."

"Be still, my beating heart!" Kit cried.

"Oh, shut up."

"Sorry," Kit said with a giggle.

She saw someone walking towards them. Was that one of the Derricks? The woman waved at Laura, who greeted her with her usual warmth.

When she'd passed, Kit whispered, "Can I confirm some crazy stories with you? I sometimes worry that Rajesh makes things up. Which is fine, I like a good yarn. But I need to know if that's all they are."

"Sure. Tell me one of his stories and I'll confirm or deny."

"Okay. Charlie Baxter trying to mediate in the Derrick-Smith family feud and ending up being vaguely and weirdly threatened with his own wheelbarrow?"

Laura tipped her head back and laughed. "That one's true, I'm afraid. We take our disagreements seriously on Greengage, especially ones regarding sexually transferable diseases. Right, the rest will have to wait if that's okay. Pub 42 is right over there and I'm starving."

Kit, still stunned that the wheelbarrow thing was legit, followed Laura. They headed inside and were met by a tall, dark-skinned butch woman somewhere in her late forties. She had a tray of empty plates that she was clearing off one of the pub's four tables.

She nodded toward them. "Hey there, Laura. You all right?"

"Great, thanks, Shannon. You?"

"Can't complain. Literally, I'm *too busy to complain*. Rachel is working behind the bar tonight. Go hug her and then tell her to stop schmoozing the customers and serve them instead."

Laura saluted. "Will do. Come over when you get a second and meet Kit. She's only been here for a few months and needs to be reassured that not all Greengage residents are geriatrics or absolutely bonkers. Or both."

"I make no promises about the bonkers bit, but sure," Shannon said with a grin. She rushed off with her tray.

Kit looked around. The pub was small but cosy, decorated in browns and greens with bronze details. Everything looked sparkling clean. There wasn't even the usual booze smell in the air, but instead a hint of something sweet, probably air fresheners.

When they got to the bar, Laura clutched the hand of the bartender and pulled her into an embrace while saying, "There you are, Rach."

Ah. This is Rachel, huh?

Kit surveyed the woman currently being squashed in a hug. She was shorter than Shannon and was light-skinned with ginger hair piled up in a complicated up-do. When the hug ended, Laura said, "Meet Kit Sorel. She's the new librarian I've mentioned."

"Aha. The famous new gay on the island," Rachel said.

Laura had the decency to look embarrassed. "That's not all I told you about her."

"No, it's not. In fact, you talked about her nonstop for about forty minutes the other night."

"Really?" Kit asked. "That must've been the dullest forty minutes of your life." She reached out a hand.

Rachel took it and gave it a quick shake. "Nah. Laura can be much duller than that. She once spent a whole dinner talking about Gage Farm's insurance costs. She likes to babble, you must've noticed that by now."

Laura took off her coat with a huff. "Must you be so rude? Kit thinks we're friends."

"We *are* friends. That's why we banter like this. And it's why your incessant chatting makes me happy and feel right at home. Like a babbling brook as background noise," Rachel said, placing a peck on Laura's cheek.

While Kit shrugged her jacket off, Laura muttered, "You should know that I now expect the quesadillas to be half off. Rudeness tax."

"Sure, pet," Rachel chirped. "You both want quesadillas?"

"I do. I'll leave Kit to order while I hang our coats." Laura headed for the hat stand with Kit's faded leather jacket and her own unblemished designer coat folded neatly on top of each other.

Rachel raised her eyebrows in query at Kit, who nodded. "I'd like the quesadillas, too. I hear this is the only place on Greengage where you can get them?"

"Yep," Rachel said as she went behind the bar again. "You can get fish and chips, chicken tikka masala, burgers, and pizzas in fifteen different places on this little island. But if you want something else… you have to take the ferry to the mainland or to Isle of Wight."

Shannon joined them. "It's a struggle. I get severe sushi cravings at times."

"I bet. I miss Thai food already," Kit admitted.

Laura came back, smiling. No, *beaming*.

Rachel beckoned to her and Kit. "Sit at the bar, ladies, so we can chat," she suggested. "The quesadillas are on the house. I'm afraid you'll have to pay for your drinks, though."

"Great, cheers for that. Have you got Diet Pepsi?" Kit asked.

Laura looked at her. "There's that Spartan drink of yours again. Don't you want something a bit boozy tonight? Or sugary? Something with more sweetener at least? Splurge a little, after all… we're eating out tonight."

"I wouldn't say *that* to this crowd," Shannon murmured, making Kit snigger.

Laura either didn't hear it or didn't acknowledge it. Her gaze was still on Kit.

"Hm." Kit scratched her head. "I know it's not a drink that screams *celebration*, but it's my favourite."

Laura's lower lip pouted out, and her eyes grew wide.

Kit shook her head, unable to keep from smiling. "Fine. Celebration it is. I'll order something with more sweetener. Do you guys have…" She trailed off when she saw Laura's face. Her lip was sticking out even further, and those hazel eyes seemed to widen even more.

Kit put her hand to her forehead. "All right, Puss in Boots! Enough with that face. I'll order a shot, too. What do you recommend, barkeep?"

"Depends on what your poison is," Rachel said with a laugh. "For example, Curly over here likes gin." She pointed to Laura.

"Don't call me Curly. But yes, I'll have a gin and tonic, Sipsmith if you have it. Kit will have a shot of your nicest vodka. I'm buying. Oh, and her sad *Diet Pepsi,* too."

Rachel bowed. "As you wish, your curly-ness." She turned to the bottle-filled shelves behind her.

"Thanks, Laura. Next round'll be on me," Kit said.

"I hope not. I'd really like to treat you tonight," Laura said distractedly, busy adjusting the collar of her paisley shirt over the V-neck of her jumper. "To thank you for helping Dylan and me."

"Stop thanking me. It was my pleasure to help."

Shannon came out from what was undoubtedly the kitchen with two plates of quesadillas. Right after that, Rachel served them their drinks.

They ate and drank in companionable silence. Kit only

burned herself on the supernova-hot cheese twice. Once on her tongue and the other when she dropped one of the quesadillas on her lap and had to try and scoop it up with her fingers before Laura noticed.

When they were finished, and Shannon had taken their plates back to the kitchen, Kit lifted her shot of vodka.

"Here's to you and Dylan. Let's hope he impressed your aunt today."

"Hope, pray, and pretty much beg the universe," Laura replied. They clinked glasses and Kit downed the vodka.

"Want a refill?" Rachel said, appearing out of nowhere.

Kit coughed. "Whoa, speedy. Give me a chance to digest the first one. I have to pace myself or I'll end up plastered and giving Londoners a reputation for being lightweights."

Rachel turned to Laura. "I like her. Good find. Let me guess, you met her when you dropped off one of those ridiculous welcome baskets?"

Laura took another swig of her G&T. "They're not ridiculous. But yes, that's how we met. Unlike the others I have given a basket, Kit and I started chatting right away and it was like we were already friends."

Kit was about to agree when Laura's phone started blaring out the theme song to *Jessica Jones,* loud enough to draw stares from around the pub.

"Oh! It's Dylan. I better take this." She walked off with her phone glued to her face.

Rachel grimaced at Kit. "So, what do you think of *Darling Dylan*?"

"Oh, thank god she doesn't only call him that in front of me," Kit groaned. "I was starting to think it was her way of saying 'no homo' to make sure I didn't hit on her."

Rachel waved that away. "Laura has self-esteem issues, she never thinks anyone hits on her. You're safe there, mate."

"You didn't answer the question, though," Shannon pointed out while wiping down the bar.

Kit played with a beer mat. "Dylan is… nice. Romantic. Obviously willing to give up his family, his cushy job, and his *inheritance* for Laura. Few people would do that at a drop of a hat."

Rachel and Shannon looked at each other.

"What?" Kit asked.

Rachel sucked her teeth. "Well, while you're right in that he is sacrificing a lot for their relationship, I'm not sure he's really thought about the repercussions enough to know what he's giving up. Stopping to think isn't something that he does. Things have always worked out for Dylan, meaning he doesn't know what failure or loss looks like."

"And what's more, the Stevensons aren't the Howards," Shannon added. "There's a reason the Howards ended up with Gage Farm. They tend to be more cut-throat. Dylan's family will be furious for ten years or so, but after that I bet they'll forgive him. His parents dote on him."

Rachel hummed her agreement. "He assumes that no one can dislike him for long. Plus, I'm pretty sure he expects Laura to provide for him no matter what. Sweet as she is, she's business savvy and can be a shark if she needs to be. He knows that and that she'd do anything to keep him happy, especially if he sacrifices his rightful place at South Gage Farm for her. Hard to believe, but he's not completely stupid."

Kit sat forward. "Wait. *Laura* can be a shark?"

Shannon topped up her Diet Pepsi while saying,

"Sure. While Sybil deals with the orchards, she leaves most of the business side to Laura. Marketing, finances, sellers, all that stuff. Sybil has no idea how much Laura does for the company or how she constantly battles the competition. Seriously, even entertaining the idea that Tom could run the company instead of her? Please."

Rachel laughed. "Tom can't run anything but his mouth off. Have you met him, Kit?"

"No. But I think I know the type."

"I'm sure you do," Rachel groaned. "Tries to look like a mix between an aristocrat and a rapper and ends up looking like a complete git. Spoiled little rich boy with mediocre looks and brains, who thinks he's entitled to everything without work or effort. Laura got all the good genes."

"You should know," Shannon said with a playful pout.

Kit pushed her glasses up. "Yeah, I heard that the two of you had a thing when you were younger?"

"Mm-hm. We were better as friends, though. Laura's great, but she's not my type." Rachel grabbed Shannon's waist and pulled her closer. "I prefer older women. With cute, short afros. Who own a pub and can get away with wearing a flannel shirt which is this tatty." She took hold of Shannon's shirt collar. "Seriously, there's the 'distressed look' and then there's the *distressingly shabby* look, babe."

They all laughed while Shannon protectively smoothed her washed-out flannel shirt.

"I have to admit, I'm so relieved to not be the only non-straight on the island," Kit said.

Shannon smacked her upper arm. "I know what you mean. Why do you think we went into business with the boys? It wasn't just to pool our cash for the down payment for this place. Outsiders have to stick together. Right, Rach?"

"Right as always, honey."

They kissed until Shannon broke it off to add, "Josh and Matt used to play rugby with Dylan, by the way. Until he decided that sports might end up injuring his painter's hands."

"Are you talking about Dylan?" Laura asked as she returned from her call.

"Yes. We were saying how *dreamy* and *perfect* he is," Rachel said before faking a swoon.

"Shush, you! I know he's not everyone's cup of tea. But he's my little lamb. That was him on the phone."

"We know," Rachel, Shannon, and Kit all said at the same time.

"Wow, didn't take you three long to get in sync," Laura said with a chortle. "Anyway, Dylan had some bad news, Kit."

Kit sat up straighter. "Okay. What?"

"The plan didn't quite work. He said that she seemed to be on the verge of taking him in and offering him a job, but at the last moment, she said she couldn't trust that he wasn't a Stevenson spy."

Kit slapped the bar. "Just what we feared. Bugger! Okay. Hm, Plan B time."

Rachel poured herself an orange juice. "I want to help. The idea is to make Sybil like Dylan, right?"

"Yes," Laura said, biting that tantalizingly plump lower lip of hers.

Kit tapped her fingers on the bar. "What we need is something they have in common. Something Dylan can use to make her interested in him. You know, to make her want to go out on a limb and give him a shot."

Shannon snorted. "I don't think they've got anything in common. Except privilege, Greengage, and Laura."

Something itched in Kit's brain. There was something that Laura had said in passing. It wasn't important at the time, but it was now.

Why does my brain do this? Remember the whole thing or don't remember it at all. Fragments are no bloody use!

Distantly, Kit registered that the others were talking about how different Sybil and Dylan were. She was still drumming her fingers against the bar and trying to remember what it was Laura had said. She needed clues to jog her memory. Where and when had she said it?

By the front door in Howard Hall. She was wearing a cashmere cardigan. She seemed nervous and happy at the same time. She took my jacket to hang it up. We spoke about Sybil and… watercolours!

Her fingers instantly stopped tapping. "Laura, did you say that your aunt likes watercolours of Provence?"

Laura stared at her. "Yes, I did, and yes, she does. Why?"

Kit banged her fist on the bar in triumph. "Because if you really like watercolours of a place and a certain painter suddenly starts to paint them. Or at least mentions liking them… wouldn't that give you something to talk about? Something in common?"

Laura's eyes widened. "Of course! Dylan can show an interest in watercolours. Perhaps even paint a set or two. Maybe going straight into ones depicting Provence would be a step too far, but he could work his way up to it."

Rachel clapped. "Brilliant! This calls for another vodka for our clever Londoner."

"Actually," Kit said. "Isn't it champagne time?"

Rachel scratched the back of her neck. "Um, I'm not

sure we have actual champagne right now. We're not that grand. We stock some cheap prosecco, though."

"Champ… I mean prosecco for everyone. My treat," Laura said, her eyes still fixed on Kit.

Rachel fetched bottles and started filling glasses. Shannon took them out to the bar's four tables. Everyone seemed surprised but happy to receive the free drinks.

Kit waited until Shannon was back and lifting up her own glass.

"Here's to watercolours!" Rachel shouted.

The four of them clinked glasses and sipped. Laura drank her whole glass in one go and then set the glass down in front of Kit with a gasp. "I shouldn't have downed that. Who downs Prosecco? I just got so excited."

"Don't worry. We won't judge," Kit said. She patted Laura's hand, certainly not noting how soft it was. Or that it was peppered with little freckles. Or how graceful it looked. Or how short Laura's nails were.

Kit breathed in rapidly. "Right. Back to the matter at *hand*. I, um, I mean the matter we should be dealing with."

"Yes, we know what 'the matter at hand' means," Rachel said with a confused frown.

Kit ignored it and kept talking. "What's the best way of going about this? Maybe Dylan should paint something? But then how would Sybil see it? It's not like he can simply stroll past her in one of the orchards with a watercolour under his arm."

Laura hummed. "No. I think bringing it up in conversation is better. How about this: tonight, I ask her how things went with Dylan. She'll no doubt tell me it went terribly. I then, without being pushy or whinging, say that I'm sorry to hear that."

She picked up the pace, warming to her theme. "I say that he's a great guy – not at all a Stevenson – and that he'll be wretched to be denied the chance to get to know the illustrious Sybil Howard. I'll add that he always admired how she ran Gage Farm and her, wait for it… collection of watercolours of Provence."

Kit played that out in her head. "That could work. As long as you don't make it too obvious. Perhaps add in a few other things he might admire before getting to the watercolours?"

"Yes!" Rachel exclaimed. "Like the leading role Sybil takes in the running of Greengage. She's in all those committees and is always trying to clean up some area or preserve another."

"And how she handles being the head of the Howard family," Shannon added.

Laura gave a thumbs up. "Those are all excellent. I'll make sure to use them."

"Be careful, though," Kit warned. "Like you said, no pushing or whinging. You don't want to pile it on too thick and seem like you're complaining about her decision to kick Dylan out. Don't annoy her."

"I'll find the right balance," Laura said. "As long as I'm not too drunk when I get home and have this chat."

It pained Kit to say it, but she knew it was the right thing to do. She pushed the nearest Prosecco bottle away and said, "With that in mind, I think we should call it an early night. Pick up the celebration another time."

Laura got up. "Probably best. I'm so excited! Thank you for coming up with a Plan B so quickly, Kit. You're brilliant!" She gave Kit a hearty peck on the cheek before pulling Rachel and Shannon into hugs over the bar. After that, she put far too many bills down, grabbed her coat, and rushed off with a promise over her shoulder to text Kit after the conversation.

After she'd gone, Kit looked at Laura's empty glass, feeling a strange fellowship with it.

"Whoosh. Gone in a flurry of auburn," Rachel said before finishing her glass of bubbly. She was clearly referring to the fact that Laura's designer coat and leather boots was the same dark reddish-brown as her hair.

"Women, huh?" Shannon said with a wink at Kit.

Kit blew out a breath. "Yeah. Well, at least she remembered to pay for the drinks."

Chapter Nine

SERIOUS PHONE TIME

T he next morning found Kit sitting behind the library counter and sneakily rereading the text Laura had sent the night before. Unaware of being found out by said morning, Kit read the message again.

> *Dearest, sweetest Kit,*
> *First of all, sorry for rushing off. I was incredibly jazzed about*
> *your clever plot (and perhaps a little tipsy.) Anyway, I talked*
> *to Aunt Sybil and her ears did prick up when I mentioned the*
> *watercolours. After that she seemed lost in thought for the rest*
> *of the night, even ignoring Tom's sucking up! We might be*
> *back in the game! I hope you had a good night with the girls*
> *and that you'll sleep well when you get to bed.*

Kit sighed as she read it for the fourth time.

Dearest, sweetest Kit.

She sighed again, more whingey this time and force-fully enough to make a Post-it note with some mystery phone number in Rajesh's handwriting blow away. She stared into space.

Who even says 'jazzed' anymore? Well, the same person who says blimey, I suppose. Argh, she's too bloody cute!

Kit hadn't stayed with "the girls" for very long. Shannon and Rachel had become busy serving the late-night clientele and Kit was still a little bothered by Laura's disappearance. She was even more bothered by the fact that if the roles were reversed, she probably would've run out, too. Love, relief, and gin would make you do that sort of thing. Still, it had upset Kit more than it should, and she was pleased that Laura had noticed her behaviour and apologised.

A new text came in from an unknown number. Kit opened it and read:

Hey Kit. It's Rachel. Relax, I'm not stalking you, I got your number from Laura. Nice to meet you last night! I'm texting cause I wanted to talk to you about something yesterday but chickened out. But it's important. And about Laura. Obviously. :) Can you ring me when you get a mo? Cheers!

Kit texted back that she'd call on her lunch break and then stared at the screen with her head tilted to the side. Important? About Laura?

"You're new."

The words broke the silence with a clear pang of incrimination. Kit shrugged off her reverie and made eye contact with an old lady in front of her. As much as she could at least. The woman had a knitted hat pulled down so far that it must've partially obscured her vision. In general, she was heavily dressed for April. Like she was challenging spring to dare inconvenience her.

Kit adjusted her glasses. "Excuse me?"

The lady pursed her lips. "It's not 'excuse me.' Or 'huh?' Or any other of these vile things you young people say. It's 'pardon'."

Kit put on her best customer-facing smile. "Okay. In that case… pardon?"

"I stated that you're new."

"Yes, I've only been here for about three months."

The wrinkle-framed lips pursed further. "Been here? As in worked here at the library or as in resided on Greengage?"

"Um, both."

"That makes sense. I've seen you here before. I come to the library twice a month. However, I haven't let you serve me. I've waited until you were in the back or out amongst the shelves. Then I've taken my books to Rajesh."

Kit swallowed down about fifty replies and settled for: "I see. Well, we do have self-service machines. In case you want the procedure to be quicker and don't want to talk to me or Rajesh. We really don't mind."

"Oh, you would like that, wouldn't you? Lazy lass. More time for you to be on your phone. That is why I came over to you now. To point out that it is a ghastly habit, especially at work."

Kit's cheeks burned. "Oh. Yeah. I'm so sorry. I normally never check my phone at work, especially not at the counter. This was an exception because I had something on my mind and the library was pretty empty. You're right, though. It's a bad habit, one I don't intend to pick up."

Please don't tell Rajesh. Please don't tell anyone. I need this job.

"I should think not! Put the contraption away. Because of your apologies and your honest face, I shall give you another chance at not disappointing me."

Kit forced her eyebrows to not rise. "Thank you... madam."

The lady's lips unpursed ever so slightly. "Mrs Baxter."

"How do you do, Mrs Baxter? My name is Kit Sorel," she said, pointing to her library badge. Then she registered the name. "Baxter? Any relation to Charlie Baxter?"

The lip-pursing returned with a vengeance. "Alas, yes. We won't talk about him."

Kit made a mental U-turn. "Right. Course we won't. So, can I help you with anything? Have you found any good books today?"

"Some. In the classics section. *Modern* books are dreadful. All violence, sex, politics, and YT."

Kit suppressed the counterargument over how many of the classics were about violence, sex, and politics and latched on to the abbreviation. "Did you say YT? I'm not familiar with that."

Mrs Baxter scowled with the intensity of a hundred suns. "YT. Young teens!"

"You, ah, you don't happen to mean YA for Young Adults?"

"I know what I mean. All these young women with purple hair who have demons for pets or mousy girls who end up having to save the world. Or sad, complaining boys who seduce other boys."

Sounds like she's read a few, though. Don't say that. You need her to like you enough not rat you out to Rajesh. More charm, Kit. More bloody charm!

"I might be able to find you a modern book that isn't just sex, violence, politics, or YA." In her head, Kit went through everything from recent bestsellers to Man Booker Prize winners and soon found that most of them had at least one of those components.

Mrs Baxter tut-tutted. "I can find my own books, thank you very much. Although, I should like you to do something about the man at the table over there."

Kit followed Mrs Baxter's steely gaze. "The long-haired man reading a Neil Gaiman book?"

"I don't care what he's reading. I care about how his odour fouls up the entire library. Bad things really do come in threes. This morning my milk had curdled, then I was forced to reprimand you on using your phone at work, and now… there's him. Handle that issue and my faith in you will be restored."

"We can't really police people's body odours, Mrs Baxter."

"It's not that he's unwashed. That I could put up with. It's that he smells sickly sweet. Probably that drug they smoke, grass, pop, or plod or whatever it's called. It comes in from the mainland, you know. This island used to be wholesome and clean. Now…" She looked Kit up and down. "All kinds arrive on the ferry."

Kit counted to ten in her head and weighed her options. There were limits for how much she could be asked to tolerate, and Rajesh would understand if she stood her ground. Right?

"Tell you what, Mrs Baxter. I'll go over and see if it's bad enough to warrant me asking him to sit farther away. But I doubt it will be. Perhaps we should all start practising the 'live and let live' motto a little?"

Mrs Baxter pulled herself up, and for a terrifying

moment, Kit thought she was going to let out an almighty scream. Instead she froze as another little old lady put her hand on her arm. "Mabel, dear. You're not troubling this lovely lady, are you? She's new, you know. And she has always been very sweet and polite when helping me."

The newcomer was of about the same age as Mrs Baxter, but shorter and with curled hair tinted powder blue. She looked familiar but not enough for Kit to place her. She smiled conspiratorially at Kit and said, "I'm the copy machine one."

Kit blinked at her a few times. "What? I mean, pardon?"

The second lady sniggered. "I'm the annoying old biddy who always needs you to help me with the copy machine, dear. Ethel Rosenthal."

Ah, that's where I recognise her from.

"I remember, Mrs Rosenthal. I've helped you copy reading lists for your book club, right?"

"Exactly. They keep wanting to read Agatha Christie novels over and over again. So I, and Mabel here, decided to take over the choosing process and give them extensive lists of books we could pick. Everything from *Wuthering Heights* to *Of Mice and Men*."

Kit refrained from pointing out to Mrs Baxter that those books contained sex, violence, and politics. Instead she asked, "And what did they pick?"

"Another Agatha Christie book," Ethel said. "They're hopeless."

"Dim-witted, annoying sows," Mabel muttered.

Ethel put a hand to her chest. "Mabel! That's terrible. Come along, we'll need to wash your mouth out with soap. Or at least get a few ginger biscuits in you to cheer you up." She looked over to Kit. "Not that she ever cheers up. Mabel's always like this. Entertaining, isn't it? We women are always told to be nice, accommodating, and pleasant. Then we get old and we can be whatever we wish. No one notices us or cares about us anyway."

Kit gaped at her. "I hadn't thought of that." She scrambled for something to say which wasn't condescending. "Well, I'm sorry you feel unnoticed, but I'm glad it gives you a kind of freedom."

"Me too, dear. Right then, Mabel, shall we go rustle up some biscuits?"

Mabel Baxter pulled her knitted hat down even further. "Yes. I'm tired of this place and the smelly men in it," she said, glaring at the long-haired reader.

Ethel giggled and pulled her friend towards the door.

After a moment of staring after the contrasting duo, Kit took some books out to shelve, passing the man reading the Neil Gaiman book. She smiled to herself as she recognised the scent as one of the new popular, unisex colognes. It had hints of grape, she figured. But certainly not of marijuana.

Sorry, Mrs Baxter. You'll have to direct your outrage elsewhere.

From behind her came a familiar voice. "Hello. I noticed you talking to our gruesome twosome. No, that's unfair, Ethel's lovely. She's just friends with one of the island's infamous battle-axes. Mabel Baxter used to terrify me when I was little. On a bad day, she still does."

Kit turned around and saw Laura standing there with a takeaway mug in her hand. The scent of strong coffee wafted forth as Laura blew on it with lips cherry red from some probably insanely expensive lipstick.

Kit's heart didn't so much skip a beat as forget how

beats worked. "Hey! What are you doing here? Shouldn't you be working?"

Laura glanced around. "Shh. Yes, but I was in town discussing prices with one of the pub owners who sells our juices and ciders and thought I'd pop in here to quickly say hello."

Kit hesitated. She'd been about to put her books down and hug Laura in greeting. Like she would with Aimee or other friends. She tried to remember if Laura was the hugging type and could recall embraces and air kisses.

You know she hugs, stop being so damn anxious around her.

Kit put the books down and embraced Laura, being careful not to bump the coffee mug. Laura smelled of the fresh, crisp outside air and faintly fruity. The latter was surely due to a perfume and not that she'd been out hugging the trees in the orchard? Her coat and cheeks were cold to the touch.

Kit stood back and said, "You feel chilly. Temperature taken a downturn?"

"Afraid so," Laura said with a sigh. "Some freezing winds to interrupt the balmy spring we've been having."

Kit picked the books back up. "Mind if I shelve while we talk? I don't have a break for another hour."

"No, go ahead. As I said, I'm only stopping by for a minute or two."

Kit read the Dewey decimal label on a book on Buddhism and then shelved it in its correct place. "So, your text said that Sybil reacted well to the watercolours thing?"

Laura swallowed a mouthful of coffee. "Yes, her ears pricked up like she was a Labrador hearing the dog bowl being moved. She didn't say anything, though."

"Great," Kit said, pointing a book at Laura. "A little at a time. It needs to happen slowly or it'll be too obvious and she'll catch on. Next, she needs to see Dylan and the watercolours together, I think. To connect the two."

"Mm. You're right. I'll think of a way to make that happen."

Kit walked to the next shelf to put another book in its home. "Great! What did Dylan say?"

Laura followed her, suddenly taking a long time sipping her coffee. "I… haven't spoken to him yet. He's not answering his phone. He probably got inspired yesterday and locked himself away to paint."

"Okay. Huh. I've never been an artist or anything else creative, but if I had someone like you loving me, I'd take a break from anything and everything to talk to you."

Laura caught her gaze. For a moment their eye contact seemed to convey something.

Something poignant.

Something vital.

Then Laura shattered the moment by staring down at her coffee and with strained cheeriness saying, "I'm meeting him for lunch tomorrow. Perhaps you'd like to join us? We can bring each other up to speed."

Kit gripped a book a little too tight. "Lunch. Yeah, why not? Our usual place?"

"Sounds great." Laura checked her watch, now completely back to her friendly, breezy self. "As great as it was to sneak in a visit, I really must get back. I have a meeting soon."

She leaned in and gave Kit a one-armed hug and an air kiss. Kit was taken by surprise and moved, making the kiss connect flush with her cheek. Laura's lips were warm, and her breath smelled of fresh coffee. Kit's heart forgot the whole beat thing again and needing reminding.

With a forced smile, Kit said goodbye to Laura and then focused back on the Dewey number of the book in her hands. Concentrating was impossible. Her cheek seemed to pulse with electricity where Laura's lips had been. She should rub at it to make sure Laura's lipstick hadn't smudged onto her, but she was strangely reluctant to wipe the kiss away. She stomped her foot and cursed herself.

Kit Sorel. You need to get laid. And you need to stop thinking about Laura.

When lunchtime came around it became impossible not to think about Laura. All because of that promised call to Rachel. Why was Laura suddenly everywhere in Kit's life? Kit squeezed her eyes closed, trying not to conjure up images of plump, cherry-red lips around a takeaway mug as she waited for Rachel to pick up the phone.

When she finally did, they had a couple of minutes of small talk about the weather and how everyone was doing.

Then Rachel coughed. "Let's get straight to the crux of the matter. I need to talk to someone about Laura. And after last night, it's clear that the person I should be talking to is you."

"Me? Why?"

"Because of how Laura behaves around you. How she looks at you."

"Uh, okay?"

"Just humour me and answer a question for me."

Kit pushed her glasses into place. "Sure. Shoot."

A beat of silence.

"Kit, does Laura strike you as… quite… well… gay?"

"Gay?"

"Yeah, as in *raging homo*. Or if not that, at least bisexual with a ninety-nine percent preference towards women?"

Kit burst out laughing. "Greengage's favourite little sweetheart? The woman who follows all traditional conventions and constantly frets about being what passes for 'normal' or 'wholesome' on this island? The woman who is tying herself in knots to get to marry a handsome, huge, hairy bloke?"

A voice at the back of Kit's mind added, *the woman who holds your gaze for too long? Who takes every chance to be around you? Who gives you intense compliments?*

Rachel sighed. "Yeah. That one. The one who is trying too hard to be what everyone expects of her. Trying to be what she thinks is, you know, ordinary. The one who mistakes caring for an overgrown child for romantic love."

"Overgrown child?"

"What else would you call Dylan? Look, Laura attached herself to him before she lost her parents, but after that, she clung on with both hands. Even though there seems to be no real love, passion, or even sense in it. She looks after him like a pet and he lets her. That's it. That's the relationship."

"I suppose I can see that," Kit had to admit.

"Meanwhile, there was plenty of passion when she dated me that summer when we were teens, despite it only being a quick crush. Her entire face lights up when she sees a beautiful woman, while sexy men leave her flat. And she's always been fascinated by my relationships with women."

Kit hummed, chewing the inside of her cheek.

There was a chuckle on the line. "And Kit…"

"Yeah?"

"There's also the teeny tiny fact that she's bonkers about you."

"What? Like romantically? No, I mean, she likes me as a friend. That's all," Kit spluttered.

"Mate, she looks at you the same way she looks at waffles with greengage jam and ice cream. Which, in case she hasn't mentioned it, is her favourite meal. I'm surprised she hasn't torn your clothes off and licked you from top to bottom yet. Seriously, I'd wear stuff with handy zips on if I were you."

Kit's phone nearly toppled out of her hand.

Rachel obviously couldn't see that and carried on talking. "That's why I wanted to talk to you about it. Not only does Laura seem to fancy you. She also respects and admires you. I think she might be falling for you, but she'd never let herself!"

Kit squeaked, but Rachel either didn't hear it or didn't want to acknowledge it.

"If you like her, too, Laura could be throwing away a chance for real love. All to spend her life supporting Dylan and trying to please Sybil. And all of blooming Greengage. She deserves better, but she doesn't know that. So, I'm asking if you agree that there is a huge chance that Laura Howard is so deep in the closet that her home address is Narnia. And that she's unwittingly crushing on you."

Kit blinked repeatedly. "I, uh, I mean…"

There was silence on the line for a while.

Rachel sucked in air between her teeth. "I've got to slow down, huh? Sorry, Kit. I didn't mean to spring all of this on you. It's just that the clock is ticking now that

Laura has gotten engaged and you're helping her relationship with Dylan along." She paused to groan. "I can't stand to see her tethered to him for life. I always thought she'd wake up one morning and go, 'Vagina! That's what I need this morning! Bye, Dylan!' But she never did. Then you came along, and she looked at you like you were waffles, like I mentioned, and—"

"And she's still forging ahead with the plan to marry Dylan," Kit broke in. "Doesn't that make you think that maybe she wants to marry him? Look, maybe she isn't straight, but in the end, she's chosen to marry Dylan. We have to respect that, right?"

"Not if it's a shitty idea and she's doing it for the wrong reasons. I love her like a sister, Kit. I can't let her make a giant mistake like this."

There was a shout in the background and Rachel groaned again. "Look, I have to go. Think about what I've said, okay? Mull it over and look for the signs when you next see Laura. Gotta go. Bye."

She hung up, leaving Kit shell-shocked and suddenly without an appetite for lunch.

That night, Kit was splayed out on the tatty sofa. Phyllis was snoring in her lap and Rajesh was singing along to his favourite Bollywood movie. They'd seen this one three times. Kit didn't mind, she loved the dancing. Besides, she was too tired from all the Laura drama and from running around in the library to focus on anything she hadn't seen before.

Kit's phone beeped. She picked it up and saw a text from Aimee.

Guess who just got off the phone with a mother complaining that George and I are sick too often and that we "need more vitamins and fresh air?" Yep, me. At least it makes a change from my dad repeating that I contact them too often and that I should be more autonomous. Shouldn't parents want you to talk to them a few times a week? I wasn't even calling to ask for help or advice, but just to see how they're doing. WTF? Am I being unreasonable here?

xo

Kit growled to herself, waking Phyllis who peered at her. She texted back.

No, you're not. They've always been harsh with you and pretty damn unhelpful but lately they seem worse than usual? Not to victim-blame, but have you upset them somehow?

She petted Phyllis with one eye on the movie and the other on her phone. Soon the reply came in.

Honestly? I think they might still be punishing me for the divorce. You know how much they liked John and how ashamed they are of having a divorced daughter with a kid and no real career. Still, no matter why they're being like this,

*it hurts. I want to have a good relationship with them,
especially for George's sake, but they make it so bloody hard.*

Kit looked at the text for a moment and then made her
mind up. "Rajesh. I'm gonna go call Aimee. Her parents
are being shitty."

He scowled. "Again?"

"Yep. Told you they were charming."

"Mm. Well, go call her, but I'm not pausing the movie
for you."

"I wasn't expecting you to, grouchy," she said fondly.
"I'll ring Aimee and then go to bed and read. Have a nice
night and I'll see you in the morning."

"Yes, yes. You, too. Now shush." He waved her away,
focusing on the movie.

As she walked off she heard him shout, "Katherine! Do
you think you'll be out any night this week? I'd like to
plan a date or two."

She chuckled. "I'm sure that can be arranged. We'll
talk over breakfast tomorrow."

"Fine. Sleep well so you can get up at a decent time
tomorrow."

"Sure. 'Night!"

When Kit was in her room, she clicked Aimee's name
in the phone's contacts list and waited. And waited.
Finally, Aimee answered.

"Sorry. I was in with George. He woke up from a
nightmare."

"No problem. Is he okay? Do you need to go back
in there?"

"Nope, he's asleep again."

Kit flopped onto the bed. "Good."

"Yep. How are you?"

Kit thought about bringing up her chat with Rachel but decided against it. They were supposed to talk about Aimee's troubles, not hers. Besides, as the hours had worn on, Kit had convinced herself that Rachel was wrong. She clearly disliked Dylan and so she probably filled in the rest of the story to have a reason to get Laura away from him.

Kit put on a cheerful tone and said, "A little grumpy at the thought that my sixty-something landlord has a more active love life than I. Otherwise I'm fine. What about you? Tell me about the call from your parents."

She burrowed in with her pillows and listened to Aimee pour her heart out. It was extremely hard to be so far from her best friend when she was this upset. That was something Kit hadn't foreseen when she moved to Greengage.

There were a lot of things she hadn't foreseen.

Chapter Ten

USE YOUR GAY LASER!

K it sat and surveyed Tea Gage, the greasy-spoon eatery masquerading as a cafe, which she and Laura usually went to for lunch. It was busy for a run-of-the-mill Thursday. Everyone on the island seemed to be here. Everyone but Laura. Kit checked her watch. Quarter past twelve.

Fifteen minutes late? That's not like Laura.

She sipped at the cup of tea she'd bought to tide herself over as she waited. Fours sips later, the bell above the door jangled, and from the corner of her eye, Kit could see a flurry of auburn.

Laura rushed over. "I'm so sorry I'm so monstrously late! First, I had to deal with an employee who's been caught stealing, and then when we were finally in town, we couldn't find a parking spot. Why is it so busy?"

Kit leaned back to accept a hug and a cheek kiss. "No idea. I hoped you'd tell me. Is there an event or something on today? There seemed to be a lot of people on the square. Oh, and who's 'we,' by the way?"

"Dylan and I. He had to park on the other side of the

square, so it's taking him a while to walk back here. He's very particular about where he parks his car."

"Ah. Let me guess, he's got a shiny, new BMW?"

It was good that Laura was busy unbuttoning her coat. It meant she didn't see Kit's rude facial expression.

Laura got the last button undone as she said, "Vintage Jaguar, actually. The vintage part is important. He says new cars have no soul and are only for the nouveau riche."

"Nouveau riche – that's the newly rich, right?"

"Yes. French expression. His words, not mine, of course. I'd quite like a new car. Safer and less likely to break down on me."

Kit only replied with a hum. She spun her cup round and round, making the tea at the bottom slosh. When she looked up, Laura was watching her.

"You… don't like him, do you?"

Kit shrugged. "He's not my type."

Laura raised her eyebrows.

"Well, yeah, he's not my type due to being a *bloke*," Kit acknowledged. "But also not my type of person. I see why he would be other people's cup of tea, though. He's good-looking, artistic, and romantic."

The bell above the café door jangled again to toll the arrival of the man in question. He sauntered over to them.

"Hello, ladies. I finally found a parking spot. Why is it so busy?"

"We don't know," Kit and Laura said simultaneously.

They smiled silently at each other, tickled by their synchronisation.

"Why are you looking at each other like that?" Dylan asked, breaking the mood.

Laura caressed his arm. "Perhaps we're simply happy to

see you? Do you mind ordering some food while we guard the table?"

His forehead furrowed. "Guard the table?"

"Yes, darling. To make sure no else takes it. Because it's so busy in here?"

His handsome face was as blank as a newly erased whiteboard.

Laura tilted her head. "You know what, never mind, I'll go. You stay here with Kit and keep her company. We shouldn't leave her all alone after making her wait for us. What do you want, Kit?"

"Um." Kit pulled on her ear. "Egg and cress on rye bread. And another cup of tea, please?"

"Good choice," Laura said, squeezing Kit's shoulder. "I think I'll have the same, but with Earl Grey. Dylan?"

He looked like he was about to ask what she wanted but then caught up. "Mineral water and a sourdough panini. Any filling as long as it doesn't give me bad breath. Wait, no, nothing too fatty, I won't have time to workout tonight. I feel a painting session coming on."

"Understood, darling. I'll be right back."

Laura went over to queue, leaving Kit and Dylan at the table. Kit sipped the last of her tea while he gazed out the window, face stoic, eyes vacant.

She waved in front of his face to get his attention. "So, a painting session coming on, huh? That's great." She leaned forward and whispered, "Going to do some watercolours to impress Sybil?"

He frowned. "No. When I feel a creative rush I want to use it to actually paint. I'm thinking—no, *feeling*—landscapes. Perhaps with a pale, blonde woman who's dying from scarlet fever in the centre. Or a duck." He nodded gravely as if something important had been settled. "I might do the watercolours afterwards. Luckily, Laura said I mainly have to *talk* about watercolours with Sybil. Which I should be able to manage."

"Watercolours aren't quite up to your artistic aspirations, then?"

He shook his head, making his long hair dance. "No. True artists use oils. Possibly charcoal. A guy on YouTube said that."

Kit wondered if "true" artists couldn't make do with whatever methods were available when pressed but decided to leave it. "I see. Still up for making a few watercolours of Provence to impress Laura's aunt, though, right?"

He placed a fist against his chest. "Certainly! I'll gladly sacrifice time and effort for romance and thwarted love."

Kit watched him for a second.

What about what you'd sacrifice just to make Laura happy?

She forced a smile. "Cool. Well, good luck with it."

"I won't need luck. Laura has prepped me for what I should talk about to sound like I'm actually interested in watercolours. And I've been to Provence, so that helps. It's all very easy, you see. I merely need to paint a few canvases and take them over to her and boom – love wins."

"Boom. Yeah. Great," Kit said, trying to not sound sceptical.

Laura brought over the drinks, Kit's sandwich, and a little black disc. "Here we go. This thing will buzz when our paninis are done, Dylan."

"Splendid," he said and began to stare intently at the disc.

Kit picked up her sandwich. "Mind if I start? I only have an hour's lunch."

"Of course we don't mind," Laura said. "Go ahead."

Kit took a bite, chewed it with delight, and then froze. Was Laura watching her mouth as she ate?

Maybe she's really hungry and jealous of my sandwich? Should I offer her a bite?

Kit kept chewing, fidgeting a little in her seat. Laura caught her eye and smiled. Kit smiled back. Then Laura's gaze went back down to her mouth. There was no sandwich there now. Laura was undoubtedly staring at her lips. Was she aware that she was doing that? While her fiancé was right there? Of course not, that wasn't something Laura would do.

Unsure of how to alert Laura to her actions, Kit groped for something to say. "Uh, Dylan's been filling me in on where we are with Plan B. Looking good so far!"

Laura had no chance to reply as a gruff voice somewhere behind Kit said, "I hope you shan't hog that table all day. Some of us are still trying to find seats and are not seventeen anymore."

Kit turned to see Mabel Baxter, knitted hat in place, scowling at her.

"Mrs Baxter," she squeaked. "Hello. You're right, you shouldn't have to stand. Maybe you could join us?"

She looked to the other two for confirmation. Dylan was still staring at the buzzer. Laura, however, nodded and said, "Yes, you should take a seat, Mrs Baxter! We don't want that new hip of yours to start acting up."

"Sit with you?" Mabel harrumphed. "I suppose I have no other choice. Unless you're up to no good, of course. I know what young people are like today. I watch the soaps. Besides, everyone says that this one," she hiked her thumb towards Kit, "prefers pies over sausages. God only knows what that lot get up to."

That's it. Time to speak up.

Kit took a breath and then held up a hand. "Before you go any further, I want to point out that comments like that, while not more ill-meant than your usual insults, can sound homophobic. I know that your generation, especially on this insular island, aren't very used to this sort of stuff, so I'm just warning you about it. Okay?"

Mabel Baxter paled, looking surprisingly abashed.

Not waiting for an apology but charging straight ahead to the now-needed icebreaker, Kit added, "Also, I'll have you know that lately I've not been getting up to anything worse than one night of drinking vodka and a few occasions of stuffing myself with Greengage's excellent fish and chips."

Laura stifled a laugh. "Yes, but when you went for the fish and chips – did you buy *pies*?"

"Well, I sure as hell wasn't going for the *sausages*," Kit replied, almost keeping a straight face.

"Why are you all talking about food?" Dylan whinged, still staring at the buzzer.

Suddenly over her worry about the moral virtues of pie-eaters, Mabel sat down. "Ethel is buying us tea and crumpets. Do please make room."

Laura moved their drinks enough to clear space on the table. Meanwhile, a stranger bumped into Kit's chair and apologised.

Mabel stared at the stranger and muttered, "Frightfully busy today. All due to that blasted fair."

"The what now?" Kit asked.

Mabel frowned. "Was I meant to understand that sentence, young lady?"

Kit prepared a few words of truth in her mind and sat

forward to deliver them. She was stopped by Laura's hand on her arm.

"Now," Laura said coolly to Mabel, "I think you know very well that what Kit meant was 'What was that you said about a fair, Mrs Baxter?' So, answer her question or I'll inform my aunt about the many early mornings when you and Ethel have been seen helping yourselves to our gages and plums. Three years running."

Mabel looked appalled. Then she crossed her arms over her chest and muttered, "There's a small jewellery and craft fair taking place at the square. Everyone who bought something from the silversmith, or that nutter who knits bric-a-brac with cows on them, received ten percent off the food in this establishment."

Laura let go of Kit's arm. "Aha! Jennie the silversmith and Holly, who knits things with cows on them, are daughters of the owners of the Tea Gage," she explained to Kit.

"Tea Gage. Ha. Ridiculous name," Mabel grumbled.

Kit scanned the mixed crowd and tried to pick out which ones might have bought silver jewellery and who bought knitted cows. On Greengage, that was hard to tell.

Ethel came over with crumpets and two mugs of tea and placed them in front of Mabel before sitting down.

"Hello, dears," she chirruped. "Guess who not only procured ten percent off the crumpets but also a lovely brooch?" She pointed to a broach in the shape of a knitted cow on her coat lapel.

In reply, Mabel snorted loudly, something which Ethel ignored with practised ease.

"It's… eye-catching, Mrs Rosenthal," Laura said quickly.

"It is an eye*sore*, you mean," Mabel muttered.

Ethel smiled. "It's meant to ward off evil spirits. It annoys Mabel and buying it made young Holly happy. You know, Holly's a lovely girl." She looked to Kit. "About your age. She has short hair and drives a jeep. And she wears dungarees sometimes."

Kit wished that she didn't know what Ethel was getting at.

"I'll keep that in mind, Mrs Rosenthal," she said weakly.

Ethel patted her hand, and Kit had to smile at how the feel of the papery, wrinkled skin reminded her of her long-passed grandmother. "You do that, petal. You should talk to her if you want some romantic lady company. See if you can use your gay laser."

In her confusion, Kit nearly dropped her sandwich. Laura once again stepped in to explain. "I think Mrs Rosenthal means *gaydar*," she whispered.

Kit put the sandwich down. "Look. It's nice that everyone is trying to make sure I'm not lonely. But my love life is perfect in its non-existence."

To her annoyance, everyone at the table looked away with a sceptical air. Except for Dylan who stared longingly at his buzzer and said, "I really fancy sausages now. Why did you have to mention them? Dear god, does no one think about my fat intake?!"

❦

After a weird lunch experience and a busy day at work, Kit hurried the few steps home. She was planning to cook up a quick stir-fry for dinner, go for a run, and then have a long bath and delve into a good book. She'd bought a nice, fluffy read with two women and a kid on the front.

Some sort of businesswoman was going to fall in love with a stewardess on a plane. The love would be requited and they, together with the cute kid probably, would live happily ever after. Heart-warming, happy, and extremely gay. Exactly what Kit needed right now.

Her phone buzzed, revealing a long text from Aimee.

Hey Sweetie,
This is sort of embarrassing, which is why I'm texting instead of calling. I've got pneumonia. I'm off work and home with George, but I'm struggling to look after him. Luckily, he's vaccinated and hasn't caught it. Still, it's all too much. John won't help with his own bloody kid. My parents say I need to learn deal with "my own issues." And the embarrassing part is that I can't afford a sitter. I haven't told you this, but I'm really strapped for cash.
I hate to ask this but, Kit, can you please help me? Please.

Kit didn't hesitate. She called Aimee to check on her while pondering how to convince Rajesh to let her take the first ferry to the mainland tomorrow morning.

Chapter Eleven

FOXTROT LESSONS AND EXCLAMATION POINTS

An hour after Aimee's text, Kit and Rajesh were eating dinner. Or Kit was trying to but struggling to get an appetite. She wanted to be with Aimee, who had pretended to be fine on the phone but sounded so small. So distressed. No matter how old Aimee was, to Kit she'd always be the bullied little girl that first made Kit learn to stand up for others. When she got home, she'd explained Aimee's situation to Rajesh. He'd nodded and said that pneumonia was "blooming awful" and that his dad nearly died from fever when he had it. Kit hadn't been sure of how to broach that she had to go to London.

Just say it, woman. He's understanding, he'll want to help.

She put the fork down. "I can't eat. I know it's silly, but I can't stop worrying about Aimee. I mean, she'll be fine, the doctors have given her antibiotics and she has a check-up booked in soon to make sure she's recovering. But she needs help, especially with George. He's her first child, and she's all alone with him. I'm worried."

He swallowed. "I can tell. Listen, you get two weeks holiday a year. Why don't you take at least one of them now? Help her out, babysit the little nipper, and make sure your friend gets to her check-up."

"Can I do that? After only having worked here for three and a half months? And on such short notice? What about getting cover?"

"I'll get by with the library volunteers. That's what I did when I was waiting for you to start. Besides, when people know that you left to help a sick friend, who's alone with a little tot, they'll queue up to help."

Kit hummed while pushing a piece of carrot around her plate. Could she do that? Was it irresponsible to simply up and leave? She thought about Aimee and little George alone.

"I'd like to go tomorrow and stay for a few days. Is that okay?"

"No, the day after tomorrow." He fixed her with a stare. "Tomorrow morning you'll go down to Dr Bowen and see if you can get some sort of vaccine. After that, you work in the afternoon while I ring around to the volunteers. Then, the next day you can take the first ferry and stay in London for a whole week. Sounds reasonable?"

"Hm." Kit tapped her fork against the plate. "Yeah, you're right. I'll try to get the vaccine and then I'll stay for a full week. Thank you."

He waved her thanks away. "I wouldn't have it any other way. Besides, it'll give me a chance to bring ladies over for romantic encounters. Marjorie has been wanting to come over for foxtrot lessons for weeks, and we both know what that's code for."

"Please say it's wanting to dance?" Kit whinged.

"Sure. The sort of dancing where the man doesn't need to worry about where he puts his feet, but where he puts his—"

"Rajesh! Stop right there!"

He sniggered. "All right. My apologies, I was only trying to cheer you up. Now, eat more. We don't waste food in this house. And you're so thin, you need every morsel."

Kit took a big bite and made herself chew it while Rajesh watched with what looked like sternness but was probably concern.

Her phone beeped. She yanked it out of her jeans pocket, terrified that it was a text saying that Aimee was deteriorating or that George had caught the pneumonia after all. Instead, it turned out to be from Laura.

Dearest, most wonderful Kit,
It worked! Dylan came by with "some presents for me."
Champagne, chocolates, and of course — the watercolours!
Aunt Sybil saw them, loved them, and started asking him
questions. He said everything I'd instructed him to say and
wowed Aunt Sybil. They're still chatting away in the library! I
just snuck downstairs to text you, but I better get up there
again before Dylan speaks out of turn. Thank you again for
this marvellous plot! I'll keep you updated!

Kit looked at the words and all the thrilled exclamation points. Despite Laura's excitement, she was finding it hard to celebrate the scheme's success. Not only due to worry about Aimee roiling her stomach, but because it seemed strange to celebrate Laura being bound to Dylan. Especially if there was even a grain of truth in Rachel's hypothesis.

Laura wants to be with Dylan. You have to respect that. You should be happy for her and proud you've helped.

That line of thought wasn't quite working.

"Rajesh, I'll have my dinner later. I'd like to call Aimee and check that it's okay that I come stay with her the day after tomorrow."

"Sure. There's Tupperware boxes in the cupboard behind you."

"Thanks."

She put her meal in the fridge and hurried to her room. For the first time, she wished she'd gotten her own flat when she moved here. Unsure of if it was concern for Aimee or unease regarding Laura which made her need alone-time, Kit stood frozen and staring into space. Listlessly, she wrapped her arms around herself and forced her thoughts towards packing.

Will I need my jacket? How cold is it in Greater London?

She picked up her phone to check her weather app and clicked away the text from Laura. That would have to wait.

Chapter Twelve

POO MACHINE

K it stood by the window, ignoring the view of Raynes Park to smile at the afternoon sunlight reflecting off George's silky black hair instead.

He was carefully putting a seventh block onto a tower of wooden blocks, his little tongue sticking out and his chubby cheeks pink with concentration. Or possibly from the stifling heat in the flat.

Kit took a step closer to her godson. "It's boiling in here. You'd think your sleeping mum is warming the whole place with her fever. You warm, Georgie?"

He crinkled his little face up and muttered, "Too hot."

"Agreed. I'm going to check if the heating is on. Your mum needs to save money, so I don't know why she'd have it on in an unusually warm April."

George hummed, probably more in regard to trying to balance an eighth block on the tower than replying to Kit. He was obsessed with those blocks lately. Kit had never seen as many towers, houses, and strange animals made of wooden blocks as she had in these past few days.

Seeing that the heating wasn't just on, it was set to 23°C, Kit shook her head.

"What the hell, Aimee?" She muttered under her breath. She punched the button to switch off the heating. "George? We should go wake your mummy and have a chat with her. I was thinking about taking you into London, but I don't know if she'll let us."

He tilted his head. "Why?"

"Why she might not let us?"

"Yes?"

Kit blew out a breath. "Well, I'm not all that used to kids. And you're quite little to be out alone with someone who barely knows what to do with you."

His brows knitted. "Not little. I big."

Kit sat down next to him. "Right, of course, my mistake. But you're not big enough to be able to tell me what I should do if you, I don't know, have a temper tantrum on a crowded train or something."

"Silly," George stated and looked back to his tower of blocks.

Kit wasn't sure if he meant her, the idea of him having a temper tantrum, or the thought of going into London. Or something completely different that she had no clue about. She was in deep, murky waters here. She could've used some of Laura's capable and patient nature.

At that thought, Kit pinched her arm. She'd promised herself to stop dwelling on Laura. She ran her hand through her hair. "No, I think we'll stay in Raynes Park, Georgie. There'll be stuff to do here, too. I just need to get out."

George watched her. "Why? 'Cause hot?"

"Yeah, that's one reason. The more important reason is that, while it's great to spend time with you and your mum, having been locked up with you for almost four days and living off what's in the cupboards is getting repetitive. And my brain is running away with me, going places I don't want it to."

He eyeballed her as if she'd started spouting Russian poetry.

Kit laughed. "Never mind, short stuff. I was more explaining something to myself than to you. Go back to your block building."

He agreed without any further prompting.

Aimee dragged herself into the room. "You're not taking my toddler into the city. You're right, Raynes Park has everything you need. I recommend the library, a place you both love." She paused to cough. A harsh, wet sound coming from her unnaturally pale throat. "There's even a good, cheap Thai place a few streets away. Sadly, no West End theatres, but then you're not going to take George to see a Noel Coward play anyway."

Kit watched the toddler, who was putting another block on the tower, making it sway dangerously. He always made her smile. "Nope. He's more of a musicals man."

Aimee coughed again before replying, "Sure. But more 'The Wheels on the Bus' than *Les Mis*."

"Fair point. Sorry if we woke you by the way. How are you feeling?"

"Like hell." Aimee shivered and pulled her robe tighter around herself. "Well enough to be on my own, though. Take my offspring out for some fresh air and eat somewhere if you want. There's a sandwich shop a few doors down from the Thai place. Get George a ham sandwich without crusts. And a banana if they have them today."

George lifted his arms as in triumph and screamed, "Banana!" in his best *Minions* impression.

Kit got up and brushed a few strands of black hair from Aimee's pasty face. "You sure that'd be okay? I really fancy some fresh air and a change of scenery."

"Of course!" Aimee managed to croak before a coughing fit. "Go for it. I'm just going to sleep anyway."

"Brilliant. We'll pop down to the library for a bit, and then I'll bring back a sandwich for the little builder and Thai food for us. I'll have my phone, so call if you need anything or if you get lonely."

"No Thai for me. I don't think I can stomach anything hot. I couldn't even drink my coffee earlier."

"BANANA FOR MUMMY!" George shouted.

They both laughed, half amused and half startled.

"Not so loud, George," Aimee chided.

"Sorry," he whispered. Then his tower fell with a deafening bang. George looked up at the grownups with a surprisingly despondent look for a two-year-old. He sighed and then said, "More sorry."

"That's okay," Aimee said. She coughed and then turned to Kit. "Can I also have a ham sandwich?"

"Without crusts and with a banana?" Kit teased.

Aimee hung her head and mumbled, "Yes. God, look at me. I'm pitiful."

"No. You're sick, mate." Kit pulled her close and kissed her hair. "When we're really ill and in pain, we all want comfort and familiar things. And easily digested food. Besides, I like looking after you. You know helping is my thing, and it's particularly nice when it's you. You know why?"

"No," Aimee said in a small voice.

"Because I love you, but also because I know that you appreciate the help. And that when the time comes, you'll return the favour. That's what we do, you plum! Now, get back to bed."

"Yes, matron," Aimee grumbled. She began shuffling back to her bedroom.

Kit turned to the boy who was restacking his tower. "Right, little builder. Leave the blocks for now. Let's go pack a rucksack with some essential Georgie stuff for an adventure. Then we need to find you a jacket and some shoes."

"We go train?" George said.

Aimee turned back so fast she nearly fell. "Nuh-uh. No trains into London, you troublemakers."

"Fine," Kit said, hands on hips. "George and I'll stay here. *South of the river* and everything."

Aimee shook her head with a smile. "Don't give me that. You're south of the river born and bred. Best place on earth and you know it."

Kit grinned, thrilled to have made her oldest friend smile.

George pulled at her trouser leg, and she focused back on him. "You heard the boss. No train. We're going to the library and then to get some food. It's going to be brilliant! Come on."

Wobbling, he got up and raced towards his shoes.

An hour and a half later they were leaving the library. It had looked so different compared to when Kit was last there, and it was making her a bit melancholic. Although George toddling along next to her and humming what was clearly Whitney Houston's "It's Not Right But It's Okay" was cheering her up.

"Nice to know your mummy still has the same taste in music," Kit said to him.

Her phone rang. She hurried to reply in case it was Aimee, then jumped when she saw Laura's name on the screen. She hadn't spoken to Laura since the trip from Greengage to London, where Kit had explained in texts what was happening with Aimee and how long she'd be gone. Laura had been extremely sympathetic and asked a million questions. She'd then quickly mentioned that Plan B was still successful and that her aunt seemed to like Dylan more each day. There'd been nothing since. Intentionally, on Kit's part.

Now Kit squeezed George's hand. "Just a sec, little builder. I have to take this call."

He shrugged and kept watching pigeons on the top of the roof ahead.

"Hi, Laura."

"Hey you! How's London?"

"Same but different. I'm out on the town with young George. Right now we're on our way to pick up some food and bring it back to the coughing victim. How's things on Greengage?"

"Not bad! Gage Farm is doing well, and Plan B is ticking along. Dylan has worked for Gage Farm for a few days now, and while he hates it, he puts up with it because he knows he'll end up with a loving wife who supports him. And all the time in the world to do nothing but lock himself away from her to paint."

Was that a slight tone of resentment? No, probably just the way it sounded over the phone.

"Cool. So, Sybil hasn't seen through the watercolour thing?"

"Not at all. Actually, I think Dylan is warming to

using them. He's working on a portrait of Aunt Sybil, in watercolour, would you believe?"

"Really? I didn't see that coming."

Laura laughed. The familiar warm sound gave Kit goosebumps. "No, I don't think anyone did, Kit."

They were quiet for a second. Kit chewed the inside of her cheek while she thought about what to ask to get a better sense of how Laura was doing and feeling. Not Dylan, not Sybil... only Laura.

In the end, Laura was the one to break the silence. "It's lovely of you to help Aimee with little George. Not everyone who doesn't have children would feel comfortable with that."

Kit chuckled. "Funny you should say that. I've been thinking about that today. Even discussed it with George." She pushed her glasses up. "I mean, I've known George all his life, but Aimee has always been there. And she babysat a lot when we were younger, so she knew what to do from the start. Teenage me made extra cash mowing lawns, not applicable to babies."

Laura laughed. "No. I'll remember that when Howard Hall needs its lawns manicured, though."

"You do that." Kit glanced down at George, who was looking away from the pigeons, lost in thought. Probably planning his next building project.

She lowered her voice. "It's tricky to look after him when Aimee sleeps or is dazed with fever, though. I'm unsure of what's the right thing to do all the time. But I'm glad I'm here. George is struggling with his mum being so different due to being sick. It scares him and, I don't know, almost makes him seem lonely. Is that too advanced for a two-year-old? Am I projecting?"

"I don't know to be honest," Laura said. "All I know is that when your parents aren't around, other adults become frightfully important. It's not comparable of course, but when I lost my parents, Aunt Sybil and many of the adults on the island rallied round. They gave me and Tom anything we needed. Time, cuddles, chances to rage and to cry. Even space if we needed that. It didn't matter to us if they were unsure or didn't have experience with children. As long as they didn't leave."

Kit felt like she'd been punched in the chest. "Laura. I'm so incredibly sorry."

"Oh, don't be. I didn't bring this up for sympathy. I'm merely saying that you don't have to be perfect around a child who's struggling, you only have to try your best and not leave them. And be affectionate and safe, which I know you are."

Kit's cheeks burned, and she scuffed her shoe against the pavement. "Uh, well, I'm trying to be. I love this kid." She looked down at George who was now watching the pigeons again. "He wakes me in the morning by kissing my nose. It's so sweet." She squeezed his hand, but he was too busy looking at the pigeons fight over a chip to care. "Sure, sometimes it's a slightly sloppy kiss, but I mean I get worse from Phyllis back at Rajesh's."

Laura giggled. "That dog is something else. Still, I'm glad you get along so well with George. He and Aimee are lucky to have you."

"I'm lucky to have them. I haven't got any siblings, I don't talk much to my mum, and my dad travels a lot for work. Aimee is pretty much my closest family, and I guess George is now, too."

"Not a bad set-up. You know, I bet I'd really like George, I love children."

"I guessed you would." Kit couldn't stop herself from smiling.

"I'm making poo," George said conversationally.

Kit looked down at him and saw that his little face was scrunching up and turning red.

"Ah. Great," she mumbled.

"What's that?"

"Oh, nothing, Laura. It's just that my plans have changed. I think I'll have to take George home to change him." She glanced down at the Curious George rucksack in her hand. "I have diapers with me, but they probably won't have a changing room at a Thai food place, right?"

"Probably not. I'd take him home if I were you. You can pop back out for food later."

Kit relaxed her shoulders. "Yeah. Good thinking. I think I'll do that."

"I'll leave you to it then. Call or text me with updates on how Aimee is doing?"

"Sure, will do."

"Great. Have a lovely holiday, even if it contains coughing and diapers."

"I'll give it my best shot," Kit promised.

"Splendid. Talk soon."

"Laura, wait."

"Yes?"

Kit froze. Had she really been about to ask Laura if she was missing her? *Holy shit.*

"Uh, nothing. I wanted to tell you to look after yourself and not to work too hard."

Laura chuckled. "No promises there! We're barrelling towards our busy period, you know. But sure, I'll try. For you, my dearest Kit."

George squeezed her hand. Kit wasn't sure if it was to

hurry her up or because he was straining. She didn't want to know.

"Great. So, um. Bye, Laura."

"Bye, Kit."

The words "*For you, my dearest Kit*" repeated in her mind, like a toy train going round and round on its tracks.

Kit put her phone away and kneeled down. "Hey, little builder. Are you finished so we can walk back to the flat?"

"No. More poo."

Kit stood back up. "All right. You take your time, mate. I'll just... think about things. And watch those pigeons. That big one is totally going to get that chip."

🐎

Back at the flat, Kit changed his diaper and together they went to wake Aimee.

"No food?" Aimee asked while rubbing sleep out of her eyes.

Kit ran her fingers through her short tresses. "Um, no. Your mix between Curious George and Bob the Builder here needed to do a number two." She smiled at him, then had to think about what else she was about to say. She snapped her fingers as it came back. "Oh, right. I can pop out and get some now. If you can babysit for a few minutes?"

Aimee stifled a cough. "Sure. I've stored up some energy."

"Great. I'll just..." Kit looked around. "Try and find my phone."

"Are you all right?" Aimee asked. "You seem a little distracted."

Kit sucked in a deep breath and decided to come clean. "Laura called. It sort of knocked me off kilter."

"Okay? What did she say?"

"It wasn't what she said so much as... hearing her voice. It makes my heart pound so fast that I get a bit dizzy and stuff. Then I can't stop thinking about her."

Aimee coughed and then gave her friend a searching look. Slowly, she raised her eyebrows and crossed her arms over her chest.

"What?" Kit snapped.

"I was right. You really *are* pining for this woman."

"No. I told you, I'm attracted to her, but that doesn't mean anything. It's a crush. It'll pass."

"Sweetheart, it's more than that," Aimee said softly. "I know that stupefied look. You're falling for her."

Kit shuffled her feet. "Whatever. So, yeah, um, if you look after the poo machine here, I'll go get us some food. You look pretty faint, I'll get loads of stuff so you can pick at whatever food you fancy. You need vitamins. And minerals. And things. Okay? Yeah, okay. Right."

With that, Kit picked up her jacket, wallet, and phone, before hurrying out to get food. And hopefully to clear her head.

Chapter Thirteen

JANE FONDA, A WANKER, AND TWO KISSES

The next morning Kit knocked on Aimee's door and said, "Hey, sleepyhead. You up?"

A foggy voice mumbled, "Sure. Been up for hours. Finished a double CrossFit workout and solved the *Times* crossword. Also, I've made a statue of Jane Fonda out of used chewing gum."

"Cool, then we're coming in."

As Kit opened the door, George barrelled past her and up into Aimee's bed. He snuggled close, and Aimee stifled a cough before kissing his head.

"There's Mummy's angel. Have you been nice to Kit? Did you wake her nicely this morning?"

He nodded. "Kissed nose."

"Well done," Aimee said and kissed his.

She pushed him to the side and started coughing. Kit wasn't sure, but it sounded less rattling than the day before. Maybe it was only because it was morning, but Kit thought she saw a little more alertness in Aimee's eyes as well.

She sat down on the edge of the bed. "I feel like a broken record, but how are you feeling?"

Aimee smiled. "Not too bad. Maybe I don't have a fever right now?"

"Let's hope not. Hey, George?"

He stopped toying with his mother's matted hair and looked up at Kit.

"Would you mind playing in the other room for a while? I need to have a quick chat with your mum before we bring her some breakfast."

Without answering, he jumped off the bed and ran out making airplane noises.

"This sounds serious," Aimee said.

"I wanted to talk about a couple of things."

Aimee coughed and sat up. "Okay. Talk."

Kit handed her the glass of water that was on her bedside table. "First of all. I think you were right about me and Laura. I have deeper feelings for her. However, it's a moot point as she's with Dylan. She's fought to be with him since she was a teenager. She's finally about to get what she's always wanted. The man, the job, the house. Full package." Kit scratched her forehead. "I can't ruin that simply because I'm crazy about her and she seems to like me. I'll have to grit my teeth through the heartache and hope it passes quickly."

Aimee sipped her water. "I'm so sorry, sweetie. At least you've faced up to it now, which means you can grieve and try to move on. There was another thing?"

Kit set her jaw. "Yeah. I've been keeping an eye on your mail like you asked and, well, this arrived this morning." She handed over the bill with red text and a threat of getting a bailiff involved if Aimee didn't pay her overdue rent.

"Shit."

"I'd say so," Kit muttered. "Why didn't you tell me it was this bad? This isn't 'finance trouble.' This is being behind on rent so badly that you risk being chucked out of here!"

Aimee rubbed her face. "Pride, I guess. And not wanting to bother or worry you. You've started a new life on Greengage, and you have enough on your plate with all of that. Besides, my parents are right. I'm an adult. I should be able to handle my life."

She had a coughing fit, and Kit stroked her back until it passed. Aimee drank more water and then carried on, "I get child support and I managed to get a part-time job, that *should* take care of the finances. But then I kept getting sick and had to be off work." She looked down at her hands. "On top of that, I was never very good at budgeting, so I found myself spending silly money on things that could probably have been cheaper. You know, phone bills, gas, electricity. Stuff for George. All those things that John handled when I lived with him."

Kit took her hand. "But between living with me and living with John, you had your own place and handled those things reasonably?"

"I had a full-time job then. And no child to support. If I didn't have the cheapest phone provider, it didn't matter. Now, every pound counts. I'm no good at that. Especially not when I'm constantly sick and I'm trying to get to work and to look after George. And childminders… man, don't even get me started on how expensive they can be."

Kit squeezed her hand. "Well, in London at least. I'm sure they're cheaper elsewhere."

"I know, I know. London prices are always higher."

"Exactly. You wouldn't struggle as much if you lived

somewhere else. Maybe move farther out? Into Kent or Sussex?"

"I'm sure I'd be out-priced there, too. Besides, I need to get into London for my job, and commuting from out there is pricy as hell," Aimee croaked out, eyes brimming with tears.

Kit leaned over and kissed her hair. "Hey. We'll fix this, okay?"

Aimee hummed noncommittally and avoided her gaze.

"Look, I'll go get you some breakfast, your antibiotics, and some paracetamol. When you have that in your system, we'll talk about what to do."

Aimee coughed while nodding. "Thanks. I'll wash up and get some clothes on."

"Whoa. You're not staying in your robe today? It's a miracle!"

"Shut up, you pillock," Aimee muttered.

Kit sniggered all the way into the kitchen.

❧

A couple of hours later, she sat by the table and spoke to Aimee's landlord, a Mr Alec Smith, over the phone.

Since Aimee was renting privately, Kit was hoping she'd be able to convince him to give Aimee a reprieve if she paid some of the money right away. That hope was currently fading.

"Do you know wha' I mean?" Mr Smith asked in a thick Cockney accent.

"Yes, I understand how late she is with the rent. But you've met Aimee, she's lovely and responsible. She's not intentionally skipping paying nor being flippant about it.

She's really struggling with being a single mum and having health issues."

"That's hardly my problem, now is it, Ms Sewell?"

"Sorel," Kit corrected.

"Yeah, yeah. My point stands. It doesn't matter why she hasn't paid… She. Hasn't. Bleedin'. Paid."

Kit took off her glasses and rubbed the bridge of her nose. "I know. Look, I'm helping her get her finances in order and from now on things will be better. She just needs to get over this hump."

He scoffed.

"Mr Smith, if I transfer over half the amount she owes today, and she then keeps chipping away at it until she's caught up, wouldn't that be better than you not getting any money at all and having to contact debt-collecting agencies and such?"

He was quiet for a long time. "Yeah. Suppose so. We'll give it a try."

Kit bit her lip to keep from shouting with glee.

"But if she falls behind again, there'll be no more chances! You hear me? Then I'll want her arse out of 'ere. Contract or not."

"Fine. Whatever it takes to make this right. You've done a decent thing here today, Mr Smith."

"Bollocks. I've had a bad case of bein' a soft touch. Trust me when I say that this only happens once every ten years."

Kit rolled her neck, feeling the tension drain. "In that case, I'm chuffed this happens to be that once-a-decade occasion."

"You wha'?"

"I'm glad that this is that time every ten years when you're a 'soft touch'."

"Oi, you calling me a soft touch?" he bellowed.

Kit tugged at her hair. "No. You did."

"Did not. When?"

"Just now," Kit replied.

"No, I said, 'Did not. When?' Can't you hear me proper?"

"Yes. You said it before that."

He grunted. "You're confusing me. Stop it. Tell your mate that there's no point in her ringing me with sob stories in the future. This is a one-off, got it?"

"Understood. I'll transfer the cash into your account right away."

"I should think so. Bye." He snorted. "What kind of bleedin' name is Sorkel, anyways?"

Kit was about to reply, but he had hung up. She stared at her phone and screamed, "SOREL! Like the surname of Charles VII's famous mistress, you wanker."

Aimee staggered in. "Pretty convinced he wouldn't know who or what Charles VII is, Kit." She coughed. "You should've said like the plant. Or the red-brown horse."

Kit smoothed her hair down. "Those both have two R's. Besides, he's already hung up. Anyway. Rude as he was, he agreed to take half the payment now and let you keep chipping away at the rest throughout the month. However, if you keep falling behind, he wants you to move out without a fuss."

Aimee rested her head against the doorframe. "Sure. I might as well. I can't afford this place."

"Don't talk like that. All you need is to be well enough to get back to work and start earning again. Considering you're improving every day, you'll be back to answering calls and doing coffee runs in no time."

"I'll try," Aimee said, putting her bravest smile on.

"Great. For now, I've made a list of things you might want to try and sell. Dusty DVDs, an old iPod, and jewellery I know you never use. We're also going to look over your bills and see if there are providers who are ripping you off and if you can get a better deal elsewhere. Okay?"

Aimee pulled herself up and cleared her throat. "Yep. Let's do it."

"Brilliant! I'll make some tea, and then we'll start going through this list of stuff to sell or pawn."

Aimee pulled out a chair. "Kit?"

"Mm?"

"Thank you."

"No probs. It's solving a sticky situation, right? My only forte, unless you count reading or messing up with women. When you feel better you can make it up to me by baking some of your mum's sesame cookies. I've missed those."

"It's a deal. I'll also love you forever, you big, bleeding-hearted teddy bear."

Kit laughed. "Sounds like your fever is back. Sit your arse down and I'll put the kettle on."

٭

Later that night, Kit snuck out of George's bedroom after reading him a bedtime story and tucking him in. She checked her phone to see what time it was and saw a text from Laura.

Hi dearest Kit,

Sorry, if I'm disturbing. It's just that talking to you yesterday made me realise how dull the island is without you. It may be selfish of me, but I can't wait to have my new best friend back. Enjoy your stay over there, but don't forget that you're missed here. Phyllis is losing weight while pining for you, she's barely even obese anymore! Look after yourself and if you're heading to bed soon — sweet dreams.

Kit closed her eyes and waited for the ache in her stomach to pass. 'New best friend.' Kit was proud to be Laura's best friend. She wasn't some wanker who'd complain about the friend zone. What bothered her was that the attraction felt less and less one-sided with every interaction she and Laura shared. But she had been wrong about this sort of thing before and was notoriously bad at identifying flirting.

She considered texting Rachel to get her to reiterate her suspicion about Laura actually being "intensely gay" and into her. But again, Rachel was biased and might be terribly wrong. If so, Kit would ruin an important friendship and come off as the predatory lesbian who couldn't stop thinking with her crotch. Besides, as she'd said to Aimee, Laura had fought for a chance to be with Dylan. Kit couldn't be the one to take that away. She couldn't hurt Laura. She squeezed the phone and then put it back in her jeans pocket.

She ambled into the living room and slumped down on the sofa where Aimee was sleeping. Some drool was trickling down her cheek and she was snoring worse than Phyllis. Kit stroked her hair and whispered, "I'll get you a tissue in a sec. There's something I have to do first." She took the phone out and hesitated over wording. Then she quickly wrote:

Hey Laura,

Missing you like crazy, too, mate. If you see Phyllis, scratch her behind the ear from me and say that I'll be back in a few days. Take care!

Kit hesitated over the *x* button. Should she really finish the text with two kisses? It was just a thing friends did, right? It didn't mean anything. Still, she couldn't manage it and sent the text without any sign-off. Then she tucked the phone into her pocket with vehemence and went to get a tissue for her dribbling friend.

Chapter Fourteen

GREENGAGE UNDER HER CONVERSE AGAIN

At the start of May, Kit was back at Greengage and busy in the library. While she'd been away, work had piled up. Work which Rajesh couldn't do, wouldn't do, or didn't trust the volunteers to take care of. In short, the technical and the tricky stuff. It didn't bother Kit, who threw herself into the job to the point where Rajesh took her aside and put a ham-sized hand on either of her shoulders.

"Settle down there, poppet. What are you doing to my nonfiction area?"

She didn't look him in the eye. "I'm checking how frequently these books have been discharged. If no one's borrowing them and they're not unique to Greengage, then I'm putting them in the 'to sell' pile. If they're in demand or of local importance – i.e. you can't borrow them anywhere else or they're needed here – I'm cleaning them and replacing their spine labels."

He sought her gaze and when he got it, muttered, "I can see *what* you're doing, you're weeding. I wanted to know why you've been doing it nonstop these past three days like the books were about to disappear. You're putting in more overtime than I could ever pay you for and dishevelling the entire nonfiction section. No one can get to the books, Katherine."

Kit looked away again at the mention of her full name. "Maybe I was speeding ahead a little. I'll slow down."

"You'll do more than that, you'll tell me what's wrong. You're running around like a blue-arsed fly." He let go of her shoulders. "Katherine, yesterday Ethel Rosenthal said you marched by so fast you didn't even hear her greet you. Anyone can see you're running, or hiding, from something."

"I…" She looked for an escape and found none. His serious eyes, framed by wrinkles and bushy eyebrows, wouldn't let her go.

She took a deep breath. "Being away, and talking to Aimee, made me realise something."

He puffed his chest out. "Good, now we're getting somewhere. What?"

"It's about Laura Howard."

"You fancy her."

Kit squirmed. "I, well, yes. That's probably obvious to everyone, including her. But what I realised was that I… feel something deeper for her."

"Feel?" He lowered his voice. "As in *feelings*?"

Kit nodded solemnly. "Yes. Feelings."

"Bloody hell."

"Mm-hm," Kit agreed.

He ran his hand over his chin. "Is that why you've not been on that phone of yours? It's been all books and no internet for you lately."

Kit shrugged. In truth, she *had* been avoiding texting or calling Laura. The last text from Laura had come when

Kit was on the ferry home. It had been strangely short, only asking Kit to call when she could. But Kit had been too upset and bewildered to dare reply. God only knows what she might blurt out.

Instead of answering Rajesh's question, Kit stepped forward and leaned her head against his chest. It was done on instinct and clearly shocked them both equally. Rajesh was stiff as a board and uttered a choked, "eh?"

She winced and was about to retreat and apologise for overstepping the boundaries of their friendship when he put a tentative arm around her and murmured, "There, there, lass. It'll be all right." He added a second arm and it became a real hug. "Feelings pass, Katherine. Although there is something you should know before you let them."

She stepped back and adjusted her glasses, which had almost slid off and gotten stuck in his woolly jumper. "What?"

"Something happened while you were away. Towards the end of the week. I've been trying to bring it up ever since you came back, but you've not been listening."

"Okay. Well, I'm listening now. What happened?"

He knitted his bushy eyebrows. "Actually, Laura may want to tell you herself. I don't know the full story, anyway. I've only heard rumours and who knows if they're true." He looked more certain now and nodded as he said, "Yes, Laura will fill you in. She came in the day before you returned and asked when you'd be back. I believe she'd been crying."

Kit gaped. "And you didn't tell me this until now?"

"I've tried! But every time I talked to you, you brushed me off or stood there with glazed-over eyes, clearly not listening. Disrespectful to your elders, that's what it is."

"Sorry." Kit chewed the inside of her cheek. "I have to talk to her. Fast."

Rajesh sighed. "It's coming up on lunchtime, and the only ones in here are the knitting group, chatting away. I can handle them on my own. Why don't you go for lunch early and head up to Howard Hall?"

"Are you sure that's okay?"

"Yes." He scoffed. "Considering you've been here until ten p.m. the last three nights and I can't pay you for it, I can give you fifteen minutes longer for lunch."

Kit yanked her library ID off and went to get her jacket. As she strode into the backroom, she heard him mutter, "Such trouble. Never should have taken a lodger. They need advice and they get in the way of your romancing."

Kit rolled her eyes, but other than a quick promise to herself to move out soon and stop cramping his style, she didn't give Rajesh another thought. Her mind was filled to the brim with Laura.

I should have called her like her text asked. Stupid, stupid, stupid.

Leather jacket half on, she rushed out the door and started jogging through town. She slowed at the square. It would take her ages to get all the way out to Howard Hall. Maybe she could take a shortcut through the orchards, but she didn't trust her knowledge of the island enough to risk it. She looked around for taxis.

This isn't London. Taxis have to be called for, and even then, the company's only four cars might be busy. No Ubers or anything like that, either. What do I do? Think!

She watched a passing car. Hitchhike? No, there'd be too many questions and gossip. Her brain couldn't make decisions. Her legs weren't much more help, anxiety made them restless with a sensation of pins and needles.

No more thinking. Move.

Kit began to run. Not jog, full-out run. She hurtled through streets which started off with people and buildings but were soon flanked only by fields and trees. She ran up the long, sloping hill towards Howard Hall. Then, finally, she felt the gravel path under her Converse.

She stopped in front of the imposing building and bent double, panting like a dog.

What if she's not here? She could be in the office. She could be up a damn apple tree for all you know! You should've texted, you idiot! She could've driven down to you.

"I say… hello there, darling. Are you quite all right?"

Kit looked up at the sound of the posh, drawling male voice. She took her glasses off and wiped away a bead of sweat which had trickled from her hairline into her eye. When she put the glasses back on she saw a man standing in the open door to Howard Hall. A smug-looking man in aviator sunglasses, a Ralph Lauren polo shirt, and tiny khaki shorts.

It's a cold day in early May and he's wearing that? He looks like a complete git.

She took a deep breath to stop the worst of the panting. "I'm guessing you're Tom Howard?"

He grinned, showing bright teeth that stood out against his unnaturally orange-tanned skin. "Guilty as charged. It's spiffing to know that the ladies hear of me the moment they arrive. You *are* the new girl, right? Kat Cyril, was it?"

"Kit Sorel, yes."

"Thought so. Nothing gets past me. The only other option was that you were some lost tourist who was beached here while trying to swim to Isle of Wight. You rather look like you could've been swimming," he said, staring at her face which was probably covered in a sheen of sweat.

"No. I'm the new librarian." She paused to catch her breath. "And a friend of your sister. Is she here?"

He ran a hand over his hair. It was shortish and slicked down with gel but as auburn as Laura's. "Yes. She's inside, waiting for lunch to be served. Shall I fetch her?"

Kit entertained the idea of asking him to invite her in, but she didn't want Sybil seeing her this sweaty and flustered. She might assume Kit had typhoid and shoot her with her fox-hunting rifle or something.

"Great. Yeah. Thanks," she said.

Tom sauntered back into the house with his hands in his pockets. When he was inside, Kit heard him shout, "Laura! Someone here to see you."

There was a muffed reply in quieter tones.

Tom shouted back, "It's the new girl. You know, nicely fit figure, and an acceptable face. Could be rather pretty if she wasn't so sweaty and didn't wear specs."

Kit sighed in disgust.

A second later Laura came flying through the open door. She ran down the stairs at a speed which Kit didn't think prudent in such high-heeled boots. When Laura was right in front of her, she threw herself into Kit's arms and held her tight.

"Whoa. Careful," Kit wheezed. "I ran here, so I'm not exactly fresh. Mind your pretty clothes."

Laura squeezed her tighter. "Who cares? I missed you so much. And I've been desperate to talk to you."

Kit returned the hug, feeling Laura's curls tickle her cheek. A strange calm poured over her.

This feels so right.

Seeming reluctant, Laura let go and stood back. She fidgeted with the top button on her suit jacket, her gaze pinned to Kit's.

Kit tried to read her facial expression but failed. "I'm so sorry that it's been four days since I got back and I haven't been in touch. Are you... angry at me?"

"No, not at all! I understood that you were busy. You needed time to get back into the normal routine and to digest everything that happened in London. It's not like I expect to hear from you every day, as close as we've gotten. We've only known each other for a few months." Laura tucked her hair behind her ear. "It's just that, well, something happened while you were away," she said in a thin voice.

Guilt tore strips off Kit's heart. "Okay. Is that why you wanted me to call you?"

Laura slumped. "Yes."

"I, um, wish you would have told me that it was serious. Or texted me again to prompt me." Kit shook her head. "No, you know what, you shouldn't have needed to. It's my fault for not replying. I'm really sorry."

"Don't be. I was being vague on purpose. I didn't want to bother you while you were away and busy helping your friend. But you see... there was a serious flaw to Plan B."

Kit's stomach churned. "Yeah?"

"Mm."

She put a hand on Laura's upper arm. "Can you tell me what it was?"

"Yes. I'm trying to." Laura gave a hollow laugh. "Funny, talking is usually the one thing I excel at. Now, however, I can't seem to get the words out."

"Take your time." Kit rubbed Laura's arm. "I'm not going anywhere."

Laura looked back at the house with its open door. "Tell you what. Why don't we go for a walk in the orchards while we talk?"

"Sure."

Laura flinched. "Oh! Unless you're tired after your run or you need to eat? How long is your lunch break?"

"I've been putting in a lot of overtime and the library is quiet today, I can take a longer lunch. I can wait to eat, too. I wouldn't mind a drink, though. Howard Hall is a bit of a run from town."

"I have the perfect thing," Laura exclaimed. She rushed back into the house and returned with glass bottles. "The last two from summer's batch of cherry cordial."

Kit took one of the bottles. "Great, thanks." She undid the screw top and gulped a third of the cordial.

Laura looked at her wide-eyed. "Oh my, you *were* thirsty. Sorry they're not cold. I picked them up this morning and stuck them in the hall to bring them with me to the office as a snack, but I forgot them."

They began strolling away from the house.

"Cold or not, they came in handy now. Delicious. Thanks again," Kit said.

"No need to thank me. It's the least I can do after you ran up here." Laura stopped walking. "Why *did* you run up here anyway? If you were worried about wasting your lunch hour, I could've come to you. Or you could have gotten a lift up here with someone."

Kit scratched her forehead. "Yeah. I, um, had…" She adjusted her glasses. "I had to see you right away and I wanted to stretch my legs."

It sounded painfully feeble, but Laura didn't question

it. She simply smiled and said, "I'm glad you were eager to see me. The feeling was mutual."

"Yes, but I bet in your case it was more because you have bad news and need my help." Kit winked. "Now, stop stalling. What was wrong with Plan B?"

Laura undid the top of her bottle of cordial but didn't drink. "The idea was to have Dylan worm his way into my aunt's withered heart, right?"

"Yep."

Laura began ambling along again and Kit kept pace.

"Well, he did. A little too well. While you were away, they spent more and more time together. Aunt Sybil would shower him with compliments and gifts. Saying that he shouldn't waste his time working on fruit farms, that he should paint full time instead. Obviously, he lapped that up and I was thrilled that they were both so happy."

Kit's breath hitched as she began to suspect where this was heading.

Laura looked down at her forsaken bottle. "The days went by and Dylan began avoiding me. When he did see me, he snapped at me. After you and I spoke on the phone, when you'd been to the library with George? Dylan pushed my hand away when I caressed his cheek, saying that I always touched him too roughly. That I should be more ladylike in my gestures, like my aunt."

"Ouch," Kit said.

"Yes. In general, he talked more and more about how she was more of a lady than I. More like the women in 'classic, romantic books that we read at school.' Strong but feminine. Misunderstood and lonely. All twaddle, of course." She paused to put the bottle top back on her cordial. "It must've been the day before you left the mainland when I walked into the lounge and saw Aunt Sybil lean over Dylan's easel and kiss him. He kissed her back."

"What?" Kit nearly tripped over her own feet. "You're kidding."

Laura looked heavenward. "I wish I was. I barged in and asked what the hell was happening, of course. They confessed that they had gone from friendly to romantic. Dylan actually had the nerve to say that he 'had thought that our dalliance was forbidden love, right out of a poem, but that it paled compared to the romance with sweet Sybil.' Aunt Sybil… sweet? Ha!"

"Yeah. I mean, has he met her?"

"Oh, she's all sweetness and light towards him. Spoils him rotten, even more than she does Tom. I think Dylan enjoys that she's a beast to everyone else but a lamb to him. Probably appeals to his male ego, having been the one to tame the shrew and all that," Laura said. There was a certain look of someone having drunk curdled milk on her face.

Kit tapped her fingers against her bottle. "I suppose it makes sense in a way."

"Makes sense?" Laura spat.

"Well, no, not to anyone sensible. I mean you're the catch of the century and your aunt is a glass of rancid vinegar. No one in their right mind would make that switch. But Dylan's… a few sandwiches short of a picnic."

"What do you mean?"

"He's, um, not the brainy type. Plus, he's self-absorbed and lives off warped ideas of medieval chivalry and Victorian yearning. He seemed more in love with the idea of thwarted, forbidden romance than in love with *you*. Which is bonkers," Kit said with a long glance at Laura before carrying on. "Sybil is not only a sugar mummy who'll cater to his every whim, but also someone who's an even better fit for the melodramatic, star-crossed lover thing. Not only is she the head of the nemesis family, she's also much older and feared by all. She's the ultimate forbidden lover, like he said."

Laura stopped dead in her tracks. Kit saw her swallow a few times, her throat bobbing. Her eyes looked like they might be filling up with tears, but it was hard to tell with the dark, cloudy skies overhead.

"So... he never loved me at all?" Laura whispered.

Kit's heart cracked into a hundred pieces. "Oh, sweetheart. I'm sure he would've if he could. But I'm not sure he can love anyone but himself."

Laura was staring down at her vice-like grip of her bottle. "I suppose that rings true. Deep down I knew what he was like. After all, everyone always told me. Rachel and Shannon more than anyone else. I simply..."

Kit wrapped her arm around Laura's shoulders. "Thought you had enough affection for the both of you?"

"Well, yes. Why not? After all, I was expecting to have to have enough *sense* for the both of us."

Kit laughed, and after a moment, Laura chimed in.

Laura leaned in closer, and Kit tightened the grip around her shoulders. They stood like that for a moment until Laura took a hesitant step and they strolled on, as close together as possible without falling.

"Sorry that my little plot backfired," Kit said quietly. "I just wanted to help."

"Please don't be sorry. It only backfired because my aunt doesn't care about my feelings and because Dylan is a selfish, backstabbing little slut."

Kit laughed again. "He is, and he never deserved you.

I'm glad that my plan, despite failing, at least showed you that."

"Agreed," Laura said with a sniff and a wipe at her eye. "It hurt like hell to lose him. But I have to admit, the heartbreak has been fading faster than I thought."

"Probably because your affection was one-sided."

Laura watched her. "You keep using that word."

"What, *probably*?"

"No, affection. Instead of love."

Kit covered her frown by adjusting her glasses. "I wasn't going to mention it, but I wondered if what you felt for Dylan was maybe more like… friendly or maternal affection than romantic love?"

"Huh." Laura's steps slowed. "You might be on to something there." She looked up to the skies for a while. "I suppose that if Dylan was my one true love, I would've been more willing to give up Gage Farm, Howard Hall, and everything else for him."

"Possibly. That would've been a real shame. Like you said, it's a legacy not only from the Howards in general, but from your parents. And you seem bloody good at your job. You shouldn't have to sacrifice that."

"Well, now I won't. I do have to decide if I want to stay at Howard Hall, though. It's not a particularly nice place to live at the moment."

"Which explains why you're walking us farther and farther away from it?"

"Mm. And why I'm working so much. I keep staying in the office or going out to schmooze customers and suppliers. I unnecessarily spent a whole afternoon with Dave, a representative for the company that supplies the jam jars. And Dave smells like pickled herring."

Kit laughed. "At least you're getting work done. Still, I'm sorry home life is so awful right now."

"Thank you." Laura rested her head against Kit's as they walked. "I've considered staying in one of the old workman's cottages down by the orchards. They used to be for the fruit pickers and the staff at the house, back when it had stables and everything. When my parents had to downsize, they tore down or sold almost everything. But not those cottages."

"Why not?"

"Firstly, there was the sentimental value in them, I suppose. A wish to one day have them filled with employees again, perhaps? Secondly, the cottages were dilapidated. They're not listed or protected, since they're patchworks of building work, from when Howard Hall was built up to the early 1970s when my family finally gave up and let them fall into disrepair." Laura moved her head from Kit's and looked down at her untouched cordial. "I don't know if any of the original bricks are even left. Shoddy work to begin with and badly maintained, it's apparent that my family cared a great deal more about Howard Hall than the worker's cottages."

Kit winced. "Sounds like it."

"I can assure you that sort of snobbery changed with me," Laura said firmly. "I care about our employees and always treat them as equals."

"I know you do."

"Glad to hear it," Laura said in relieved tones. "Anyway, I might have one of the cottages renovated. One or two of them aren't in such horrible nick. If I'm lucky, some quick structural work and a lick of paint might do it. I could live close to Howard Hall and bide my time until it passes to me."

Not having a clue about building upkeep, Kit merely nodded. They walked on in comfortable silence.

After a while, Laura tucked some hair behind her ear and mumbled, "Thank you for what you said before, by the way."

"Which part?"

An irresistibly bashful smile played at Laura's mouth. "That I'm the catch of the century."

"It's true. You're smart, sweet, funny, generous, and so attractive it kills my little lesbian libido."

"Are you sure that it's so little? You strike me as quite the amorous type," Laura said with a slight smirk.

Kit gasped. "You mean to tell me that you've noticed? I thought I hid that so well."

Laura bit her lip. "Afraid not. Not with the way those eyes of yours smoulder."

"Maybe that's just when I'm looking at you?"

Stop. She only broke up with Dylan a few days ago.

Laura took a long gulp of her cordial, nearly halving its content.

Kit smacked her own bottle against her leg. "Sorry. Ah! That was too flirty."

"No, it's fine," Laura said after quickly swallowing. "I think I might have started it."

They were quiet for a moment. Kit retracted her arm from Laura's shoulders and they put some distance between their bodies. They walked on, both finishing their drinks. Tasty as the cordial was, it wasn't enough to quash the hunger growling in Kit's belly.

"Um, unless there was something else you wanted to talk about, I should get something to eat before my lunch hour is over," Kit said.

"Yes. Me, too. Lunch at home is… interesting now.

Aunt Sybil pretends like nothing ever happened. The sadder I look, the more theatrically jovial she acts. It's disturbing. Tom doesn't notice or care about anything but himself, as always."

"He'll make a great playmate for Dylan if he and Sybil move in together."

Laura groaned. "Gosh. I hadn't thought of that possibility. Well, no matter how much I love that house, I'll move goddamn *miles* away if Dylan moves in."

"You can come live with me and Rajesh. Phyllis has room in her giant, slobber-covered dog bed."

"Smashing. Thanks," Laura drawled.

Kit sniggered. Then Laura's phone rang. She looked at it and sighed out the word, "Tom." She answered it and Kit heard her snarl, "Yes, I'll be there in a minute. Start without me."

"Eek!" Kit exclaimed. "Looks like my plan to trudge all the way back and hurriedly shove a cheap sandwich in my face is actually preferable to your luxurious, comfy lunch."

"Probably is. I'd invite you in, but I like you too much to put you through that. Want to borrow my car?"

Kit looked up at the sky where the clouds seemed to be clearing. "No, thanks, I've got some stuff on my mind and a walk usually clears things up."

"As you wish."

As Laura put her phone away, Kit couldn't help herself. "I've got to say, the *Jessica Jones* theme song as a ringtone – bit of an unexpected pick for you."

"Is it?"

"Mm. I'd expect either something more neutral and business-like or something, well, cutesy."

Laura shrugged. "It's my favourite show and people

around here don't have a clue what it is. Furthermore, quite a few of them have the theme song to *Only Fools and Horses* as theirs, and can therefore not complain."

Kit chuckled. "Agreed. Wait, *Jessica Jones* is your favourite show?"

"That surprises you?"

"Yeah. I guess I thought you'd be more into rom coms or documentaries. Or, you know, less dark shows."

Laura surveyed her for a while, then she smirked. "Maybe I like *Jessica Jones* because I have a thing for women with black hair and equally black leather jackets?" They both laughed as Kit adjusted her jacket and hair. Laura's laugh faded away and she fixed her gaze onto Kit's. "Also, people aren't only one thing, you know. Not only light or dark. Not just sweet or tough."

"Of course," Kit broke eye contact and shoved her free hand into her pocket. "I know you're not only sweetness and light. In fact, Rachel said you can be quite the shark at work."

"She did? Oh. Well. I mean, you sometimes have to be. I might have mentioned that it's not easy keeping this kind of business afloat in today's market of big brands and cheap imports. I'm never nasty or ruthless, but I do have to be a businesswoman."

"Makes sense. Hey, don't look embarrassed. It's wasn't criticism, in fact I think she meant it as a compliment. I know I certainly did when I brought it up."

Laura surveyed her again. "In that case, thank you." She cleared her throat. "Right, I should probably be getting back to the awkward lunch."

Kit shuddered. "Yikes, poor you. How about lunch tomorrow? We can save you the awkwardness for one day at least. Unless I put my foot in it, of course."

"Trust me, I'd much prefer that to lunch with Aunt Sybil. Shall I swing by the library at noon and pick you up?"

"Oh rather, I think you *shall*," Kit said in her poshest voice.

"Shush you. I was going to buy you lunch, but since you mock me you can very well pay for your own."

Kit grinned. "Totally worth it."

Laura shook her head with a smile. She leant in to give Kit another tight hug. In place of her usual air kisses, there was a kiss firmly placed under Kit's cheekbone. "See you tomorrow, dearest, sweetest Kit."

After that, it was quite a relief for Kit not to have to use her feet to get home. Instead, she floated the whole way on cloud nine, with a head and heart full of Laura Howard. It wasn't until she'd scoffed down lunch and was about to start work that she noted she was still dragging around an empty bottle of Gage Farm cherry cordial.

Chapter Fifteen

PERFECT AMOUNT OF BUM

During lunch the next day, Kit peered over her teacup at Greengage's favourite daughter. Laura was blowing on the liquid in her own mug, some sort of sweet coffee. Vanilla-caramel-foamy-marshmallow-pixie-dust macchiato, or whatever. Sweet tooth or not, Kit had to admit that it looked and smelled amazing.

Like Laura.

She coughed and scrambled for something to say to shake the thought. "This sandwich tastes like it was made last week."

Laura looked it over. "It does look a little soggy. Shall I go ask them to make you a new one?"

"Nah. I'm too hungry to wait."

"Suit yourself," Laura replied with a smile.

"So, was yesterday's lunch as crappy as you thought it would be?"

"Worse. They were both grumpy because I was late, especially Tom."

"You did tell them to start without you."

"Yes, but Aunt Sybil says that is not proper etiquette."

"For Christ's sake."

"Exactly. They're driving me mad. I did contact contractors to have a look at one of the old cottages in the end. But until they come back to me with an estimate, I'm stuck. It's fine when I can work, but weekends and evenings are awful."

Kit scratched her neck. "Well, when I got back from London, I was kinda avoiding some of my own problems and started a lengthy project – weeding out the nonfiction section. Which is huge for a small island! I still have some to do. And after that there's the stock of nonfiction in the basement. You wouldn't believe the amount of duplicates down there. So," she adjusted her glasses, "if you want a project away from home, you could lend me a hand. I'm mainly doing it when the library is closed. Since there isn't enough budget to pay me for my time, I treat myself to cheesy music and sweets while I do it."

Laura smiled impishly. "Hm. Which sweets?"

"I brought chocolate last time, but we can expand the selection to anything your sweet tooth desires."

Laura held out her hand. "Deal. When do I start?"

Kit shook the hand, exhilaration bubbling in her blood. "Tonight?"

"I'll be there," Laura vowed. "Right after the library closes."

"Brilliant!"

"Kit?"

"Yeah?"

She seemed to hesitate. "May I ask what you were avoiding?"

Kit blew out a breath. "Um, partly Aimee's sticky situation and partly something more personal. It's a long story. I'll tell you later, promise."

Laura beamed, and it hit Kit straight in the chest.

"All right. I'm nothing if not patient," Laura said. "After all, I was in a secret relationship for a little over a decade."

Kit sipped her tea. "Yeah. Crazy-pants."

Laura playfully slapped her arm. "For that, you're not going to get any of my superior library-sorting treats tonight. Now, eat your manky sandwich before we both have to get back to work."

❧

That evening Kit hurried to hug Laura hello. As they parted she got a closer look at Laura's face. It was blotchy, the eyeliner and mascara smudged around puffy eyelids.

Kit held her by the shoulders, examining her. "Hang on, you've been crying."

"No, no. It's my delicate upper-class eyes reacting to the socialist dust of the library."

"Laura, come on. None of that 'stiff upper lip and laugh it off' business. We're not *that* English. Something's wrong, talk to me."

She wiped away some misplaced mascara. "Fine. I… I didn't want to bother you with more Dylan stuff."

Kit squeezed Laura's shoulders through the thick coat. "You're never a bother. Tell me."

"Dylan came over for dinner tonight. Thankfully, he sat on the other side of the table from Aunt Sybil, but they kept exchanging loving glances and laughing at each other's stupid jokes." She grimaced. "Honestly, neither of them are funny. Even Tom couldn't make himself suck up enough to laugh at their limp banter."

"Ah, mate. I'm sorry. Why didn't you excuse yourself? Say you were having dinner with me?"

Laura laughed mirthlessly. "Aunt Sybil didn't actually bring him in until we were seated at the table and about to start eating. I thought about causing a scene and walking out, but it's not the Howard way. Besides, I'll have to get used to it. I assume he'll come over more often from now on."

"Yikes. You should pay those contractors a little extra to fix up the cottage quickly. Or maybe go on holiday for a while? Until the worst of the wounds have healed, if you know what I mean."

Laura ran her hand over her curls. "I can't leave. We're in the investigating stages of expanding our range of drinks to wine. Aunt Sybil can't be bothered with that sort of thing and the only interest Tom has in wine is showing off expensive ones to his dates."

"I see." Kit pushed her glasses up. "Maybe it's for the best. Even when you leave, Greengage seems to stay on your mind. I noticed that when I went to help Aimee. And I've only lived here for a few months. You've been here all your life."

"Mm. Well, except for when I went to business school."

Kit's head jerked back. "Business school? Huh. I never thought about that. I guess there's not much further education on the island. Where did you study?"

"Southampton University. I lived there for a while. Then I came home and took up the business side of Gage Farm right away. That's all I've done since."

"There you go, I've learned something new about Laura Howard tonight. Cool."

"I don't know how *cool* it is, but I do know that there's

plenty left that we can learn about each other." Laura undid her coat. "Oh, speaking of the mainland. I wondered if being back in London would tempt you to stay there. Did it highlight all the things you miss out on here on Greengage?"

Kit hooked her thumbs into the back pockets of her jeans while mulling that over. "When I first came to Greengage, I struggled with it being so small and not having the stuff I wanted, but—"

"Stuff? As in objects or amenities?" Laura interrupted.

"Amenities," Kit clarified.

"I see. Sorry, carry on."

It's not half as annoying when she interrupts as when Aimee does it. Man, I really do have it bad.

Kit tapped her foot. "Where was I? Right, yes, I realised that it has most things I need and that the mainland isn't that far away if I want something else. What Greengage lacks in shops and restaurants, it makes up for in fun and nice people. I'll give up Thai food to watch Mabel and Ethel quarrel. Or hear about Charlie Baxter's wheelbarrow."

Laura chuckled. "Glad to hear we haven't frightened you off with our quirkiness."

"Nah, you lot aren't that scary."

"Me? Not scary? Remember what Rachel told you. I can be quite the shark." Laura quirked an eyebrow with a devilish smirk.

Kit's knees wobbled. She swallowed any comments about wanting to be bitten or eaten and said, "Only in business. As long as we stick to a personal relationship, I bet I'll be safe."

"Not if you eat all the purple chocolates in the box of Quality Street I brought with me."

Kit put her hands up. "The purple ones are all yours as long as I get the green triangles."

Laura squinted at her. "Hm. Fine. It's a deal."

"Brilliant. That's the chocolates sorted. Onto the job then, those nonfiction books need our full attention."

"See, now that sounds like we're working together. Mind your extremities, these shark teeth are sharp." She snapped her jaw closed, and the sound was surprisingly scary.

Kit laughed. "Point taken."

Laura smiled at her before flinging her coat over the counter and saying, "Ready when you are."

Together, they walked over to the nonfiction shelves. Slowly, Laura ran her hand along the spines, and Kit tried in vain to not watch her fingers caress the books.

It was strange, all of a sudden, Kit's ribcage seemed to tighten.

Oh god. I'm not going to survive this night.

"So, what are we doing with these?" Laura called over her shoulder.

Kit shook her head to clear it. "You see the book with a pink Post-it note underneath it? That marks how far I've gotten on my own."

"I see it."

"Great. I'd like you to pick out a handful of books after that one, check them on the library system – I'll show you how to do that – to see if they've been borrowed in the last year. If they haven't, we need to check if there are others copies in the country that the Greengage residents could request. If there aren't, we have a duty to keep the book. If there are other copies, we can probably put it on the 'to be sold' pile."

Laura pouted, her plump lips unjustly distracting. "Getting rid of books seems so… severe. I feel bad."

Kit drew in a quick breath.

Finally! I've actually fallen for a woman who appreciates books.

"Yeah. But overfilling shelves damages the books and means that people can't find the ones they want. Also, we can't get new books in. You have to cull. Rajesh, however, hasn't been arsed to do it for years."

Laura dipped her head. "I see your point."

"Besides, like I said, we have duplicates in the basement. So you can sell one copy with a clear conscience. Especially as the money will go to maintaining the library. Speaking of the duplicates, after these shelves are tidied, it's time to venture down into the great, dark, and dusty basement," Kit whispered with a theatrical shiver.

Laura scrunched up her freckled, button nose. "Are you thinking spiders?"

"Yep, and possibly mice. I'll need you to deal with all of that. I'm a city girl, I only handle pets."

"I'm glad my vermin expertise will come in handy," Laura said with a laugh. "Actually, I had pet mice when I was twelve. Mickey, Minnie, and Winnie."

Kit leaned against the wall, hoping it looked casual and cool. "There you go, then."

"Until Aunt Sybil convinced my parents to make me get rid of them."

"Whoa. That woman seems worse with every story I hear. What did you do?"

"The only thing I could do. I released them." Laura looked mischievous. "Into *Aunt Sybil's bedroom*. She was furious! She tried to stomp on them, but they were too quick. Aunt Sybil was never athletic, I knew she couldn't catch them in a million years."

Kit laughed. "Good for you. Did they end up living in her bedroom, or did they escape out a window or something?"

"No, they were tame mice, they'd never survive in the wild. I snuck them back out when she left, then I gave them to Imelda Smith."

"Your cook?"

"Yes, well, I didn't exactly give them to her, but to her young son. Remember Jason from the pizzeria?"

"Sadly, yes," Kit muttered.

"For all his faults, he became a good mouse owner. With help from his parents and older sisters, of course, he was far too young to do it alone. He'd take pictures of them and show me. They all died of natural causes at a ripe old age in a loving home."

"Phew! Hang on. I get why two of them were called Mickey and Minnie, like the Disney mice. But why Winnie? Because it rhymed with Minnie?"

Laura bit her lip. "Not exactly."

Kit grinned. "Aha! There's a story here. Spill."

"Must I?"

"Yep."

"Fine, I... might've been under the illusion that Winnie the Pooh was a mouse."

Kit put her hand to her chest in feigned shock. "Laura! Everyone knows he's a bleedin' bear! He even brings that up in the stories, like, frequently."

"Yes, well, I suppose I wasn't listening properly. Anyway, let's move on. Show me how to check the books on the library system."

"All right. But after that I'm gonna find all our original

Winnie the Pooh books and your homework will be to read them cover to cover."

Laura smiled at her. "Tell you what, when we've finished for the night, why don't we take the chocolates and Winnie books over to those sofas and you can read them to me?"

"Only if you read some, too. Like I said that night on the way to Pub 42, I really like your voice."

Laura opened and closed her mouth before hoarsely whispering, "Thank you."

"Was that, um, inappropriate?"

"I don't think so." Laura avoided eye contact. "If you said you liked my ample arse, now that would be inappropriate."

Kit almost choked on air. "Hang on. Did the woman who usually says 'gosh' just say 'arse'?"

Laura sniffed. "I told you, there's more to me than you think."

"*More* to you? Is that why you said '*ample* arse'?"

Laura picked up a book about Norse gods and slapped Kit on the leg with it.

"Ouch," Kit exclaimed. "Sorry! I couldn't resist. No offence meant, you have the perfect amount of bum. Let's leave it there before I definitely say something inappropriate. Come over to the computer and I'll show you how to check the books."

Laura replaced the Norse gods tome and followed Kit. Subtly, Kit glanced back at her. Gone was any trace of dejection or crying. Laura was back to her normal open, sweet, beaming self.

At the sight, Kit walked a little taller.

Chapter Sixteen

WE KNOW WHERE THIS IS LEADING

Over the following week, Kit and Laura had spent their evenings finishing up the nonfiction section upstairs and were now working on the shelves down in the basement. There had been some distractions, like *Winnie the Pooh* reading, chocolate box comparisons, and play fights with bookmarks as weapons. All Kit's ideas. And all ending when Laura said they had to get back to work.

Now, on this rainy Sunday morning, when the library was closed as usual, they had decided to roll their sleeves up and get the lion's share of it finished. Laura's idea. She'd been so energised lately. Kit didn't know if it was because her heartbreak was fading or because them spending time together made Laura feel as good as it did Kit.

Now Laura was surveying the dusty, dim basement. "You know, I meant to ask when we first got down here. What are these shelves called? Not the plain ones in the corner, but these ones here, the ones with the lever you spin round to make them move back and forth? I don't think I've ever seen them anywhere else."

Kit racked her brain. "Mobile aisle shelving or something like that. They're mainly used in libraries and archives. Since you can roll them all together, I suppose they give you a lot of room to work with."

"Mm. Which means they've managed to store all the more books down here."

Kit sighed. "Yup. I'm sure there'll be some gold nuggets down here, but I think there's gonna be lots to cull as well."

Laura smiled. "More culling means more sales, which means more funds for the library."

"True. Actually, this basement isn't too bad. I've seen worse in some of the London libraries." Kit smoothed her hair, wondering if there was dust in it. "However, I've seen better ones, too. You know, modern, *clean* ones."

"At least your worries about spiders and mice have so far been unfounded," Laura said.

"True. Hey, what's in those?"

On the far wall, she had spotted a stack of large boxes.

Laura followed her gaze. "No idea."

With the help of the library's only pair of scissors, huge and blunt as they were, Kit opened the top one and whispered, "Whoa."

"What is it?" Laura asked.

"Looks like old vinyl records."

"Gosh, really?" She came over and began leafing through them. "These all begin with A or B. Do you think all the boxes are filled with old, alphabetised vinyl records?"

"Seems like it."

"What are we going to do with them?"

Kit scratched the back of her neck. "Well, I'll check if they're on the library system, but I bet they aren't." They both stared down into the box. Kit said, "Either way, by the looks of them, no one's touched them for years. We should try to sell them."

"Here or off-island?" Laura asked.

"What do you mean?"

"On Greengage we have a large elderly population, which are not known for embracing modern technology but are likely to keep something like an old record player," Laura said with a smile. "So, I'm certain you'd find buyers. However, they'd be buyers with shallow pockets. I'm willing to bet that the library will get far more money for these on the mainland, selling them to some hipster music shop or to a collector."

Kit pointed to her. "See! This is why you work with business stuff and I stick to books. What do you think I should do?"

"The side of me that you refer to as 'Business Stuff' says flog them off-island. The Greengage girl in me says sell them here, where they came from. In the end, I'd recommend leaving it up to Rajesh."

Kit slapped her forehead. "Ah, I forgot that this isn't my problem. I am but a humble minion, freed from all serious decisions," she declaimed.

Laura laughed and helped Kit close the box back up.

While Laura was searching for something in her pocket, Kit had her hands above her head, stretching out her back while breathing in deep. Yes, it was dusty and stuffy down here, but more prevailing than mustiness that was the scent of books. Shelf after shelf of leather-bound tomes.

Kit closed her eyes. "God, I love the smell of old books."

She stepped back when something overpowered that scent. Something she knew well and soon placed – Voyage

176

d'Hermès. Kit frowned. She hadn't put perfume on this morning. She opened her eyes and saw Laura standing right in front of her, observing her with lips slightly parted.

"I, uh, I mean, what are you looking at?" she spluttered.

"Oh! I didn't mean to scare you, Kit. It's merely that standing there with your eyes closed, stretching like that, with that look on your face, you looked so…" Laura trailed off and cleared her throat. "Never mind. I'm sorry if I startled you."

"You didn't. Just confused me. Because, um, did you spray my perfume a moment ago?"

"Well, technically I reapplied *my* perfume as *I* bought it." Laura fidgeted with her hair. "But yes, it's the one you have. The one you let me sample."

"Yeah. Voyage d'Hermès. The one I always carry with me because it's like *my trademark fragrance*?" Kit wasn't sure why this had her in such a possessive huff.

Laura looked away. "Well, I suppose so, yes. The truth is…" She paused. "The truth is that while you were in London I bought a small bottle for you. To thank you for helping me and Dylan. Then he tumbled into the arms of my blasted aunt and in my mind, the perfume was connected with that, so I put the bottle in a drawer and avoided it."

"Okay. I guess that makes sense. But then, why are you wearing it now?"

Laura kept her eyes averted, focusing on the wall. "Last night, I found the bottle again and was going to bring it to you this morning. After breakfast I opened it to sniff it and it reminded me of you, and I… wanted to wear it. Wanted to keep smelling it. I don't know why."

Kit tried to get the sensation of the ground bouncing like it was made of rubber balls out of her wobbly knees. She had a pretty good idea why Laura would feel the need to spray Kit's scent on herself and walk around smelling it all day and night. Kit had done that with nearly every crush she had ever had.

Her mind borrowed some expressions from Laura and tried them all out in shock.

Gosh. Golly. Blimey.

Then, because Kit was still Kit. Her brain settled on…

Bugger me.

She swallowed. "Um, well, it's a lovely perfume. It suits you."

Laura shrugged, gaze still on the wall. "I prefer it on you. I have the bottle with me. I'd like you to have it."

Without thinking, Kit reached out a hand and gently took hold of Laura's chin. She turned Laura's face towards her and looked deep into her eyes. "If you want me to have it, then sure. If you want to keep it, though… I'd be honoured to share the same scent as you."

Laura groaned quietly. "You have to stop being so perfect," she whispered.

"What? I'm not—"

Laura pulled away, eyes big and hands wringing. "Right. We should get back to work. We'll leave the vinyl for Rajesh. Let's carry on with the shelves, shall we? Where were we up to?"

Kit, sincerely shell-shocked, shrugged the emotions off best she could. "Um, over here," she said and led the way.

꧁

It was five-thirty p.m. Laura had been right, putting their

backs into it had resulted in the bulk of the work being completed. An hour or two after the perfume incident, they'd even cleared some of the awkwardness and tension that had built up. Some banter had come back during lunch, and through the afternoon, things had settled back into comfort.

Laura was presently popping out from her row of rolling shelves, holding up a book for Kit to see and asking, "Why on earth are there so many books on the mating habits of beetles here? Who even bought all of these?"

Kit's reply of not having the faintest idea was pushed aside by the basement's only light source, a naked light bulb high in the ceiling, going out.

Shrouded in darkness, Kit swore repeatedly and banged her hand against the wall.

"It's all right," Laura soothed. "It's only that ancient light bulb giving up the ghost. I left my phone over there on the boxes, do you have yours so we can use it as a torch?"

Kit shook her head before realising that Laura couldn't see her. "No. It's in my jacket up there somewhere."

"Hm. Then I suppose we'll have to feel our way towards the stairs."

Kit groaned inwardly.

Fumbling about in the dark with my crush? Fanfics and romantic comedies have taught me where this is going.

She took her glasses off and put a hand over her eyes.

There's no way I can be in a closed library, down in the pitch-dark basement, with my stunning crush – who probably feels the same but is only a couple of weeks out of a breakup – without the two of us colliding in some embarrassing way.

She rubbed her face hard and sighed.

What's it going to be, fate? Huh? Hands touching each other as we grapple blindly before us? Bumping into each other? If so, chest to chest or arse to arse? Which is worse? Which is more tempting to you, fate?

"You're awfully quiet," Laura called. "Are you okay?"

"Yeah," Kit muttered. "I'm not great with the dark. Spooks me a bit."

That wasn't a total lie, she was quite frightened of the dark.

"All right, well, you just stay there then. I'll make my way to the stairs."

Kit straightened up. Maybe this would be fine after all. She'd stay here until Laura had gone up the stairs and opened the door, letting the library lights beam down here. Or maybe even picked up a phone to light Kit's way. Yeah, this was going to work out without any inappropriate, romantic entanglements.

Ha! Take that, fate!

Naturally, it was during those thoughts Kit felt something against her shoulder. Thinking Laura far away somewhere by the stairs, Kit shrieked her lungs off.

"Sorry! Don't scream. It's only me," Laura's warm voice reassured her. "Now, please don't panic, but when I was on my way to the stairs, something ran over my foot. I think you were right. There are mice down here. Or rats."

Kit wasn't sure which was most disconcerting. That there were rodents surrounding them. That it was so dark. Or that Laura's hand on her shoulder was currently caressing up and down, feeling so incredibly good that Kit wanted to purr and lean into the touch.

There was a squeak on the floor, making Kit scream and jump forward, thereby bumping her body right against Laura's. But instead of leading to a smouldering moment of passion, or a hilarious slapstick scene, it simply led to Laura grabbing her and holding her for a brief second while softly saying, "It's okay, dearest. Everything's fine. They're as frightened as you are."

Kit made a noise somewhere between a hum and a whimper. Laura released her but kept a hand on her upper arm, rubbing it in a soothing rhythm.

"Breathe slow and deep. I'm going to uphold my end of the bargain and be the one who deals with the animal situation. Rats or not, I'm going for those stairs again. You stay here. Stomp your feet if you want to scare the rodents off. Okay?"

"Okay. Wait, Laura?"

"Yes?"

"Please hurry back," she whispered.

"Of course. Everything's going to be fine, honey. I'll be back in a jiffy."

Laura's voice had never sounded softer nor warmer than during those sentences.

Kit wanted to wrap up in those words and hide from the dark and the squeaking rats. And the mice. And the slimy creatures with giant teeth, rotting eyes, and hairy toes that her brain was currently making up.

She heard Laura's slow steps, as always loud in those high-heeled boots, grow quieter as she moved farther away.

Hang on. Did Laura call me honey? Bugger it all to hell. I want her to be with me so bloody badly. Stupid Dylan. Stupid Sybil. Stupid heartbreak. Stupid everything.

Laura's steps sounded different now. Kit guessed she was on the stairs. Then the door opened and light from upstairs spilled down. It wasn't bright by any means, but Kit could at least see where she was putting her feet.

"Kit, you okay?" Laura shouted down. "Do you want me to get a phone to light your way?"

"No, it's okay. I'm almost up now."

Kit climbed the last few steps and flung herself up into the safe library. Laura was waiting for her and gave her a quick hug before letting her catch her breath.

Leaning against the wall to hide her slight tremble, Kit tried for a natural-looking smile. "Wow. Sorry for getting so rattled."

"Don't worry about it. No one likes old, pitch-black basements with rats running over your feet."

"I'm still telling myself that they were cute little mice."

Laura nodded. "Naturally. They were descendants of my Mickey and Minnie, I'm sure."

"And Winnie," Kit added. "I'm sure some of them were weirdly yellow with red T-shirts and pots of honey under their little mouse arms."

"Oh, shush you! I'm trying to make you feel better and all you do is mock me."

"Sorry. Thanks again for being so sweet and reassuring down there."

Laura played with the hem of her turtleneck. "No need to mention it. I can't stand the idea of you ever being frightened or uncomfortable."

"Likewise," Kit said, her voice sounding as shy as Laura looked. "So, we should try to find a new light bulb and a ladder."

"Yes. First, though, I think we should eat." Laura stepped closer. "It's dinner time, you know."

"Really? Man, time flies when you're inhaling dust. Okay. Pizza?"

Laura grimaced. "No, thank you, not in the mood for that. Fish and chips?"

"No, too greasy. Pub 42? Those quesadillas were nice."

Laura bit her lip. "I think that if we… show our faces near Rachel and Shannon, we might get teased."

"Teased?"

Laura looked down while tucking hair behind her ear. "They seem to think we're on our way to becoming a couple and take every chance to either encourage it or tease me about it. If I even mention you, which I constantly seem to do, they make jokes. If we tell them that we spent the whole day alone in that basement and then the lights went off…"

"They'll make assumptions and tease you so much it'll make you break out in a rash," Kit finished for her. "Gotcha."

They looked at each other, unspoken things floating in the air between them like the dust motes from the basement.

Laura kept tucking away hair that was too thick and curly to ever stay behind her ears.

Kit blew out a breath. "So, burgers from that place by the ferry dock?"

Relief seemed to cure Laura's fidgeting. "Yes! Good idea. They have excellent chicken burgers."

"I'll go get our coats," Kit said.

When she was in the other room, she allowed herself a shaky little smile.

She's into me. She's got to be. Now what? I guess I wait for her to be ready? When she is… please let her ask me out because my silly arse sure isn't going to know how and when to do it.

She clenched her fists as her mind added, *Oh, and please don't let her be put off by the fact that I'm a woman or have her fall back in love with Dylan or something.*

Kit picked up the coats and hung them over one arm. Then she faced the ceiling and mumbled, "God, I haven't believed in you since I was a kid. But if you're listening, please give me the chance to make her happy. If you don't, I'm going to start worshipping pixies and fairies. Just so we're clear."

She paused to make another decision. Then, with firm resolve, she undid another button on her shirt, revealing enough of her humble cleavage and the top lace of her bra to draw attention from even the politest love interest. Then she strode back out to Laura.

Chapter Seventeen

TRYING NOT TO FLIRT. FAILING MISERABLY

The evening passed in an atmosphere of flirtatious joy, which was occasionally broken by how tentative they were around each other.

After dinner they decided they were both too tired to face more work or the ordeal of locating a ladder and light bulbs. Kit walked Laura home instead.

When they got to the door of Howard Hall, Laura pulled Kit into a goodnight hug. The embrace was tighter and lasted longer than usual. Long enough for Tom to shout, "Are you two glued together? Shall I call 999 and request an ambulance?" through a window. Laura had promised Kit she'd sneak laxatives into his evening cup of chai tea as punishment.

The next morning in the library, Rajesh and Kit had replaced the bulb and watched the basement light up, ready for the final session of sorting and culling later that night.

A tingle coursed through Kit as she envisioned another evening in Laura's company. This time she'd be smoother and figure out how to put Laura at ease. How hard could it be?

Kit worked through the day, helping people with books, magazines, reservations, computers, and occasionally taking money for fines. An average Monday in the library. Still, it didn't feel average to Kit. Every hour brought her closer to Laura. Closer to hearing that soft voice, to seeing those cute freckles which make-up couldn't quite hide, to knowing how Laura's day had been, to stealing glances and touches whenever appropriate.

When Rajesh told her to "stop walking around grinning like the bloody Cheshire cat," she couldn't really blame him. Nor could she stop that smile from tugging at the corners of her mouth.

❧

Finally, the day agreed to bring about closing time. While Rajesh was getting ready to leave, Laura arrived. In her hand was a basket filled with sandwiches, snacks, and Gage Farm apple cider.

Rajesh inspected it. "Looks lovely. I'd stay and try some of that if I didn't have a promising date," he said as he put his cardigan on.

"Goodnight, Rajesh, have a nice time with Mrs Shaw," Kit mumbled while also examining the picnic.

Laura gave him a set of air kisses and informed him that the way to Mrs Shaw's heart would be a box of Turkish Delights, as they were her favourite treats.

When he'd gone, Kit was still busy inspecting the basket. "She likes Turkish Delights, huh? I can't believe how well you know everyone."

"Side effect of being a Howard," Laura said with a shrug.

"Doubt it, your brother wouldn't know. You take an interest in this place and its people, that's where the whole 'Greengage's favourite daughter thing' comes from." Kit prodded at the picnic pieces. "I also can't believe how bloody organised you are. This is as neatly packed as that welcome basket you got me when I moved in."

Laura joined her. "I like doing things like this. Life is messy. At least when I arrange a basket I can make it beautiful and tidy. It should have everything we need and fancy, which is yet another way my basket is superior to life."

Kit smiled, making certain they had eye contact. "Oh, I don't know. Life seems to be bringing me what I *need and fancy* lately. I can't complain."

Laura blushed, making Kit's heart soar. She must have felt her cheeks heating as she covered them and whispered, "Please say my cheeks aren't bright red."

"Hey, there's worse things than pink cheeks," Kit reassured her. "I mean, I have them all the time."

"Actually, I have always wondered about that. I never knew if it was rouge or if you were born with it."

"I rarely wear make-up unless it's for a party," Kit said. She tapped her cheeks. "These things are always pink. Like I've been out playing in the snow or something. Ridiculous."

"Beautiful," Laura amended instantly. "Goes well with your... sharply blue eyes. To paraphrase someone I admire, 'What do you call it when eyes are that shade of blue? There's a precise word for that.' Hm?"

Kit shoved her hands in her pockets, remembering that day when she was meant to be comforting Laura and instead started geeking out about words and Laura's hazel eyes.

"Aimee says they're cornflower blue," she murmured.

Laura inspected her eyes long enough to make Kit squirm, then said, "Yes. Cornflower. That's the exact word. How is Aimee, anyway?"

Kit pushed her glasses up, noting that her hands were trembling a little. "Pretty much recovered, all that's left is feeling run down and sleeping a lot. The financial situation is a different picture. Things look pretty bleak, so she'll have to move somewhere cheaper. The question is when and where. She wants to stay within easily commutable distance of her job and the childminder."

"Makes sense."

"It would, if her boss hadn't been grumbling about her being sick so much. Which means she feels like she's on thin ice at the office, wondering if she'll get fired. I keep telling her she'd be better off finding a new place to settle, including a new part-time job."

"Why doesn't she?"

"What, move? Or get a new job?"

"Both."

"She won't move because she says she wants to stay, and I quote, 'Where there's civilization and you don't need to own a car.' I can't really imagine her in anything smaller than Raynes Park." Kit scuffed the ground with the tip of her shoe. "Job-wise, like me she knows what it's like to be unemployed and live on porridge, getting job rejection after job rejection. She can't handle that anxiety again, especially not now that she has George."

Laura fished out a neatly folded blanket from the basket and spread it on the floor by the lending counter. "I didn't think of that. Gosh, I'm so privileged. Since

Southampton, I've never had to interview and worry about rejection. And when I did get part-time jobs in Southampton, I knew that if I lost the job and ran out of money, Aunt Sybil would save me with a bank transfer. Even if it did come with weeks of lectures and guilt-tripping."

"Yeah, my family wasn't well off, but my dad would've pitched in if I was starving," Kit said quietly. "Aimee's parents have money, but they also have this weird thing about being a survivor and being independent. They both had to make their way on their own and think it's a character flaw to need help. Which would make sense if they had a kid who needed tough love, but Aimee isn't lazy or weak, she's just had bad luck and needs a hand."

Laura put the picnic basket on the blanket and sat down. "Poor Aimee."

Kit joined her. "Yeah, she has a toddler, a low immune system, anxiety, unhelpful parents, and a useless ex-husband."

Laura moved a little closer. Kit pretended not to notice and kept talking. "She might have to leave London for George's sake. If she was on her own, however, she'd rather starve there than move to some quiet town. She needs to live in the bustle, where people are open-minded, and leave you alone, let you be anonymous, you know?"

Laura chuckled. "As a Greengage girl, I can certainly see why that would be appealing."

"Speaking of Greengage, I did tell Aimee that if everything fell apart she should grab George and come stay at Rajesh's. She actually scoffed at me. Said she'd be so claustrophobic here she'd swim all the way back to the mainland."

"Thinking about how much swimming that would take makes me hungry," Laura said.

"Really?"

"No, I was trying to switch the focus back to my picnic basket. I'm famished."

"Ah." Kit shook her head with a smile. "Wow, I was being really dense there. I'm hungry, too. Let's empty that basket before we brave the basement!"

Laura awkwardly held up her hand, and this time Kit knew she expected a high five. Their hands smacked together, and Kit let her fingers caress Laura's as they let go. That wasn't pushing it, was it?

"I'm afraid there's far too much cheese on the sandwiches," Laura said. "Our cook made them, and she knows I love cheese. Which explains the chubbiness, I suppose."

Kit started digging through the basket. "I still don't think you're chubby. You're curvy and healthy."

"Use whatever adjective you wish," Laura muttered. "I just want your fit body."

Kit looked up at her, freezing in the middle of picking up a jar of jam.

Laura stared back. "I, oh, gosh. I didn't mean it that way. Not that I 'want your body' like that, but that I'd rather *have* a body like yours. Not have it as in have it sexually, you understand." Her eyes widened. "I don't mean that I wouldn't desire your body because it's undesirable. I mean, it's a smashing body and anyone would want it. Either to look like that or for... um, sexual purposes. Wait, that was an awful expression. I meant for erotic use. No, hang on, I..." She trailed off, burying her face in her hands.

Kit grinned. "Do you want a shovel to dig yourself further into that hole, mate?"

Laura gave her a playful smack on the arm. "Shush. You know what I meant."

"Yes. You don't want my body for erotic use," Kit deadpanned.

Laura hid her face in her hands again and groaned.

Kit sniggered but decided to let her off the hook. "Change of topic. This gage jam looks great. What are we having that on?"

Fanning her heated face, Laura mumbled, "There are scones in the Tupperware box at the bottom. And there should be a jar of clotted cream somewhere. I prefer that jam on waffles or crumpets, but I didn't know if you had anything to heat them."

Still holding the jam, Kit bumped Laura with her shoulder. "You're a crumpet. A really hot one."

Laura laughed while opening the box containing scones. "Surely that's as bad as my 'want your body' comment?"

"Nope, mine was intentional. Yours was innocent on the surface but naughty underneath."

Laura reached out and snatched the jar from Kit. "Exactly like me, then," she said in a deep voice. "Now stop hogging the jam."

Kit watched Laura with open-mouthed admiration as she ignored the sandwiches and salad and went straight to slathering jam and clotted cream on a scone. She looked blissful as she prepared the unhealthy thing which had now replaced a nutritious dinner. Then she took a big bite and smirked at Kit as she slowly licked clotted cream off her lip.

Sweet with a sprinkling of wicked. Exactly what I've always wanted.

With a smirk of her own, Kit grabbed the scone out of Laura's hand, making her gasp and exclaim, "Hey!" Laura's features softened as she watched Kit nibble her stolen prize. "Fine. Have it. I suppose I should have some salad anyway. I'll need the vitamins if we're going to be in that sunless basement for the next few months."

"Nah, you're too efficient for it to take more than one more session. I've never seen anyone learn a new task so quickly and then race through the job without messing stuff up. With you helping me, I bet we'll finish in a couple of hours."

Laura smoothed down her dress. "Unless I slow down to make sure it takes all night."

"To punish me for stealing the scone or because you like being in my company?"

Laura smiled. "Wouldn't you like to know?" She reached out and ran a finger under Kit's lower lip. "You had some jam there."

She put her finger in her mouth, sucked the jam off, and then started to unpack some plastic cutlery and the salad. All while Kit sat there, trying to remember how to breathe.

✤

Around three hours later, they'd not only eaten but also finished clearing the basement stock. They were now back in the library and inspecting the fruits of their labour.

Laura wiped her forehead. "That's an impressive 'for sale' pile you have now."

"Yeah, it's brilliant. Rajesh is quite the salesman, he'll make all the library users cough up a quid or two and leave with purchased books on top of their borrowed ones."

"No doubt! And what won't sell can be recycled, right?"

"Yep." Kit put her hand on Laura's shoulder. "Thanks again for all your help. This would've taken me ages on my own."

"You're very welcome. As you know, I needed the distraction. And the excellent company!" She hesitated before adding, "Will you tell me why you started the weeding project in the first place now? You promised you would."

Kit removed her hand. She considered lying, but the truth was stinging on her tongue, wanting out.

"Yeah. I, uh, had some romantic feelings I was avoiding. Or processing, I guess."

Laura's forehead furrowed. "Oh."

"Mm."

They stood in painful silence for a while.

Slowly, Laura began packing away the empty containers and leftovers from their picnic. Kit helped, staying inches away from Laura's hands and body at all times. The tension was so thick she wouldn't even need a knife to cut it, she could grab a slice right out of the air.

When everything was tidied away, and they were standing face to face, Laura bit her lip and murmured, "Kit?"

"Yes?"

"Tell me honestly. Do you think it's too early for me to date?"

Kit shifted her weight from foot to foot, trying to

pretend that she wasn't pleading with fate, God, and the damn pixies that she was the one Laura wanted to date.

Don't be presumptuous. No one likes that.

"I don't know. It's been a little more than two weeks since the breakup. Does it feel too early?"

"No. Yes. Maybe. I don't want to rush into anything, even if I feel ready. I don't want you to be a rebound."

Kit's breathing halted. That last sentence echoing in her head. *'I don't want you to be a rebound.'* There was the confirmation she'd needed so much it had been suffocating her. She had assumed, of course, but hearing it was so much more powerful than she could've guessed. Butterflies filled Kit's stomach to the point where she wondered if they were about to fly out of her mouth and ears.

"Well, um, I'm willing to risk that if you are," she began. "I've been a rebound before, and it ended in a six-year long relationship. Probably would've lasted longer if she and I didn't want different things."

Laura tucked hair behind her ear. "Do you... think *we* want the same things?"

"Depends. How does a quiet life sound? With lots of nights at home, cuddling while reading, or cuddling while cooking, or cuddling while watching movies."

"Heavenly."

Kit licked her lips. "Okay. What about an occasional holiday somewhere? See some nature and a few museums but mainly chilling in the sun or in a snowy cabin?"

"Also heavenly."

Kit's heart was racing. "All right. Um, what else? You pick something."

Laura tapped her fingers against her lower lip. "How about staying on Greengage and one day moving in with me? Either in the renovated cottage or taking over Howard Hall?"

"Perfect. I'm totally in love with this island."

"Great!" Laura clasped her hands in front of her, then her hands dropped while the glee on her face was replaced with something *intense*. "What about most of those nights at home ending with… you know?"

Kit made her face blank. "No. What?"

"Copious amounts of…" Laura smiled self-deprecatingly. "…erotic use."

Kit didn't know whether to laugh at Laura poking fun at her earlier mishap, or to try to be sexy about the offer of copious amounts of sex. Either way, she was buzzing.

"Laura. I'd be overjoyed, thrilled, proud, and fifteen other words for 'incredibly chuffed' to get any amount of lovemaking with you. I don't think I've ever wanted someone the way I want you."

"The feeling is very much reciprocated." Laura beamed. "Anyway. More questions to check if we can pass the test. How about getting a dog at some point? And discussing children – but I'll say right now that I can go either way on that."

"Me, too. Oh, and yes to the dog. But I'd rather have a cat," Kit said eagerly.

Laura stepped forward. "Yes! We'll have both. I'll buy you any pet you want and love it almost as much as I—" She stopped with a panicked look.

Kit's cheeks burned. "Okay. Um. We've established we're probably compatible and could survive a rebound start. Let's not steam ahead too much. We shouldn't go too far into the U-Haul lesbian stereotype."

"You mean the 'bring a toothbrush and ask for your own key on the first date' syndrome?"

Kit laughed. "Ah, you know it? I knew you were gayer than you seemed."

"I certainly seem to be anytime you're near," Laura purred.

Choking on her laugh, Kit gawked at her. Then she swallowed and whispered, "Please don't."

"Don't what?" Laura asked softly.

"Don't take my breath away like that."

Laura looked like she was about to say something, but then she closed her mouth.

They stared at each other and the seconds ticked by. Laura's eyes flashed. Her lips were slightly parted, but there was a line between her brows that spoke of worry. Kit wondered if her expression was a perfect mirror of Laura's.

With agonising effort, Kit forced herself to break the spell. She took her glasses off, pretending that she needed to polish them. In truth, she couldn't watch Laura's beautiful face anymore. Not without kissing her or saying something they weren't ready for.

"I should go close the door to the basement," Kit said. "We're letting all the dust up here."

"Hold on. I never got a chance to tell you why I brought up dating."

Kit wanted to kick herself. "Right. Soz."

"Soz?" Laura quirked an eyebrow. "Look at you with the modern slang. What's next? 'Totes'?"

"Don't tell me 'totes' made it out here on Greengage?"

Laura put her hands on her hips. "We're not in the Stone Age you know. We use abbreviations and slang. We've heard of stuff like Tinder, WhatsApp, and Uber. We even have running water and penicillin."

Kit extended her hand and wobbled it in a "the jury's still out" gesture.

"Anyway," Laura said in an admonishing tone, "I wanted to ask you to come with me to the opening night of the Greengage Theatrical Society's new play on Friday night. It's a big deal because the theatre has been closed for renovations for two years. It'll be—"

"Yes."

"I haven't given you all the details yet."

"The answer is still yes."

"Great!" Laura said, beaming. "I need the moral support. It's the first public event where Aunt Sybil is bringing Dylan. They're officially coming out as a couple. It's vile. Naturally, I had to bring someone to show that I'm over it and doing fine."

Kit stiffened. *What? This seems less about us and more about trying to prove something. Wait. Where does that leave us? Is it still a real date?*

She tried to look casual. "Sure. That makes sense."

"Oh, I'm so relieved. You're so helpful."

Helpful? She sounded like she was about to profess love a few minutes ago and now... she seems to be asking a friend for a favour. She isn't putting the brakes on, is she? Ask her! Ah, why is it so hard to get the damn words out?

Kit rubbed her left eyebrow. "Not a problem. I've never been to a Greengage event like that before. Should be interesting."

"That's one word for it," Laura droned. "Right, I should get home, shower, and have an early night. I'm sad to say I have a meeting at seven tomorrow morning."

"Okay. Text me with details about the theatre? Then maybe we can discuss it over lunch tomorrow?"

"Absolutely, I'll send you all the details as soon as I've gotten home and double-checked the times on my tickets.

I have to text you goodnight anyway. I can't go a day without talking to you anymore, Kit."

"I know the feeling."

Laura smiled. "So, lunch tomorrow, did we say?"

"Any day you want."

"We'll aim to make it a daily habit, then." Laura buttoned up her coat. "Unless I get held up at work or have a lunch meeting, of course."

"Yeah, of course," Kit echoed.

They hugged and said their goodbyes. As she watched Laura walk out, Kit swore to herself that at some point during this week she'd clarify where they stood and if Friday night was a "real" date or not. If it wasn't, she was asking that woman out on a real, one hundred percent romantic date and even pre-booking a kiss goodnight. If Laura said no, at least Kit would know what was what.

She nodded to herself and began locking up.

Chapter Eighteen

IN AND OUT

L ater that night, Kit was on the phone to Aimee, giving her a recap of the evening. She was pacing back and forth with Phyllis on her heels. The dog was panting at the unexpected exercise. Or maybe it was something else. Phyllis had a master's degree in panting and wasn't afraid to use it.

"So, that's how we left it," Kit wrapped up. "What do you think?"

Aimee blew out a breath. "Well, I can't really help you as I didn't hear the tone of her voice or see the body language. And I don't know her."

Kit whinged. "Aimee. Please guess."

"All right, all right, don't get your knickers in twist." She hummed. "I'd say wanting to prove something to Sybil and Dylan wasn't Laura's main reason for asking you. Not after all that romantic gubbins about having copious amounts of sex and getting a dog. Not to mention the flirting over the scone. By the by, the whole 'jam and scone' thing is so Olde Worlde Britain that it makes me dizzy."

"Yeah, that's Greengage – all croquet and cucumber sandwiches. Never mind that, back to Laura's reason for asking me out."

"As I said, considering everything that's happening between you, I'm convinced her main reason was wanting to ask you out."

"You think? It wasn't just to have a lover to show off? Or to not have to face the evening alone?"

"You muppet! If that was all it was she wouldn't have been talking about you not being a rebound first, would she? She could've simply asked you to come with her as a friend and pretend it was a date. Instead, *she asked you to date her.*"

"I suppose," Kit mumbled.

"Also, remember that her best friend said weeks ago that Laura fancies you. So, you know, maybe time to get your head out of your arse?"

"Rude."

"Uh, yes? That's my personality, remember? I'm only looking after my best friend, though. As you yourself said when I visited, you're rubbish at hitting on women and knowing when they're hitting on you. You asked for my opinion? Here it is. From what you've told me about your interactions, Laura is committed to you guys and fancies the pants off of you."

Kit took her glasses off and rubbed the bridge of her nose. "I guess. If she does want to be more than friends, I have to make sure that she's emotionally ready and that she's really attracted to *me*, not to the attention and the fun of flirting. Or to the first person who treats her well." Kit paused to put her glasses back on. "Also, is she sure about the whole woman-loving-woman thing? She's only been with a woman once and that was when she was young. Is she ready for a life of being different and having homophobia lurk around every corner?"

"There's a way to sort all this out."

"Asking her," Kit groaned.

"That's the one."

"I will. But I'm… scared of rejection, I suppose. I really like her, Aimee. Really, really like her."

"Yes, you muppet! I told you that, remember? You were here, running around with my angelic son while I was dying from tuberculosis in my bed."

"You mean when I selflessly looked after your pooping womb nugget while you acted like pneumonia was worse than being eaten alive by piranhas?"

"Ah, you *do* remember."

Kit laughed. "Piss off."

"Now who's being rude? Remember what that scary teaching assistant we had used to say? 'Language, Miss Sorel. You will fail at life if you use foul words.' Remember her? Did she really come to school in a hearse or did I dream that?"

"I think you dreamt that." Kit leaned her head against the wall. "I miss having you around."

"I miss having you around, too, you berk."

Aimee's voice had been quiet and seemed so frail that Kit's heart stung.

She tried to sound chipper for them both. "Enough about me. Have you thought any more about what you're going to do about the moving thing?"

"Not really."

"Aimee, you can't keep burying your head in the sand. It'll only make it worse. You need to act before everything comes toppling down."

"I know, I know. Stop bloody berating me. I get enough of that from my parents."

"Sorry. Hey, you know I love you, right?"

"Yeah. I love you, too," Aimee whispered.

"Cheer up, sweets. Everything's going to be okay."

There was a long sigh on the line. "Maybe if I could bounce ideas off someone. I've got a map of Greater London here. Before you called I was making notes on it while checking online for places to live, seeing where I can afford and all that. But I need someone to help me reason out which areas would be too unsafe or too far away from the office."

"Sure! I'd love to help. Let's FaceTime and you can show me the map."

"Cool. Can I also show you where George drew a princess slaying a dinosaur on my hip this morning? It's pretty special stuff. Other kids just draw dinosaurs."

"Not if it means taking your jeans and knickers off. I don't need to see all that."

"Oi! What's the point of having lesbian friends if they don't fancy you?"

Kit shrugged. "Sorry. You're too rude to be my type. Now FaceTime me."

"All right, I'm doing it! Keep your hair on, woman."

Kit smiled at the glee in Aimee's voice.

About two decades of solving each other's problems. Laura's right, I'm lucky to have a best friend like Aimee.

⁊⁌

Friday night came around without any warning. Typical Friday to be so inconsiderate.

Kit was standing in the middle of a dressed-up and

incessantly chatting crowd. They were all in the theatre's foyer, mingling over drinks, killing time. Apparently, there was about an hour until the play started.

She blinked repeatedly. Wearing mascara and eyeliner always made her eyes dry. She wanted to rub them but didn't want to ruin her make-up and didn't have a free hand with which to do it. One hand held a champagne glass and the other a bag, or rather a clutch, which Laura had lent her to go with the pencil skirt Kit had borrowed. Along with a pair of barely fitting heels. And a pair of uncomfortable tights. At least Kit was wearing her own shirt. And knew she looked absolutely smashing, which had been the goal and would normally make her happy. Right now, though, she was too annoyed at herself to be happy. She tapped the clutch against her thigh, harder and harder.

Idiot. You've had a week to confirm where you stood and what this date meant. All those lunches, texts, and even two bloody dinners. Did you ask her? No. Because you're a twit.

Laura leaned in to whisper, "Are you all right?"

Kit gripped her glass hard at the smell of her own perfume. Laura had bought a new bottle for herself after giving Kit the little one. It was still strange to smell her unusual signature scent on someone else, even more so on a woman as extraordinary as Laura. Especially tonight when she looked brain-meltingly astounding in a curve-hugging burgundy dress and what looked like diamonds in her ears and around her neck. That diamond in the neck-lace, dipping dangerously low into her generous cleavage, hypnotised Kit.

Don't look. Deep breaths. Stay calm.

"Uh, yeah, just a bit frazzled. I'm, uh, going to go walk it off. Be right back."

She marched off and went through the first door she found, assuming it was the bathrooms. It wasn't. It turned out to be a kitchen.

Dammit. Well, if you go back out, everyone will know you got lost.

Kit looked around. At least it was empty. If someone came in, she'd tell them she was looking for someone. She put her glass down and saw that champagne had dribbled down the side of it. She quickly checked her white shirt.

The sound of an opening door made her jump. She turned and saw Laura step into the kitchen.

"Kit? Ah, this is where you're hiding. You okay?"

"Yes," she lied. "I'm making sure I haven't spilled champagne on my shirt. I seriously can't wear light colours without being covered in stains in two seconds."

Laura looked her up and down. "I can't see any stains."

"No, I think I dodged a bullet there."

"I love this shirt," Laura said. She placed her hands on Kit's waist and smoothed the fabric. "Nicely fitted but not too tight to move and breathe in."

Breathe. Bad word to bring up. Kit's breathing had already picked up when Laura was checking her torso, those hazel eyes gazing at everything the shirt covered. Breathe. She had to remember to breathe correctly. But how could she when Laura was staring at her chest with a playful, wicked smile on her lips? Her hands were warm and steadying on Kit's waist, lingering there, holding Kit in place. Almost as if she was staking a claim.

Kit now saw confidence in Laura, something that was usually saved for her work life.

Her breathing sped up again. Laura had to stop looking at her like that. Like she was older, more experienced, and preparing to seduce a young ingénue. Kit was the one with experience here, she was meant to do the seducing, wasn't she?

"Beautiful," Laura said, her warm voice lower than usual. Firmer.

Was she still pretending to admire the shirt or was she talking about Kit? Either way, Kit's breaths were coming in fast and hot. How long were breaths meant to be?

Make a joke to break the tension, her brain hissed. *Or kiss her. Do something!*

Laura's gaze founds hers. "Calm down, dearest. You're breathing too fast, you're going to hyperventilate."

Her hands moved from Kit's sides and up her belly, over her breasts, stopping right above them, her fingers resting on Kit's collarbones and her palms flush to her chest.

"Calm," she repeated softly. "Breathe deeper."

"I-I can't."

"Then you'll have to copy my breathing. Look at me."

Kit watched Laura take long, slow breaths. Her face still smiling, but kinder now, less seductive. Somehow that was even more irresistible.

"Watch my chest and time your breathing to mine," she said. "We don't want you fainting and hitting your head. I invited you to this nightmare evening, I'm responsible for seeing you survive it."

Kit's gaze dipped obediently. Laura's generous breasts meant the pinstriped blouse she wore fit snugly. Kit tried not to think about that as she watched Laura's chest rise and fall with every breath. She concentrated on matching the rhythm.

"Good. That's it," Laura said. "In. Good. And now out. In. And out," she said in time with their breathing. She repeated it again, but this time, her eyebrow arched, and that wicked smile was back. "You're doing so well. In and now out. Slowly. Yes. Just like that, honey. In and back out."

There was no mistaking the second meaning of those words and every time Laura said them, Kit knew that they were both thinking about the sexual double entendre. Unable to stop herself, Kit found herself changing her stance by spreading her legs. Laura looked down and groaned a little.

"Yes! That's right, my dearest. In and out."

Kit couldn't help the moan sneaking past her lips. How could breathing with someone be this intensely erotic? It took everything she had not to move her hips, rocking them back and forth to the unhurried rhythm of "in and out" that Laura was now whispering.

Slowly, oh so slowly, Laura's hands lowered until they were cupping Kit's breasts.

"Oh god," Kit mumbled.

"I want you so much it's killing me," Laura whispered back.

Her hands squeezed and Kit moaned again.

A loud cough came from their right. "Pardon the intrusion."

They broke apart and both stared at the doorway where a man stood.

"Hello, Mr Baxter. How are you?" Laura croaked.

Kit put her hand to her forehead. "Shit. This is too much. Baxter? There's about six thousand people on this island and you're telling me I've been caught in an intimate situation by another person related to Charlie Baxter, the wheelbarrow guy?"

Laura shook her head. "No, dearest. You've been caught in an intimate situation *by Charlie Baxter*."

"The wheelbarrow guy," he provided helpfully.

Kit gaped at him. It was hard to determine his age, but his dark hair and moustache were streaked with grey. He was a thin man with an animated face, which would probably be quite jovial when it wasn't painted with embarrassment.

"You're Charlie Baxter? The bloke who was harassed with his own wheelbarrow for trying to mediate in the STD feud?"

He furrowed his brow. "I've never heard it summed up like that. And to be frank, it's not what I'd like written in my epitaph. But yes, I suppose I am. I'm also in charge of this event and you're standing in the way of the trays of hors d'oeuvres which waiters will soon come in to fetch."

"Ah, so you weren't stopping us because you disapprove?" Laura asked.

"No! Certainly not. You've had enough heartache with Dylan Stevenson and deserve someone who'll appreciate you. From what I hear, the famous 'lesbian Londoner' would fit that bill. Even Cousin Mabel, who usually only criticises, says you two are a good match and a nice couple. Her words, not mine."

"Whoa," Kit exclaimed. "*Mabel Baxter* said that? I didn't know she even had words that could be strung together to form positive sentences."

"You've met my cousin Mabel?"

"Yep."

"My apologies," he said.

Kit shrugged. "She's not your fault."

"No, but I tend to still apologise on behalf of the entire Baxter family. Rather like Laura tends to apologise for her aunt, Sybil—"

"Or Tom," Laura muttered.

"Yes, or him," Mr Baxter said with sympathy. He addressed Kit again. "On an island where everyone knows everyone, and each family has several black sheep, you end up apologising and rolling your eyes over relatives quite a bit."

"Sure." Kit realised she was gawking. "Sorry, Mr Baxter, I'm still shocked that Mabel said something so kind about us."

"Call me Charlie. Oh, and it's not only her," he said. "A number of people have mentioned you two being a good match."

"I should've known that everyone was talking about us," Laura muttered. "Good news that some support our relationship, at least. It means we should have less malignant gossip than couples who are generally disliked."

"Like Sybil and Dylan?" Charlie asked with a grin.

"I hadn't thought about that," Laura said with a stunned look. Then she stood taller. "And I shan't do so in the future because as of right now – I'm done thinking about them. They don't deserve that power over me!"

Certain she was still two steps behind in this conversation, Kit cleared her throat. "Good, they sure as hell don't! However… can we back this conversation up a little? Laura, you said 'our relationship' and 'other couples' earlier."

Laura looked like a deer caught in headlights. "I did?"

"Yes. Are you referring to you and me as a couple?"

Laura paled. "I'm so sorry! I didn't mean to rush you. You're still new to this island full of odd people, and I know we've been taking it slow so you don't become my rebound. And you said we shouldn't be such a lesbian cliché and steam ahead. However, I…" She wrung her hands. "I like you so awfully much. No, more than that.

I'm falling in love with you. And I can't imagine not being with you. I'm sorry, I didn't mean to be presumptuous in calling us that, I simply—"

She didn't get the chance to say anything else as Kit had rushed her and kissed her square on the mouth.

Pulling away a second later, Kit panted, "Ah, bollocks! Sorry! I didn't mean to do that movie thing where the woman never gets to finish her sentence because some bloke kisses her to shut her up. I never want you to shut up, I only did it because I've wanted to kiss you for so long. I'm falling in love with you, too, head over bloody heels."

There was a discreet cough. "Ladies. I truly hate to break up such a lovely scene. However, you've now both apologised, you both know what the other one feels, and you've shared a kiss. Superb! Now, could I trouble you to move along? The servers are waiting on the other side of this door, and the guests are growing impatient."

Charlie looked so apologetic that Kit had to smile. Laura patted his shoulder and thanked him.

Then she took Kit's hand and together they sauntered past him and out through the door. Although saunter was the wrong word, Kit thought. It was more like floating on air. Or clouds. Or rainbows made of spun sugar.

They parted crowds of staring people, they might've even passed Sybil and Dylan, but they only had eyes for each other. Then they were out of the stuffy building, still walking and holding hands.

Laura leaned in to kiss Kit's cheek and say, "Well, this went south. We better plan another date. A better one."

Kit looked up at the starlit sky. "Hmm. What about Pub 42? Let's give Rachel and Shannon something to really talk about!"

Laura chuckled. "Why not? Tomorrow night? Then we can make it a late night since we are both off on Sundays."

"It's a date. Literally."

"Wonderful," Laura sighed.

A few seconds later, Kit looked back at the theatre. "There's one thing I regret about what happened in there."

Laura's face fell. "Oh. What's that?"

"I didn't have the frame of mind to ask Charlie why he thinks they concentrated on his wheelbarrow."

Laura laughed, and Kit's knees made a strange transition to something liquid. "God, Laura, can I please kiss you again?"

"No, because it's my turn to kiss you," Laura said.

She took hold of Kit's glasses and gently tugged them away. Kit was about to say that she could kiss perfectly well with specs on, but somehow... the way Laura took them off was strangely intimate. And erotic. Like she was undressing her. Laura carefully put the glasses in the pocket of her suit jacket and then placed her hands on either side of Kit's face. Inch by inch that beautiful mouth approached. It took all Kit's patience to not lunge forward straight into the kiss, but she let Laura set the pace.

It was worth the wait. Laura's lips were hot in the chilly evening air and her mouth tasted sweet, of apple juice. When her tongue slid between Kit's lips, it was as if someone had set off fireworks of pleasure in Kit's every nerve ending. She was giddier than any kiss had ever made her, and she had to hold on to Laura's rounded hips for support, something which set off a different, *less wholesome* sort of giddiness.

The kiss ebbed out, and they drifted apart, staring into each other's eyes as if they'd uncovered some secret miracle.

"That was some kiss."

"Yes," Laura breathed.

Some moments of blissful gazing later, the magic broke as Kit shivered. "I wish we hadn't left our coats in your car."

"Let's go get them. Then we can stealthily kiss in the backseat before I drive you home. Don't worry, I didn't have any champagne, I'm fine to drive."

"You'll have to get drunk off me, then," Kit said with a wink.

Laura took her hand and began leading her towards the car. "I already am."

Chapter Nineteen

DATE NEAR BAD-TEMPERED COWS

K it smoothed down her ironed white shirt and black chinos, groaning at having to be dressed up again. At least this time it wasn't to impress all the Greengage toffs. Only one *special* Greengage toff.

Laura had clearly made an effort as well. In her case that meant leaving her suits and serious dresses at home and wearing grey skinny jeans and a blue cashmere jumper. Kit peered at it. Was that… cornflower blue? Was that intentional?

"It's busy in here tonight," Laura pointed out.

Kit looked around. Pub 42's tables, and almost all spots at the bar, were occupied.

"Yeah. Good thing Rachel and Shannon saved us a table."

"Mm. Even if it comes with them looking over at us and smiling like proud parents every two seconds."

Kit leaned forward. "Shh, one of our new mums is on her way with the drinks."

Rachel arrived at their table with a tray, a huge smile, and what Kit had seen described as 'heart eyes' on Twitter.

"Hello again, ladies. Here's a Sipsmith gin and tonic for Curly. And a Sipsmith vodka with diet Pepsi for Pixie Cut. Your food is being prepared by the boys as we speak."

Laura pursed her lips. "Are the nicknames necessary?"

"Yep. I'm afraid they are," Rachel said with a grin.

Laura breathed out an ironic "great."

Kit accepted her drink with relish. Nickname or not, she was feeling her nerves and wanted the vodka to calm them.

Rachel cradled the empty tray, still with a thrilled grin. "Soooo, anything else I can get you ladies?"

Kit was busy drinking so Laura replied, "Peace and quiet. That's all I can think of right now."

"All right. Oh, and I wanted to say, you both look so extremely nice tonight and you make *such* a sexy couple. Your styles, colourings, and your body types - you contrast and complement each other perfectly."

"Thanks. You cruising for a foursome?" Kit joked.

"What? No!" Rachel exclaimed. "Can't I compliment someone without wanting to sleep with them? Look, I'm only proud and smug because I called it on day one. As soon as I saw you two together, I knew there was a love connection. And here you are, blushing and starry-eyed, on a real date, right here in my pub, under my care. I feel like a lesbian fairy godmother!"

"Can you please get back to work and leave us alone?" Laura whinged.

"Fine! I'm going. But do shout if you need anything else. I want to help make this the best date you've ever had."

"Thank you so much for that," Kit said.

Rachel bowed theatrically and walked off swinging her tray.

Laura sipped her drink and then said, "Maybe we shouldn't have come here after all? Perhaps we should've settled for a walk or something?"

"Nah, it'll be fine. She's just being a proud match-maker and..." Kit dithered. Should she use the word lesbian or the more wide-ranging sapphic? She didn't want to label Rachel's sexuality without knowing it, she might be bi or something, but also wasn't sure if Laura knew what sapphic was. She decided to risk the confusion and finished the sentence with "honorary sapphic older sister".

Laura's well read, she probably knows who Sappho was. If not she'll ask.

A man suddenly appearing at her elbow stopped Kit's train of thought in its tracks.

"Hi there. Kit Sorel? We haven't met. I'm Josh Cullen, one of the other owners of this place. I wanted to pop by to introduce myself and say welcome to Greengage. And mention that my husband, Matt, and I are chuffed to bits that you two are dating!"

"Cheers for that," Kit said. "It's nice to finally meet you."

Josh put one hand on Laura's shoulder and the other on Kit's and squeezed before letting go. "Right, I'll leave you alone now." He smoothed his already flawless hair and said, "Matt will have finished your food in a few minutes and then the girls will bring it out to you."

"Oh, I'm sure they will," Laura muttered.

He inspected her with raised eyebrows.

Laura took a deep breath. "Never mind. Thanks for stopping by."

"Of course. You two are so cute!" He waved enthusias-tically and walked towards the kitchen.

Laura and Kit looked at each other and smiled.

Then they sat there in silence, sipping their drinks and watching each other over their glasses.

Kit put her drink down and said, "So, here we are."

"Yes. Here we are. Alone at last."

"Um, what do we talk about?"

Laura chuckled. "Well, we can plan our thirtieth birthday bash."

"Told you, I'm not having one."

"Fine, *my* thirtieth birthday bash where I will make a point of everyone celebrating yours, too. That's more than a month away, though. Isn't your birthday coming up soon?"

"Monday, next week."

"Oooh. I'm going to get you a smashing gift. What would you like?"

"I'm not that much into things. I prefer experiences. What about you?"

Laura tapped a finger against her lips. "Hm. I enjoy getting things, but yes, you're right, experiences can be better."

The front door opened with a whoosh and in came Mabel Baxter, dragging Charlie Baxter along by his jacket sleeve.

Mabel came to a halting stop in front of their table. Charlie bumped into her with a thud.

"Hello?" Kit said, annoyed at herself for sitting up straight and taking her elbows off the table at the sight of Mabel.

"Good evening, Ms Sorel and Ms Howard."

"Titles and surnames? We mean business tonight," Kit mumbled under her breath.

Mabel's gaze bored into hers. "Pardon?"

Laura tried to hide a smile. "Kit was merely saying that

it's nice to see you tonight. How may we help you, Mrs Baxter?"

"My cousin here has come along to explain something to you."

Charlie groaned as Mabel pushed him forward. His brow creased and his moustache twitched. "I'm terribly sorry to interrupt your evening. I'm here to clarify that my apology for my cousin yesterday was uncalled for and could perhaps be seen as a form of…" He paused to grind his teeth. "A form of slander."

Mabel nodded curtly, making her knitted hat sink yet closer to her eyes. She was about to speak when Charlie put a hand on her arm and said, "There, all clarified as per your instructions. Let's leave these lovely ladies to their dinner."

Mabel showed every sign of being about to disagree when the door whooshed open again. This time it delivered Ethel Rosenthal who quickly approached them with small steps and a big smile.

"Good evening! Sincerest apologies, girls. I had to come and explain." She gripped the table to steady herself. "I mentioned to Mabel that Charlie had informed me that he apologised for being related to her. I thought it was hilarious, and in a moment of feeblemindedness, I thought Mabel would find it amusing also. As you can tell, she did not."

Charlie ran a hand over his face. "I still cannot believe you told her!"

"I can hear you both, you know," Mabel snarled.

"Only because I bought you new batteries for your hearing aid, dear," Ethel countered. "Now that all clarifications and apologies are out of the way, we should leave.

Charlie has to run the bingo tonight and I have to win it, so hurry up."

She turned and stepped out in her unique way.

She's so cool, Kit thought. *I want to be like Ethel when I'm old. Happy, funny, clever, and walking like an adorable penguin.*

The other two followed her, Mabel finally letting go of Charlie's jacket sleeve. He gave them a sheepish look and a wave as he left.

Laura groaned. "I'm so sorry. As I said, we should have gone somewhere with fewer Greengagers."

Kit noticed that Laura was eyeing the people at the table next to them as she said it. It wasn't the first time she'd focused on them. Kit took a closer look at the two people, who were glancing back at Laura quite a bit. They had lush, honey-blonde hair and were built on the large side. They reminded Kit of someone.

"Kit? Are you listening to me, dearest?"

The term of endearment made her snap her head back towards Laura.

"God, I love it when you call me that," she gushed.

Laura's smile was shy, but her eyes glittered. She reached out a hand over the table, and Kit took it. It was warm and perhaps the tiniest bit damp.

Good, I'm not the only one who's nervous.

At that moment, Shannon came over with their food. She smiled but said nothing as she put the plates down.

Kit pulled her plate of cheeseburger and chips closer and inhaled lungfuls of the delicious smell. She groaned. "Man, I didn't realise how hungry I was."

"Being stared at and interrupted by the whole damn island will do that to ya," Shannon said with a wink.

"Oh, thank heavens, someone reasonable!" Laura said. "Thank you."

"No problem. Do you need any sauces or anything?"

When they both said no, Shannon smiled, stepped back and left with a simple "enjoy!"

Kit popped a small chip in her mouth, realised it was too hot and had to swallow it down with her drink.

Laura sniggered a little. "Careful. I might need that mouth later."

Kit quirked an eyebrow at her.

"Not for that, you gutter brain! I meant for a good-night kiss."

"Oh. Right, that. Well, I suppose that sounds nice, too."

Kit had expected a light slap on her arm or leg, but Laura merely smirked and said, "Blow on it, honey. Or learn to wait for your treats."

Kit nearly choked on her drink and had to put the glass back down.

"I told you to be careful," Laura said with a cheeky grin.

Kit leaned forward, making sure Laura could see down her shirt. "Since it's you, I'll try to do as I'm told."

"Gosh. That's the same white lacy bra you wore that night when we were clearing the basement stock, isn't it?" Laura whimpered.

"You noticed, then?"

A naughty smile tugged at the corners of Laura's mouth as she said, "Of course. It was the least I could do after you'd gone to all that effort to make sure I did."

Kit sat back and playfully pouted. "Are you complaining, baby?"

"Certainly not! Nor will you hear me complain about

you calling me baby. No one's ever done that. Honey, darling, sweetie, babe, and sugar tits – yes. Baby – no. I think I like it."

Kit put her hands one the table. "Hang on. Who the hell called you sugar tits?"

The door opened again. This time it revealed Tom Howard. Laura threw her napkin on the table while cursing under her breath and got up to head him off. She didn't have time as he dashed towards them. The siblings met right next to Kit, Laura scowling and Tom looking unfazed by her ire.

Kit noticed a bulky blonde couple at the table next to theirs whispering loudly. The woman said, "Another Howard. It's like an infestation."

Tom put his hands in the pockets of his coral-pink khakis and grinned. "Sorry to disturb and all that. Figured I'd pop in and say well done on getting over that Stevenson git. Ruddy shame that he's now bagged Aunt Sybil, but what can you do? Gold diggers were always a risk." He clicked his tongue. "Still, while I hoped you'd get yourself a sugar daddy to bring some bullion into Howard Hall, at least you did the second-best thing and fetched some eye candy to pretty up our dinner table."

Laura squeezed her eyes closed. "You..." She scrunched up her features. "...absolute, stinking fopdoodle! Try to not be a shallow chauvinist for once in your life."

He chuckled. "Excuse me?"

"Tom, it's long overdue that you learn to show women, and everyone else, some respect. If not, I'll have to thrash you like I used to when we were little."

"Ha. You wouldn't dare. Aunt Sybil would hand me Gage Farm on a plate if you hurt me."

Laura stepped closer to him. "I don't think she would anymore, *Sweet Little Thomas*. She's more likely to want to give it to Dylan. Watch yourself. You've been replaced as the favourite."

If he was worried, he didn't let it show. "Look, I merely wanted to congratulate you on upgrading your bit of fluff. No need to be a bitch."

Laura's mouth dropped open. "Did you actually call me a bitch? If either of us should be compared to a dog, it's you. You'd spend all day licking your testicles if you could. Get out of my sight!"

He seemed to be about to retort, but when he saw her take another step closer, fists clenched and jaw set, he snapped his mouth shut, backed up, and mumbled, "Fine. I've better places to be tonight than this unsophisticated, weird little island anyway. I'm taking the next ferry out. I might not be back for days."

"Promises, promises," his sister hissed. "Get out!"

He ambled towards the door but hurried up when Laura followed him with loud steps.

Meanwhile, Kit, who was busy wondering what the hell a fopdoodle was, overheard the honey-haired couple say, "Causing a scene and hogging all the attention. Typical Howards."

That was it. She waved at them. "Hi. Considering your shitty manners, blondness, hatred for the Howards, and that you look like giants, I assume you're the Stevensons. Dylan's parents, yes?"

They recoiled but didn't reply, so Kit carried on. "Now, I've been told to not take sides on Greengage, but as I'm in love with a Howard and you're clearly awful, consider me having taken a side. Also consider me thinking you should bugger off. Or at least stop talking about us behind our backs." As she was about to turn back to her plate, she remembered one last point. "And stop staring at Laura! You're making her uncomfortable."

Laura returned right at that moment. She gave Kit a wan smile. "Thank you, dearest. I'm not used to someone defending me." Then she addressed the Stevensons. "And yes, do please keep your opinions and bulging eyes to yourselves. Have a nice evening."

The pair huffed and looked away, beginning to loudly discuss last night's play.

Laura slumped down on her seat. "This… isn't working, is it?"

Kit sucked in air between her teeth. "Well, I've had two bites of food. You've had none. We've drunk all the booze to be able to put up with the interruptions. And I think we've said about eight sentences to each other."

"In short, a disastrous first date," Laura summarised.

"No, I wouldn't say that." She reached across the table and put her hand over Laura's. "It's just I didn't know I'd be dating all of Greengage."

"I see your point. You're being surprisingly patient."

She shrugged. "Patience is easy when you're happy. After all, I'm spending time with you, and I finally know that you're interested in me. All this craziness can be sorted out, as long as I know that we'll sort it together."

"I absolutely agree," Laura said.

"Good. I'm so glad you want to date me. You'll let me know if you have any concerns, right? We sorted the rebound thing, but we haven't talked about if you're comfortable dating a woman. Society doesn't make that as easy as straight relationships."

"I know. Don't worry, those concerns I already handled when I developed that crush on Rachel. It's worth the trouble. You're worth it. Society can—" She was interrupted by a rap on the window. When they looked out, Rajesh was standing there with a big bouquet of red roses.

"Oh, for crying out loud!" Laura squealed before burying her face in her hands.

Looking from the exasperated Laura to the clueless Rajesh made Kit laugh so hard that her stomach hurt.

This whole evening is bloody surreal.

After a moment, she managed to gather herself enough to wave at Rajesh to come in. He shuffled over to them.

"I didn't want to disturb, but Shannon called me to see if I could help. She said half the island has been in here to poke you with sticks."

"Pretty much," Laura said.

"Well, I'm here to fix that. Katherine, take these." He shoved the roses towards Kit, and she took them.

She stared at the bouquet. "Thanks. Um, you... shouldn't have?"

Rajesh snorted. "They're not for *you*. They're for Laura. I can't believe you didn't buy your lady flowers. I thought I'd set a better example than that, Katherine. Where's the wooing?"

"First of all, I wouldn't call her 'my lady.' Secondly, I —" Kit broke off. She turned to Laura. "Should I have bought you flowers?"

Laura toyed with her earring. "Oh. Hm. I don't know. Not more than I should have bought you flowers, I suppose?"

Kit shook off her worry. "Never mind all that. We were finally alone, Rajesh, so tell me about this fixing you're meant to be doing."

He crossed his arms over his chest, resting them on his potbelly. "Not until you follow through."

"What?" Kit tracked his gaze down at the roses. "Ugh. Right. Laura, these are for you."

Her date accepted them, feigned a gasp, placed a hand on her chest, and chirped, "Oh my! How chivalrous of you, my knight in shining white shirt."

Kit gave her a look and then turned back to Rajesh.

"There. Flowers delivered to lady. Lady wooed. Now what?"

"Hurry up with the meal, but make sure you eat it. No wasting food," He paused to look them both in the eye and then continued. "Then pay and come home, where people can't bother you. I have set the place up for you, and I'll make myself scarce when you show up. I have a date of my own planned, anyway."

Kit looked to Laura. "What do you think?"

Laura threw a glance at the Stevensons, who were both glaring at her from under bushy blonde eyebrows while ruminating their food like bad-tempered cows. "I think it's a splendid idea," she said.

Rajesh gave a thumbs up. "Good. Don't dawdle. I don't want to keep Widow Caine waiting too long."

With that he rushed off.

"Better do as the man says." Laura placed the roses on the table and began eating.

"Yeah. Don't want to keep Widow Caine waiting," Kit grunted. "Seriously, how much and how often does Rajesh get around?"

Laura pointed her fork at Kit. "Don't slut-shame him. He keeps a lot of lonely women happy on this island."

"Fine. As long as he leaves me one woman. A Howard one to be exact," Kit said before taking a bite of her burger.

Laura stabbed a piece of tomato with pretended bitterness. "Great. You want to date Aunt Sybil, too?"

Kit swallowed the food. "Yep. It's the shrill, nasal voice and the dislike of women. Really makes me wet."

Laura nearly choked on her tomato. "You're terrible."

"In the *dearest* way, though… right?"

"Absolutely," Laura said on an exhale.

Chapter Twenty

THE COMPLICATED DATE THAT KEEPS GIVING

F ood eaten, and the bill paid, Kit and Laura walked hand in hand towards Rajesh's maisonette. They passed the library, making Kit reminisce about weeding the nonfiction stock together and falling more in love every minute. She squeezed Laura's hand and placed a kiss on her soft cheek.

At Rajesh's place, romantic sitar music was playing. They walked in and found a bottle of sparkling wine resting in a plastic bucket filled with ice cubes and splotches of frozen water clearly scraped off the freezer shelves.

Kit shook her head. "That's the bucket we use for mopping the floor."

With a giggle, Laura said, "Give him a break, look at the effort he's gone to. He got you wine even though he doesn't drink. There's even strawberries!"

"You're right, he's being sweet. We'll ignore that he's not unpacked the berries but plonked the whole plastic box in the bowl."

"Yes, and that he bought imported berries for a British

fruit farmer who's spent her whole adult life fighting to make Britons eat only locally grown fruit."

Kit winced. "Mm. Maybe he should've stuck to chocolates. Still, he tried. Where is he, by the way?" Kit put her hands around her mouth to make a makeshift megaphone. "Raaaaaajesh?"

He appeared from the bathroom, splashing Old Spice on his cheeks. "Hello again. I heard you arrive, so I went to put the final touches on the 'Rajesh Singh Lover Man Package.' How do I look?"

"Handsome as ever," Kit said.

He grinned. "I do, don't I? I see you got here without being mobbed. Well done." He put his coat on and then searched the floor around his feet.

"Thanks," Kit said while pointing to his shoes behind him.

He grabbed them as if he'd known where they were all along and began putting them on.

"And thank you for all of this, Rajesh," Laura said, pointing to the bottle and the berries.

"You're both very welcome. I'll deduct it from your next paycheck, Katherine."

Kit noticed Laura edging closer to her. Soon they were right next to each other, both leaning against the table and watching Rajesh whistle while tying his shoelaces. Laura's body radiated heat. There was no mistaking the responding warmth beginning in Kit.

She's so hard to resist. I bet her whole body is as soft as her hands and tastes as sweet as her lips.

Kit grabbed the table to keep her hands from straying to where neither she nor Laura were ready for them to go. Yet.

Rajesh checked his reflection in the hallway mirror.

"There we go. All ready to charm and satisfy an amorous widow."

"Ugh. I do not need to hear that," Kit said with her lip curling.

He snorted. "Bah! Don't be such a prude. Tonight, we're both getting lucky. It's about time in your case."

Kit wheezed. "Rajesh!"

"No, Katherine. I mean it. You must keep your machinery in working order." He held up his hands. "Some people don't want to use their machinery and that's their business, but I know you want yours to be in use, and that means giving it a good run-through once in a while. You're long overdue."

He looked so serious and concerned that Kit didn't know what to say.

Luckily, Laura stepped in.

"If you make Kit anymore embarrassed, I think her machinery will break down out of pure panic. Best get to your date instead. Tell Mrs Caine that Laura Howard said hello."

"Fine, fine." He waved his hand dismissively. "Have fun and be careful. I don't know what sort of protection ladies use with each other, but make sure you use it. No babies, pox, or crabs under my roof."

Kit wrapped her hands around her head and mumbled, "Please just go, Rajesh."

He squinted at her. "Pardon?"

Laura draped an arm around Kit's waist and said, "She was indicating that you know very well that we can't get each other pregnant. And that I've been in a long, monogamous relationship and she's been celibate for quite a while, so STDs are unlikely."

He appeared unconvinced. "You can get them, though?"

"Yes," Laura replied, as cool as if they'd been talking about the weather. "It's apparently rarer that women who sleep with women get them, but it is possible. Rachel is always going on about that."

Rajesh hummed. "Will you be all right, then? I have condoms. Do you want one? The package says they're ribbed. Which I assume is some sort of medical function. Perhaps the ribbing means the diseases can't stick to the smooth surface?"

A strangled noise worked its way out of Kit's throat. She removed her hands and fixed him with a stare. "You know what, if it makes you leave us alone faster, I can put your mind at ease. I was tested before I moved here and I'm clean. Now, if something were to happen between us tonight, which I wish you'd stop assuming, I promise to book us both in for tests tomorrow. Okay?"

"All right. I'm only looking after you since neither of your parents are here," he grumbled.

"Thanks, but we're both *thirty years old*!" Kit cried.

She stormed to the door and opened it for him. He smiled at her with a certain glint in his eye and then slipped outside, laughing as he strode off.

Kit faced Laura. "Hang on, did he do all that to mess with me?"

"Mess with *us*, I'd say. I think he was genuinely worried about us, but he was also having some fun with the... tension between us. That's why I was trying to act unfazed. So he'd stop teasing and leave us alone."

Kit deflated. "While I played right into his hands."

"It's not all bad, dearest. At least now I know you've been tested not too long ago and that you won't get me in a family way." Laura caressed her stomach as if she was pregnant, making Kit laugh.

"Oh, for crying out loud, don't start."

"Okay, I won't." Laura picked up a colander from the drying rack. "If you bring me the strawberries, I'll wash and hull them while you open the champagne."

"It's sparkling wine," Kit corrected before stopping mid-movement. "Did you say Hull? As in Kingston upon Hull?"

"No, you numpty. Not the town. Hull, as in removing the leaves and stem of the berry."

Kit picked up the box of berries and noted the little green bits. "Aha. I clearly have a lot to learn from you fruit farmers."

"I'll teach you about fruit if you teach me what lesbians do in bed," Laura purred.

Kit barely caught the berries before they slipped out of her hands.

Laura bit her lip around a smile. "I'm always making you nearly drop things, aren't I? Sorry, dearest. You're just so easy to tease. I'm not…" She paused, and her expression softened. "Not expecting anything like that to happen tonight. All I've been hoping for is a goodnight kiss. Anything else would merely be a pleasant surprise."

Kit's shoulders settled back down. "Right. Good. I, um, feel the same way. We'll play things by ear."

"No pressure," Laura said, opening the pack of strawberries.

"Exactly. Anyway, I was meant to be serving the drinks."

Kit fetched the sparkling wine, popped the cork, and was ready to pour it into the two glasses Rajesh had supplied. She froze as she looked at them. One of them was a plain highball glass and the other a wine glass that said "South Gage Farm Cider" on it.

A glass from her family's vicious main competitor. Really?

Laura was hulling the strawberries with her back turned to Kit but mumbled, "I don't hear pouring. If you're worrying about that South Gage Farm glass, don't. I saw it right when we walked in. I told you, he's teasing *both* of us."

Kit put the bottle down. The smile on her face almost made her cheeks hurt. She walked up to Laura and put her hands around her waist. Tentatively, as this was new territory after all.

"How are you so wonderful, Laura? Why is it so comfortable to be around you? Why does it make me so bloody happy?" she whispered into the auburn curls.

Laura reached over her shoulder and fed Kit a strawberry. "All I know is that I feel the same way. I so desperately want you to like me and this mad island, because I don't want to ever be without you."

Kit swallowed the strawberry a little too quickly, needing to reply right away. "Don't worry about me liking Greengage, love. Unlike with Dylan, you won't have to worry about giving up Gage Farm or Howard Hall to be with me. You can have it all. I'd never take you away from where you're happy. Where you belong."

Laura stopped hulling. "You know what?"

Kit eagerly nuzzled into the curls. "No, what?"

"I think the place I belong might just be in your arms."

With that, Laura turned and kissed Kit. It was a kiss which went deeper than mere sexual attraction. It seemed to cement the fact of their flirty crush turning into deep affection. It made it all real. Certain. Permanent.

Kit reeled, holding on to Laura for dear life as their tongues touched and strawberry sweetness filled their mouths. She heard a moan and wasn't sure if it came from Laura or herself. Her heart pounded so hard she was sure Laura must feel it. Her grip on Laura's waist was probably too tight. She loosened it and let her hands begin to wander. Every part of her was now ready to admit that Rajesh was right about what her machinery would want. She needed everything Laura could give her. Heart, soul, mind, and body.

When Laura ran her hands through her hair and grabbed on to the short tresses, Kit worried that her brain was short-circuiting. Her hands were by the button of Laura's jeans, and the temptation to undo it was growing harder to resist.

A sudden high-pitched noise broke them apart.

Kit used every swear word she had ever heard, some of them not even English, as she recognised the noise as the doorbell.

Laura was breathing heavily, her hands still on Kit's collarbones, clearly on their way down to her breasts. "Ignore it."

Kit groaned. "No one ever rings that doorbell. What if it's Rajesh who lost his key and had a sudden pang of his heart problems?"

Laura leaned her feverishly hot forehead against Kit's. "Fine. We'll go check. But I swear, if it's Carla the island's only Jehovah's Witness come over here with a pamphlet, I'll make her eat it."

"I'll let you," Kit promised.

With her arm around Laura's waist, they walked to the door. Kit trying to ignore how Laura kept raking her eyes over her body.

She let go of her date to open the door. Outside was a man she knew quite well but couldn't quite place. In the end, she didn't have to since Laura exclaimed, "Steve? What are you doing here?"

That's it. Steve Hallard who runs the newsagent by the library. Why is he here? Now's not the time for chocolate bars and a magazine!

He coughed. "I'm sorry to bother you girls, but I've been told what's going on here tonight and I have to speak my mind. It's not right."

Kit stiffened and held her breath. She had heard similar words before.

Don't let this be homophobic! We were so happy, and Laura is so new to being out. Should I slam the door in his face now? Just in case?

He took his cap off and twirled it in his hands. Kit chewed the inside of her cheek.

Say whatever it is, man. I want to get back to the wine and the kissing.

"Please tell me this isn't about our gender," Laura snapped. "Or the class divide between us."

"Course not," Steve snapped. He twirled his cap another couple of seconds. Then he pointed to Kit. "This is about you! You come to our home as a stranger. Jabbering about fancy food and posh plays that Greengage doesn't have. Making jokes about us being inbred."

"I didn't do that last thing," Kit pointed out.

His face was reddening to an unhealthy purple now. "Maybe not, but I reckon you thought it!"

He's got me there.

Laura stepped closer to him. "Wait. So, she's an off-islander. What does that matter? We have people who have come here from places further away than London. Rajesh

Singh, Siobhan O'Shaughnessy, and Zhang Ying, to name a few. You've been fine with them."

"Sure, but they haven't wanted to court one of the island's most important daughters. A person who's a key part of the island's history. Who's got power as well as our love and respect."

Kit rubbed her forehead. "I still don't get it. Do you want me to stop dating Laura?"

He stood up straight. "No. I want you to be careful."

"This can't be about safe sex again, can it?" Laura whispered to Kit.

Kit didn't reply but went straight to the source instead. "Steve, what do you mean by careful?"

He squeezed his cap in his big, calloused fist. "I mean that if you hurt or use our Little Laura Howard, you'll answer to me! I know what you Londoners are like. I lived there for a spell back in the seventies, I did. You court people and then you leave 'em heartbroken." He spat on the ground. "Laura had enough of that with the Stevenson lad. She's a dear heart and both the history and future of this island. You can't cause her grief. Or try to take her back to London with you!"

"Okay. Wasn't expecting that," Kit mumbled towards Laura, who was standing frozen with her mouth slightly ajar.

Carefully, Kit put a hand on Steve's shoulder. "Please don't worry. I don't *use* women, and I certainly try my best to never hurt them. I'll treat Laura the way I'd want to be treated myself. Hell, even better than that."

"That is, if she ever gets the chance to do anything around me without being interrupted," Laura grumbled. Seeing how crestfallen Steve Hallard looked at that, she added, "Thank you for worrying about me, but I'm an adult and not the public property of this island. Firstly, Kit is sweet and harmless. Secondly, neither of us is moving to London."

He was about to speak, but she cut him off. "And if you want to lecture someone about hurting me, you don't need to be talking to a newcomer. Dylan is your man. You'll find him in the arms of Aunt Sybil. Go knock on the door of Howard Hall. Or go home and watch *Springwatch* as usual."

"It's not on right now," he said sheepishly.

Laura sighed. "Well whatever *is* on, then. Thank you, Steve, and goodnight." She banged the door shut and leaned against it.

Kit laughed under her breath. "I was really worried that was going to be something more serious."

"Me, too."

Neither of them went into details, but the silence spoke volumes.

Phyllis came trudging out into the hallway, sat down in front of them, and began licking her bum.

Kit and Laura looked at each other for a while before Kit stated the obvious. "This isn't happening tonight, is it?"

"Not tonight, no." Laura moved closer, cupping Kit's cheek with her hand. "I don't think either of us is in the mood anymore. Too many interruptions and emotional ups and downs. But I can make it up to you."

Kit's heart lightened. "Really?"

Laura touched her lips to Kit's, the ghost of a kiss. "Absolutely. Remember what we said about your birthday?"

Kit wracked her brain. "That... I prefer experiences to gifts?"

Laura nodded before placing another peck on Kit's lips. "Mm-hm. How about I take the day off on Friday and we go to London? You can show me some of your favourite spots and I'll arrange some expensive and exclusive experience for you as an early birthday surprise?"

Kit grabbed Laura's waist, unable to get over how those mind-blowing curves tapered in like this. "Sounds amazing! You sure about this, though? Travelling there takes a while and getting around London takes ages. After I'd shown you a favourite spot or two, we'd be out of day and have to catch the last ferry back. No time for birthday experiences."

Laura leaned in and Kit expected another ghosting peck. Instead, she ran her tongue along Kit's upper lip. Then she whispered, "I suppose we'll need two days then, honey. We should arrive on Thursday evening and spend the night."

Kit moved away, looking into those hazel eyes framed – like the artwork they were –by black make-up. There was a definite promise in those eyes, one that caused a pulling sensation in Kit's lower stomach.

She forced her suddenly dry mouth to reply, "Yeah. Right after work on Thursday night and then we'll take the last ferry back on Friday. I want as much time alone with you as I can get." She slid her hands down to grab hold of Laura's hips. "And if you're the one who books a hotel room, ask for one that's as soundproofed as it can get."

Laura beamed. "Consider it done. Now kiss me goodnight."

"Bossy," Kit joked before leaning in.

The liquid-heat kiss buzzed all the way down to Kit's toes, making her quiver.

How the hell does she kiss like this? How does she make me feel this way?

Lust mixed with bliss so that when Kit opened her eyes again, all colours seemed a little brighter.

"I adore you, my dearest," Laura whispered while adjusting Kit's glasses, which had gone askew.

Then she placed her hands on Kit's shoulders and gently manoeuvred her away from the doorway. She grabbed her coat off the hook, stepped into her shoes, and opened the door, all while holding Kit's gaze. Kit couldn't look away either, marvelling at the wonder and anticipation she saw in those radiant eyes, assuming it was mirrored in her own.

Laura stepped out, looking over her shoulder and gifting Kit with a smile. "Remember, everything good is worth waiting for. And what we have is better than anything I've ever known. Good night."

"Good night, Laura." Kit reached out and brushed her hand before adding, "Make sure you have some islanders walk you home, so you're not mobbed by Londoners wanting you to move there."

Laura waved that away while laughing. The warm sound haunted Kit as she shut the door and leaned against it. She closed her eyes and pondered how long she should wait before texting Laura about lunch tomorrow, to avoid the clingy woman cliché. She decided that four minutes was probably enough. It ended up being closer to two and a half.

Chapter Twenty-One

EXTREMELY HOMOSEXUAL

K it wondered if the idea of pinching yourself to see if something was a dream actually worked. Here she was. Thursday night. The first evening of their two-day London birthday trip. In a hotel which was the poshest thing she'd ever seen. It made Howard Hall look like a potting shed. The suite they'd been given fifteen minutes ago was bigger than the first flat she had shared with Aimee, so much so that the concierge had come up with them to show them around and explain all the amenities. Or maybe they always did that? Kit blinked and shook her head as she looked at the antique furniture, lush fabrics, and tasteful decorations in cream, oak, and gold. The Dorchester. She was actually staying at the bloody Dorchester.

How did someone like me end up here?

Coming up behind her, Laura caressed the column of her throat and then over to the side by her pulse point. "You've got such a strong but slender neck. I need to kiss it."

Oh, yeah. That's how I ended up at the Dorchester.

"Sure. But only if you do it like you mean it," Kit flirted.

Laura's breath tickled her neck as she whispered, "I don't know of any other way."

She kissed Kit from shoulder to ear, soft kisses with the occasional brush of a tongue.

Kit closed her eyes and relaxed into it, noting tingles of arousal travelling throughout her body.

She'd been considering trying out the big tub in the extravagant bathroom. Or maybe checking if anything in the big minibar was free. Or the third option of stealing all the soaps, shampoos, and conditioners right away so she didn't forget later. But these kisses, which were now covering the shell of her ear, reminded her that there was an even bigger treat in store.

Priorities rearranged, she turned into Laura's embrace and kissed her hard.

Soon clothes began to shed like leaves and Kit's glasses were dropped onto the bedside table with such force she was impressed they held. Laura's hands roamed like greedy explorers, and Kit let herself be thoroughly studied.

Before she knew it, Kit Sorel was on her back.

On the widest bed she had ever seen.

Underneath her were the softest sheets she had ever felt.

On top of her was the most wonderful creature she had ever met.

If there was a heaven. It'd be like this.

Laura showed no signs of needing directions on what to do with a woman, she simply opted for doing it all. Soft touches mixing with hard. Gentle kisses interspersed with rough sucking. Every part of Kit was surveyed, from the crease behind her knee being licked to the nipples being bitten, increasing the sensation of being thoroughly explored.

Fleetingly, Kit was grateful they'd eaten before they came up. They were going to be here for a while. She pulled Laura to her, breathing in the scent of her skin and kissing everything she could reach. Laura tasted sweet, was incredibly soft, and her touch was so warm. Soft, sweet, warm – the three words Kit most connected with Laura Howard. The three things that had first made her fall for Greengage's most famous daughter.

Once again, Kit considered the idea of pinching herself to make sure she wasn't dreaming. She decided there was no point, what Laura's mouth was currently doing was close enough to pinching that it surely would've woken her. This was real.

The last thought in Kit's mind before she was swallowed up by the intoxication of making love to someone she adored was nine words long.

This is the best birthday present I've ever gotten.

❧

Coming up for air some time later, Kit grabbed her glasses from the bedside table and wondered what time it was.

Time you get a watch, as Rajesh would say.

She noted that she was hungry and that about every third muscle in her body was thrumming with extended strain, while the rest were relaxed by sexual satisfaction. The hunger meant it must be quite late, right?

Laura was laying with her head on Kit's chest. It was hard to breathe. Not because of the weight of Laura's head but because the joy surging through Kit was hitching her breathing. She couldn't see Laura's face to check if she was sleeping, though, no matter how she craned her head.

"Laura? Are you asleep?"

With a quick movement of the head, Laura looked up at her. There was an alert, on-edge sort of vibe to her.

Kit was suddenly fully awake. "Whoa. Hey. You okay?"

"Yes. That was just…" Laura swallowed visibly. "Illuminating."

'Illuminating?' I give her multiple orgasms and she says illuminating?

"Uh. Thanks? I'll put that on my sexual CV."

Laura's eyes widened. "No, no. I didn't mean the sex in itself. That was the best and most satisfying sex I've ever had, wild and sweet all at once. That was what was illuminating. Because…" She paused to bite her plump lower lip. "Kit?"

"Yes, sweetheart?"

"I… think I might be gay. I mean, utterly gay. Intensively gay. Not even bisexual. Just… extremely homosexual."

Kit remembered Rachel's words. *Raging homo.*

She made her voice as soft and reassuring as she could. "I think that could be possible. Rachel put that theory out there after the first time I met her."

"What?!"

"Yeah. She asked me if I thought you might be gay and in the closet. Maybe fooling yourself that you were in love with a man for, well, different reasons."

Laura glowered. "That little minx knew and never said anything? Well, I think she might have been right. The way you made me feel, how aroused your body makes me and how good the sex felt…" She closed her eyes. "All those perfect curves fitting together. All that welcoming softness and wetness. The complete reciprocity of all the acts. Everything smelling and tasting so good. It felt so natural to me, so right. It's never been like that with a man. Not that I have much experience, of course."

"Oh baby, I don't—" Kit had brushed her fingers through Laura's tangled curls and was now regretting the act of comfort as her fingers were stuck and Laura was wincing with pain.

"Sorry!" Kit exclaimed. "Crap. Hang on, let me just get my fingers free. There we go." She coughed to hide her embarrassment. "Um. Where was I? Right. I don't know what your sexual orientation is or what it has been before. But I'm here for you if you want to explore it. I'm also okay with it if you never figure it out. As long as you like and want *me*, I'm happy."

Laura took Kit's recently freed hand and brushed it against her cheek, then kissed the palm. "How could I not want you? After all, like I told you once, I always go for the sweetest option. And that, my dearest, is you." She kissed Kit's hand again, this time letting the tip of her tongue brush over the sensitive skin of her palm. "It's never felt this exquisite," she added in a whisper.

Kit's cheeks tugged into a smile she could only guess looked as goofy as it was huge. "Do you mean the sex or the cuddling?"

"Both. Top marks! How do you do it?"

"A proper London education. I failed maths but got good grades in shagging and cuddling."

Laura groaned. "You're a plum."

"From a fruit farmer who specialises in plums, I'll take that as a compliment."

Laura opened her mouth to reply when she was cut off by Kit's stomach growling loudly.

"Hm. The beast that lives in this unfairly flat stomach needs feeding," Laura said, caressing Kit's tummy.

"Yeah, I'm starving. How long did we… you know?"

"To use your charming expression, shag?"

"Well, it was either that or the F-word and I wasn't sure I could use that word in this hotel. Or with a woman like you."

Laura knitted her brows. "Don't say 'woman like me'."

"It's not a bad thing. I only meant that you're—"

"Rich. Yes, my family has always been affluent, but those funds are dwindling. I'm rich by Greengage measures, but I'm not a millionaire or anything."

"I was going to say posh," Kit said soothingly. "But sure, I know what you mean. Nonetheless, anyone who can afford to pay for a hotel like this is rich in my book."

Laura bit her lip and hummed.

Noting the tone of the hum, Kit craned her neck further to look Laura fully in the eye. "What? We're gonna leave without paying?"

"No, of course not! It's already been paid for." Laura dodged the eye contact, instead drawing little patterns on Kit's breast with her fingertip.

"Baby, what aren't you telling me? I know something's up. You have no poker face."

"Well," Laura sniffed. "I might have used Aunt Sybil's credit card to pay for the hotel."

Kit guffawed. "Sneaky little vixen! That's perfect! That'll teach her to steal your fiancé."

"Dylan wasn't stolen. He's not a gold watch." Laura lowered her voice to a grumble. "He's a pretentious, vain, selfish, untalented…"

"Fopdoodle?" Kit suggested.

"I was going to go with 'prat', but sure, that works, too."

Kit kissed the crown of her head and then leaned her head back on the ridiculously comfy pillow. "Good thing he's out of your life. And now that you think you're probably, what was it, *extremely homosexual*? You shouldn't have to worry about that tosser ever again."

"If this is being extremely homosexual – winning you and escaping Dylan Stevenson – then being extremely homosexual is the best thing ever!"

"No arguments here. Anyway, you never answered my question about how long we were at it."

"A couple of hours or so. Why do you need to know that?"

Kit shrugged, moving Laura's head up and down as a side effect.

Laura leaned on her elbows on either side of Kit's torso. "Wait, let's examine the evidence here. You're clearly hungry and your voice sounds drowsy. Are you, perchance, checking if it's socially acceptable to eat and then go to sleep?"

"Not *socially* acceptable," Kit grumbled. "If it's acceptable for someone trying to impress the woman she's dating. And on that note, if you want to go again – we can."

Laura laughed. "Now there's a charming expression. Go again? Ha! Easy there, stud. You'll want to save some energy for your birthday surprise tomorrow."

With that, she got up and padded naked over to the minibar. Relishing the view, Kit sat up and mumbled, "What is my birthday surprise, anyway?"

Laura returned with a gourmet-brand bag of salt and

vinegar crisps, a bottle of Coke, and a chocolate bar. "Should I really tell you? Don't you want to be surprised?"

"No, tell me. I've been dying to know all week!"

"I know. I doubt we've had a single lunch or dinner without you begging for hints. You've always seemed more patient than this."

Kit opened the chocolate bar. "Not when it comes to birthdays. I have a bit of a thing about birthdays. Comes from when I was little."

"Really? Tell me."

After swallowing a bite of chocolate, Kit replied, "Okay. Um. Well, my dad was a consultant, which meant that some months he made decent money, but others, he had no clients. Those months we had to scrape by until someone wanted his services."

"What about your mother's income?" Laura interrupted while opening the bottle of Coke.

"Mum didn't work. Anyway, some birthdays fell on a good month and then I'd have great birthdays. But more often, they fell on one of the lean months and I'd make do with whatever we could afford in the way of birthday cake and presents."

Kit stared at the chocolate to avoid the sympathy in Laura's eyes. "Don't pity me. It wasn't that bad, we weren't starving or anything. It just meant that it was a bit of a luck of the draw what kind of birthday I'd get. Which led to me always being curious about what's happening for my birthday. Tricky habit to shake."

"I see." The pity on Laura's face was, clearly deliberately, replaced with excitement. "Well, there's a reason why I picked a hotel so close to the West End."

She let a hand caress up Kit's arm, over her shoulder, and then up to play with the little hairs on her neck.

Goosebumps immediately pricked up on Kit's skin, and, to avoid teasing, she distracted Laura by feeding her two squares of chocolate. "I won't be the only one eating. Have some."

Obediently, Laura parted her lips. Kit forgot to breathe while slipping the chocolate between those full, kiss-swollen, rosy lips.

Look up the word sex in a dictionary, and there'd just be a picture of that mouth.

Kit cleared her throat. "Yeah. Uh, what was I going to say?"

Laura kept chewing slowly and even licking her lower lip, completely unnecessarily for chocolate-cleaning purposes, Kit noticed with a needy whimper.

She squeezed her eyes shut to concentrate. "I was going to say something. Stop scrambling my brain, you annoyingly sexy woman."

She heard Laura laugh and tried not to smile. There really was something she was going to say. Going to ask.

She opened her eyes. "Got it! What were you saying about picking a hotel close to the West End?"

Laura washed the chocolate down with some cola. "I spent days scouring the internet for experiences in London, ones that were rare or expensive enough that even a London girl wouldn't have done them fifteen times." Her free hand went back to playing with Kit's hair. "I found the most exclusive spas, hot-air balloon rides, renting a whole capsule on the London Eye, getting a private tour of some of the famous museums, but in the end… the thing that came back to me was how often you mention West End plays."

"Oh! You got us tickets for something? What are we gonna go see?"

Laura retracted her hand from Kit's hair and began fidgeting with the chocolate bar wrapper instead.

Kit tried to catch her eye. "What now? Did you make Sybil pay for the tickets or something?"

"No, it's not that. It's just that going to a play is something you could've done yourself."

"Not in your wonderful company, but okay, I get your point. So, what did you do differently?"

"I didn't book you tickets for a show tomorrow. I booked you tickets for *three* different shows. VIP seats. Champagne and truffles whenever possible."

Kit's mouth worked wordlessly.

Laura tucked hair behind her ear and said, "That isn't too much, is it?"

Kit's mouth gave up and simply fell open.

Laura held three fingers up and ticked them off. "One early matinee, then a late matinee, then an evening show. It's a lot of sitting, but we'll have time to stretch between the shows."

She waited for Kit to speak but then seemed to lose her nerve and carried on talking.

"I'm buying you lunch at whatever your favourite Thai place is, and we have a dinner reservation for Spring, a restaurant in Somerset House. My recluse uncle always books a table there when he's forced to go to London. I tried to get something even fancier, but most of those places you have to book six months ahead."

Kit's jaw dropped further, causing it to click disconcertingly. She snapped it shut. "Laura. That's... I... I'm speechless."

"That's all right," Laura said timidly. "I'm the chatterbox in this relationship."

Kit marvelled at the rush of joy starting in her

stomach and spreading through her. "I love it when you talk about 'our relationship.' Makes me so proud."

"Me, too."

Laura beamed and then nibbled her lip shyly, ensuring that any part of Kit which had been held back at the fear of another failed relationship surrendered completely.

Katherine Sorel was now one big ball of hopeless infatuation, fully committed to Laura Howard.

And damn happy about it.

A wrinkle appeared between Laura's brows. "Do you like the sound of the birthday treat? I know there'll be a lot of traipsing and traveling about. And, of course, a lot to process with so many shows in one day. But I thought it would be special."

Kit tucked some of Laura's hair behind her ear and smiled when it sprang back out again. "So very special. Although, I have to say, tonight was bloody special, too."

"Utterly," Laura whispered.

Kit switched to caressing her cheek, running a finger along Laura's jaw. "Thank you, baby. I'm so bloody grateful."

"No need to be grateful. Simply be *happy*. And if possible, horn... I mean randy."

"I can be all three, sweet cheeks. Just watch me," Kit growled, moving in to join her mouth to Laura's.

Their kiss wasn't so much a kiss as an excuse to allow their tongues to do lewd things to each other. Before things escalated and all conversation would be forgotten, Kit stopped the kiss to happily mumble, "As incredible as this early birthday treat will be, next time maybe we should skip the London outing?"

"What would we do instead?"

"Maybe go to a hotel in Southampton or on the Isle of

Wight? It'll be equally without Greengagers, but we won't be stuck on public transport for as long." Kit grinned. "We wasted so much time today in places where you couldn't run your hand up my thigh without having to pretend to be wiping off crumbs. No one bought that, by the way."

She leaned into Kit's hand, making her cup her cheek. "Next time, we can hopefully be in the cottage. It's pretty much down to interior work now. I think they said they're skimming the walls on Monday. Soon we'll have a quiet place, away from prying eyes. Then I'll be putting my hands wherever I, and you, like," Laura said with raised eyebrows.

"I can't wait."

Kit leaned in for another kiss, taking her time to savour the taste and feel of her newly appointed girlfriend.

After a few moments, Laura broke away. "Sorry, now it's *my* stomach churning. Pass me the last bit of chocolate, please. The one that's probably melting since you tried to hide it in your hand."

Kit grumbled but opened her fist, revealing the last square of chocolate.

"The things I do for love. Have it, then."

Laura leaned over and ate the solid chocolate. Then, with a smirk, she licked the half-melted chocolate out of Kit's palm, not stopping until the skin was clean. When she was done, Kit was a whimpering mess who was trying to hide her sexual thirst by quenching her actual thirst. She drank about half of the cola while Laura rolled off the names of the three shows they were seeing tomorrow.

One Kit hadn't heard of. The second was a musical she'd seen once – which she didn't tell Laura – and the third a play she had always wanted to see. When Laura mentioned that one, Kit swallowed the fizzy drink so fast she coughed and then spluttered, "We're actually seeing Ingmar Bergman's *Fanny and Alexander* at the Old Vic? Right when I thought I couldn't fall deeper for you."

Laura stopped reaching for the bottle. "Do you… worry about it being too soon for us to be talking about falling in love?"

Kit thought, *Falling in love – no. Maybe wait with saying 'I love you,' though?*

Out loud she said, "Not really. Sure, it's early days compared to some couples. But not for woman-loving-woman couples. Also, technically, I have a head start on you. I was crushing on you while you were still trying to deal with Dylan. It's been like two months for me."

"True. Where does that leave me? I was platonically drawn to you when I was with Dylan, but I didn't let myself even think about crushes or love until I'd been single for a while. I haven't had months, only weeks. Am I rushing into things?"

Kit began peeling the label off the bottle. "Do you feel like you are?"

Laura seemed to ponder it, then she shook her head so forcefully it made her big curls dance. "No. Be it in a friendship or a relationship, I knew I had to be around you from the moment you set those dirty Converse on Greengage soil."

"They're not dirty, only worn."

Laura raised her eyebrows.

"Fine, okay, so they could use a little scrub," Kit muttered. She looked around the extravagant room. "Considering what this place is like, I bet they have a Victorian urchin down in the basement who'll clean shoes for a bowl of gruel."

Laura merely rolled her eyes and grabbed the Coke bottle for a big gulp.

Kit picked up her free hand and began kissing the freckles on her wrist. It was still such a rush to Kit that she could kiss and caress Laura if she wanted.

Laura screwed the top onto the bottle before asking, "Why is it so relaxing to be here with you? Not only in a post-coitus and on-holiday way, but in general. You make me so calm."

"Well, first of all, I think you like me," Kit joked. "Secondly, here you don't have the pressure of: One, pleasing the Howard clan. Two, being a charming and respected member of Greengage society. And three, portraying the sharp yet approachable businesswoman that Gage Farm needs." Kit ran a finger over Laura's left deltoid. "You have a lot resting on these sexy, freckled shoulders. I'm an outsider who has no expectations of you. With me you can shrug it off. Like you did with your skirt over there, which by the way, is now more wrinkled than Phyllis."

Laura looked over at it. "Don't worry about that. I wasn't going to wear it tomorrow anyway."

Kit opened the crisps. "Shame, it's short enough to show off those amazing thighs of yours."

"Amazing in their wobbliness," Laura sneered.

"No! Amazing in that they're soft. Perfect for wrapping around my head," Kit said around a mouthful of crisps.

Laura covered her eyes with one hand, barely stifling a giggle.

Kit's heart missed a beat. "There, I bet that feels nicer than having to constantly be Greengage's perfect champion – the wholesome and capable role model, right?

While you're here with me, you can chill and be a blushing, giggling woman who's about to get laid."

"About to get laid?" Laura's forehead creased. "You mean who recently got laid?"

"Nope. Meant what I said. Unless you have other plans?"

Laura smirked. "If I did, consider them all cancelled." She put the bottle away and threw herself on top of Kit.

Now it was Kit's turn to giggle as crisps went everywhere on the bed and Laura's mouth went everywhere on her.

Chapter Twenty-Two

MASSIVELY RUDE AND ANNOYING

L ate that Friday night, Kit and Laura stepped off the ferry, buzzing and chatting about everything they'd seen and eaten that day. Kit fell silent as she perused Greengage Dock.

There was a crowd waiting. Like a bunch of cats who'd heard the sound of a box of treats being rattled.

Kit's shoulders sagged. "Don't these people have jobs? Wait, don't say it, most of them are retired. I know."

The Greengagers were all milling around, pretending to be looking out at sea or fussing with their dogs. But Kit felt their glances stick to her like mud, so different from how the Londoners' gazes had simply slid right off.

Laura sighed. "Welcome to my world, dearest. My apologies."

Kit planted a full-on kiss on her lips. "Don't ever apologise. No matter the side effects, being with you is absolutely brilliant."

They heard a passing senior citizen with a terrier say, "Aww," and both laughed.

Hand in hand, they strolled towards Laura's car. If

everyone on this damn island knew they were a couple, they might as well demonstrate exactly how happy a couple they were.

Kit kissed Laura's cheek and said, "Thanks for one hell of a pre-birthday celebration. I loved all three shows."

"No, thank you. They were great, and without you, I wouldn't have seen them." Laura clicked her tongue. "Granted, I wouldn't have overeaten so much at that Thai place either."

"I warned you about that. Naff as it looks, they have the best food north of the river."

"You'll have to show me whatever place has the best food south of the river next time."

Kit kicked a pebble, watching it roll away. "That would be my mum's house. If she could be bothered to cook for me. Or talk to me."

Laura squeezed her hand. "If you want, I can try to charm her? To make her come round? After all, if you have to put up with Aunt Sybil and Tom, the least I can do is see if I can improve your relationship with your mother in any way."

Kit scrambled for a way to change the topic. "Family is bonkers. Speaking of family, will I ever meet your uncle and cousins? Are they nicer than Sybil and Tom?"

Laura winced. "Not really. They, well, they have their own eccentricities."

"Like what? Being hermits?"

"Tell you what, I'll let you find out for yourself. When you're deeper into our relationship and can't simply run back to Raynes Park."

Kit settled for kissing her as a reply. The problem was that when you started to kiss Laura Howard, it was extremely hard to stop. Or see where you were going.

Meaning that they stumbled about until Kit's bum hit a bench.

"Ow," she cried. "See, now some padding would've been good. Being thin and muscular is useless when it comes to stuff like this."

"Agreed. Next time, *I'll* bump into the bench," Laura said before playfully adding, "clumsy."

"Oh, you will, huh? You can't if my hands are on your arse," Kit roared, before grabbing Laura's bum to prove her point.

"Which they shouldn't be in public," a passing man said.

"Noted. Now please mind your own business, Mr Wrexham," Laura called after him.

Kit sniggered. "You tell him!"

"I will. If anyone on this island bothers you, let me know and I'll handle it. They have to learn to behave around newcomers. What's acceptable on Greengage isn't in most other places."

Kit took Laura's hand again. "You better walk me home, Ms Howard. To make sure no Greengagers bother me on the way to Rajesh's."

Laura nodded. "I think that's best. I'll protect you and your honour."

Kit chose her new go-to reply, a kiss. She wasn't usually a woman of many words, especially not when action could show her feelings much better.

Fortunately, Laura didn't seem to mind.

§&

After having kissed and cuddled their way across town, Kit grudgingly moved away from Laura long enough to open the door to Rajesh's place. She blinked at the brightness of all the lights being on.

Weird, he's always lecturing me about wasting electricity.

"Rajesh? Why is every light you own on?" she called out.

"Because the little nipper was a bit uncertain, and I thought he'd be happier if it wasn't dark," Rajesh shouted back from the kitchen.

Kit looked to Laura who shrugged. "Don't look at me. I have no idea what he's on about."

When they entered the kitchen, they saw Rajesh standing stoically with a child on his shoulders, Kit's godchild to be precise.

Kit stared at the toddler. "George? What are you doing up there, mate? Where's your mum?"

"Over here, Kit."

Aimee came into view as she closed the fridge door and opened a can of Diet Pepsi before handing it to her best friend. "And here's a peace offering."

Kit looked from the can to Aimee. Then over to George who was currently examining the hair sticking out of Rajesh's ear.

"Leave that alone, George," Kit said.

"Thanks," Rajesh muttered. "He's taken a fancy to the hair in my ears. And in my nose. And on my knuckles. I never knew my furriness could be so appreciated."

Aimee went over and grabbed George, who clambered into her arms. When she sat down, however, George quickly left to toddle over to some plastic bags, a holdall, and a suitcase. He grabbed a fire truck from one of the plastic bags and began racing around the kitchen with it, promptly crashing into Rajesh's slipper-clad foot.

"Hrmgrhpf," Rajesh said as he retracted his foot.

"Since you're here now, Katherine, I think I'll head over to Marjorie's for dinner. She always makes enough for two and won't mind the surprise visit."

With that, he escaped to his bedroom, probably to get changed into something more appealing. Or to trim his ear hair.

Aimee watched him go and whispered, "I think we might've freaked him out." She rubbed her forehead. "We were on the doorstep with all those stupid bags when he got home from the library. I thought you'd be here. I must've gotten the dates you said you were in London wrong. I thought you'd arrive back yesterday, not tonight. Sorry."

There was a stab in Kit's chest at Aimee's quietness and shamed expression.

This isn't my Aimee. Not even when she was about to pass out from fever earlier this month. Or when she was sixteen and threw up all over my new dress and suede shoes.

Kit crouched down by Aimee's chair. "It's okay, sweetie. He'll recover. Even from having his slipper hit by a fire truck. You all right, though?"

"Not really." Aimee sniffed and blinked away tears. "I made a mess of things. And as usual when I do that, I ran to you. George and I left the flat. Those bags have the clothes and stuff we needed most. Everything else I sold to the neighbour, threw away, or left."

Kit put the full can of drink on the table. "What? The furniture, too?"

Aimee wiped her nose with her hand. "I rented the place furnished, remember?"

"Oh, yeah. Sure." Still crouching, Kit rubbed Aimee's knee distractedly and added, "If you'd waited, you could've packed in real bags and sold stuff online, though. Why did you leave in such a hurry? Why did you leave at all? Was it that wanker of a landlord?"

Aimee looked down. "No, not exactly. I bailed before he could throw me out. We're still behind on the rent and none of the measures you set in place have helped. Plus, I kinda made it worse."

"Huh? How?"

"After you left… I wanted to show you and my parents that I could take care of myself. I took one of those loans over the phone."

"Aimee! The interest on those things—"

"I know," Aimee snapped. "I quickly realised that and paid it off with the cash you'd lent me. I used the rest to clear my debt to the landlord. Then I moved out, not owing anything anymore, but also not having more than about seventy quid to my name. I swallowed what little pride I had left and went to my parents, but…"

Kit sighed. "As usual, they said something along the lines of being unable to help because you had to learn from your mistakes and be independent?"

"Yeah. They said that if it got to the point where I'd need to be on benefits, they *might* help a little. But if that happened, they'd break contact with me after I'd received the cash."

Laura gasped audibly, apparently reminding Aimee that she was there, too.

Aimee inspected her, some of the sadness on her face being replaced by curiosity. "Auburn hair, lesbian-enticing curves, and cute chipmunk cheeks… oh, and I think I see freckles. You're Laura!"

Kit stood up in panic. "I never said Laura had chipmunk cheeks! I said, slightly plump cheeks."

Aimee grinned. "Well, they're great cheeks no matter

what you call them. And unlike Samara, she knows how to apply make-up without looking like a goth version of a clown. Nice!" She smacked Kit on the leg and then switched her gaze to Laura. "I hear you're smart and nice, too. Phew! I spent years barely getting along with Kit's cultural snob of a girlfriend. But from what I've heard about you, we should be able to be friends."

"Thanks?" Laura said, looking to Kit for what else to say.

Kit winced. "I told you that she's honest to a fault. To the point where she's sometimes *massively rude and annoying*." The last words were said through gritted teeth while glaring at Aimee.

"I meant no offence," Aimee said sheepishly.

"None taken," Laura said. "I've heard so much about you."

"Same here. Only good stuff, though! I mean, how often do you hear a brilliant story like yours?"

Laura looked at her quizzically. "Story?"

"Yeah!" Aimee squealed. "A woman has a secret relationship with a man for like a decade. Then, with the help of a meddling lesbian, plots to endear him to her dictator aunt, only to do it too well, making the boy-crazy aunt fall in love with him." She clapped. "It's bloody great. Your life is like a cheesy, quirky comedy or something. You should write this shit down. Not that anyone'd believe it, of course."

Kit groaned and slapped Aimee's arm before saying, "Sorry, Laura. What she lacks in a social filter, I promise she makes up for in loyalty and fun."

Laura chuckled mirthlessly. "Well, she has a point. It's a ridiculous thing to happen to a person."

"By normal standards, yeah," Aimee said. "But from what I hear, it's pretty regular stuff here on Greengage."

"Greengage isn't that odd, really," Laura said.

Kit scoffed. "Aimee, ask her about the kitten races."

Aimee's eyes widened. "The what?!"

Laura put her hands on her hips. "All right, that might be a tad… different. We're well aware of that, though. It's supposed to be a fun, eccentric event to gather attention, since all the bets go to a local cat charity."

Aimee fixed Kit with wide eyes and said gravely, "Important update. I need to see these kitten races."

"Kitten!" George shouted from the floor, probably agreeing with his mother. Or maybe asking for a kitten.

"Yes, my sugar-dipped angel. Not so loud, though," his mother admonished.

He ignored her and went back to driving his fire truck around a chair leg.

Laura tapped her fingers against her hips. "Hm. There is a way we can solve your living arrangement issue and you can see the kitten races. Stay here at Greengage."

Aimee winced. "That's really kind of you, but I've already discussed moving in with Kit. I'd go bonkers after a month."

"Then stay less than a month," Laura suggested. "Why not live with me at Howard Hall? I'm stuck there for the next couple of weeks until my cottage is renovated. While the size of the place means I don't have to see my family much, I do still have to eat with them. Only wanting to keep away from gossip and prying islanders has stopped me from moving into the hotel and—"

"*The* hotel? There's only one?" Aimee interrupted.

Laura lifted her head high, a stalwart champion of her

home. "And a bed and breakfast on the other side of the island."

Kit kicked Aimee's leg, which made her friend paste on a smile and say, "I guess you wouldn't need more than that on a petite island. Sorry for interrupting. Go on."

Laura smiled graciously. "To summarize, I think you should come stay with me."

Aimee sat still and unblinking. "Whoa. That's so generous. You don't even know me! I… can't accept an amazing offer like that."

"Of course you can," Laura said. "It can actually be beneficial for all of us. Think about it. Kit gets to be around her best friend. You and George get a free place to stay. You can give me all the gossip on Kit. You'll distract me from the Dylan-Sybil affair in Howard Hall. And…" Laura's sweet face took on a devilish aspect "…having a toddler around would annoy Dylan, Aunt Sybil, and Tom no end, giving me some revenge."

Aimee grinned. "Now you're speaking my language." She picked George up and sat him on her lap. "Sweetie pie, would you like to go live in a big house and play with all your *noisiest* toys?"

George tilted his head. "What toys, Mummy?"

"The hippo that makes that screeching noise over and over again. Maybe your xylophone and that little plastic trumpet your dad gave you? Oh, what about the little Curious George doll who laughs and makes monkey noises? You like him."

George clapped. "Yes, yes. Love him. Battery all better now?"

"Yes, I think his battery will be all better by the time we move to Howard Hall. I bet he'll have had a battery transplant by then." Aimee winked at Laura, who did a brief victory dance.

George looked up at Laura. "I named by George."

Aimee kissed his head and translated, "Yes, you're named after Curious George because as a baby you always looked curious. And cheeky."

"And cute," George added, clearly having heard this story as many times as Kit had.

Laura bent over so she was at eye level with him and whispered, "You're cuter than Curious George. But don't tell him I said that."

George giggled while Aimee muttered, "He's more curious, too," under her breath.

Kit put a hand on Laura's arm. "Getting back to the living arrangements for a moment. Aimee's right, it's really sweet of you to offer up your home. I have to ask, though; can you convince Sybil to let you have houseguests for, like, two or three weeks?"

Laura crossed her arms over her chest. "She's still being disconcertingly pleasant and accommodating. Especially now that Dylan visits more. I'm not sure if the pleasantness is out of guilt or merely wanting me to stop sniping at her and go back to happily following her orders." She shrugged. "Either way, I don't think she will deny me having a friend over for a while. We have five guest rooms, after all. I simply won't mention that there's an adorable little George coming along. When they're in, Aunt Sybil's upbringing will stop her from throwing them out without a stone-clad excuse."

Aimee raised her hand. "Important question. If I only stay for a few weeks, will I still see the kitten races?"

"Stop raising your hand," Kit teased. "I've told you, this isn't school."

Aimee put a hand in front of George's eyes to hide the fact that she was sticking her tongue out at Kit.

There was a moment of much-needed cheerfulness before Laura picked up the conversation again.

"Regarding the kitten races. I'll make sure it takes place while you're here. I'm on the events committee and have the ear of the other committee members. If I say we should have the kitten races on a certain date, they will take place on that date."

"My powerful baby," Kit crooned and kissed Laura's cheek.

While Kit was still close, Laura whispered, "There's that term of endearment again. I still really *enjoy it*."

Kit swallowed at the commanding tone in Laura's voice and then croaked, "Noted."

They heard George and Aimee laughing at something. Kit looked over and saw George rolling his fire truck over Aimee's head. Seeing the three people she loved most in the same room was making her choke up with affection.

Trying to get a hold of herself, she said, "It's settled then? Laura, you'll let Aimee stay at Howard Hall until we figure out where she can start her life over?"

"Gladly."

Kit strode over to Aimee and George. "Sound good to you guys?"

Aimee turned to Laura with a downward gaze. "If you're sure that's okay? I don't know how I'd repay you, but I promise to keep George out of your hair and keep a lid on my rudeness."

Laura dashed towards her. "Please don't worry about that, your frankness is funny. If it ever hurts or offends me, you'll know and be able to address it, since I have no poker face. So, keep being you. And certainly, let George be George. He's marvellous." She finished with a melting look at George, who was trying to open one of the fire truck's little windows.

"Not when he wakes up at five a.m. and wants to watch cartoons, he's not," Aimee muttered.

Laura hummed a little laugh. "You know, one of the guest rooms is quite close to Aunt Sybil's room. I'll ensure it has a bed for George and plenty of storage for whatever toys he brought. But most of all, I'll make damned sure there's a TV with powerful speakers in it."

"TV in bedroom?" George asked.

"Absolutely," Laura said with an evil smirk.

Kit intervened before Laura suggested something like George waking Sybil with his plastic trumpet. She had heard that thing. It sounded like a dying walrus, and as much spit as sound came out of it.

"Great. That's all sorted, then. I'm sort of jealous of you all living together."

Aimee moved George to sit more comfortably in her lap. "Well, I *do* need to get to know your new lady love without you censoring me."

Kit gave her a look.

Aimee grinned. "Unless this is your way of telling Laura you're ready to move in together? The way you two are speeding along, you might as well start nesting."

"What? I... No, I..." Kit spluttered.

Laura was blushing and tucking hair behind her ear as if her life depended on it.

"I'm joking!" Aimee roared. "Although I'm betting five quid that in half a year you'll be living together." She put George down on the floor. "For now, we've gotta hunt for food. Then, we need to get my little munchkin and all our bags up yonder to Howard Castle."

"Howard Hall," Laura corrected.

"She knows," Kit said. "She was ribbing you for having a posh home."

Laura's shoulders slumped. "Blast, I missed that one."

"Don't worry," Aimee said. "You'll be up to speed no time and giving me hell right back." The smile she gave Laura sparkled. Kit recognised that smile as well as that particular brand of ribbing banter. Laura had been accepted.

George parked his fire truck by the oven. "Food now?"

"Sure," Kit said. "We'll find some food for all my fave people. But first…" She crouched down. "George?"

He tilted his head. "Yes?"

Kit glanced up at Aimee and then back down to the boy. "Have you met… Phyllis?"

Aimee groaned. "Great. Now he'll want a slobbering, snoring fur heap with flatulence. Thanks, Kit. Now who's being massively rude and annoying, huh? I'll make you pay for this!"

Chapter Twenty-Three

HOME A.K.A. FANCY GINGER BUM

Nearly three weeks later, Kit and Aimee stood outside Howard Hall. George scurried around them with a knitted squirrel that Ethel Rosenthal had made for him. Mabel Baxter had taken one look at it and deemed it unfit for human eyes. George, however, loved it, despite that it was a sickly orange colour and cross-eyed. Or perhaps that was why he liked it.

Kit put her hands in her pockets. "Sorry. I don't know what's taking Laura so long."

"I do," Aimee said. "Living here, I've seen how much work Laura does when she's not romancing you. First off, there's the employees and pickers. Sure, Sybil bosses them around, but if they want anything else besides orders barked at them, they come to Laura. Then there's all the marketing, the finances, networking, and keeping up with the accountant who seems to be overcharging and—"

"Wow. You're knowledgeable. Sounds like you could jump in and be her assistant."

"Don't try and deflect from the fact that I know more about your girlfriend's work life than you do."

Kit bumped her with her shoulder. "Hey, I know plenty! It's just that you live here and hear the day-to-day dinner chat about work."

"And at breakfast. And lunch. It's the only thing they can stand to talk about. Well, when I say 'they,' I don't mean Tom. He's only interested in how much money they're making."

"Yeah," Kit groaned. "I've noticed that even at the few meals I've been invited to. Remember what he said when I came over for that birthday dinner?"

Aimee frowned so Kit added, "When he asked if they could save money to buy a Jacuzzi by making the labels on the jars and bottles smaller?"

"Right, yeah, then when Laura said no, he suggested they could make the font on the labels smaller instead, to save ink? Mm, hard to forget that kind of head-up-arse stupidity." Aimee curled her upper lip. "Anyway, when they finish talking about Gage Farm, they all sit there in painful silence. Thank goodness the cottage is finally done, and Laura can move out."

"Yep, you've got to admire her commitment to Gage Farm. To put up with her aunt and Dylan cooing like love birds – and living with Tom – that takes some determination and patience."

George ran past with his squirrel held aloft. Aimee prodded his head, making him giggle.

"Yeah. Laura does seem to love this place. Not just the farm, but Howard Hall, too. Not sure why. It's cold, far too posh, and stupidly big. Even with a cleaner and a cook, I wouldn't want to be responsible for a place of this size," Aimee said.

Kit looked up at the elegant, tall building with its clean lines, oblong windows, and faded sandstone. "I don't know. I see the appeal. It's got character. It's not big to show off, it's big because… that's its personality."

Aimee scrunched up her nose. "Its personality? You've lived on this weird island too long."

"Maybe. I've really grown to like Greengage, though."

"It's got its charms, I suppose," Aimee admitted. "I'm still happy I'm moving."

"I'm not. I'll miss you."

"I know." Aimee smiled. "That's why you found me that flat and part-time job in Southampton, though, right? Plonk me a quick ferry ride away so you can keep an eye on me?"

Kit leaned her forehead against Aimee's shoulder. "I found you that place to have you close by, yeah. But not to keep an eye on you, dopey, to have you near for when I need my best friend and adopted little sister."

"You adopted me as your sister?"

"Yeah." Kit moved away and feigned surprise. "What? You didn't get the paperwork?"

"No, George must have eaten it."

At the sound of his name, George came over. "What I eat?"

"Not enough carrots last night," Aimee replied.

He frowned. "They had leaves."

"I told you, sweetheart, that was parsley. It's a herb and completely fine to be used when cooking carrots in butter."

"Leaves," he intoned with a disgusted expression.

He ran off again, making train sounds while swooshing the squirrel along.

"Wait, is the squirrel *on* a train or *is* it a train?" Kit whispered.

"No idea. This island is getting to him, too."

The front door opened and shut with a bang. Laura came out, ashen-faced and with her hand on her head.

Kit hurried over to her. "Baby, what's wrong?"

"Aunt Sybil said she had to speak to me about something. I thought it was about the issues with the cherry trees. But it was about Howard Hall."

Aimee came over, George perched on her hip. "What about Howard Hall?"

Laura's eyes were wide as saucers. "She's… leaving it."

"Leaving it?" Kit and Aimee both said.

"Yes. Apparently, Dylan has had enough of the enemy farm. Enough of Greengage in general. He claims the reason everyone treats him and Sybil badly is that they're a Stevenson and a Howard in a relationship. Aunt Sybil said he can't focus on his art because of it."

Kit did a double take. "He really thinks that *the feud* is why people don't like them? He doesn't realise that it's because Greengagers love you and hated what he and Sybil did to you?"

Aimee sneered. "Mate, Dylan still thinks he's going to be the next Rembrandt. I mean come on, George paints better than he does. Dylan doesn't live in the same world as the rest of us."

"Well, his parents are still freezing him out," Laura said. She glanced up at a window, from which electronic house music was blaring out. "And Tom up there gives him a terrible time over being a gold digger and a Stevenson. Dylan doesn't really interact with anyone else, so he has no idea what the island in general thinks."

"Laura, honey," Aimee said pityingly. "The world could give him a full thesis on its thoughts and he still wouldn't get that they disliked him because of his actions. He has no self-awareness. He reckons he's a misunderstood genius and that people hate him for things he can't control. Your aunt isn't much better. Which is why they work so well together."

"I don't know," Laura said with a sigh. "Either way, they're moving! To Provence. Aunt Sybil feels it'll be a good place for Dylan to paint and for her to start preparing for retirement. Sadly, she's not completely retiring yet. She says that she'll be back to check on Gage Farm once a month. Other than that, it's mine. So is Howard Hall."

Kit grabbed Laura's shoulder. "Oh my god! Just like that?"

"No, there's a caveat," Laura admitted. "It's all on a trial basis. If anything is out of order when Aunt Sybil comes for her monthly check-up, she'll give it all to Tom."

"And he'll bugger it up further," Aimee muttered.

"Probably," Laura agreed. "Then I suppose she'll have to give it back to me. But I'm not letting any of that happen. I'm going to work my fingers to the bone to ensure both Gage Farm and Howard Hall are in the shape of their lives." A dreamy look came into her eyes. "I can finally try all my ideas and invest in the business and the house without Aunt Sybil holding me back. Then, when she sees that everything is going well, she won't feel the need to keep checking on me."

Kit adjusted her glasses, suppressing any questions about what happened if Dylan's career failed or Sybil grew bored.

"Great news! So, when are they leaving?" she asked instead.

"In a week." Laura ran a hand over her brow. "It'll be so strange. First you and George move out, Aimee. Then

Aunt Sybil. It'll just be me and Tom. And god knows what I'll do with the cottage."

"Yeah, you have to love your aunt's timing. Telling you all this when you've just finished renovating the cottage and were taking me and Kit down to see it," Aimee said.

"Mm. I was going to surprise you with all the new furniture that arrived yesterday," Laura said dazedly. "I suppose I'll give the place all the last finishing touches, paintings and such, and then try to rent it out."

Aimee was looking from Laura to Kit and back again. "You know what?"

Kit squinted at her, worried where this was going. "What?"

"Laura, why don't you rent the place to Kit?"

"Huh?" Kit asked.

Laura followed up with "What?"

"Well, Rajesh's love life gets cramped by Kit living with him in his tiny maisonette, right? Meanwhile, you'll go bonkers rattling around in Howard Hall with only Tom for company, Laura. This is perfect! You can see each other all the time without having to move in together. Saving that for, oh, I don't know, another five months or so? I'm still going to win that bet I made, the one about you both living together in half a year."

"No one took that bet, Aimee," Kit said.

"Doesn't matter. I gamble for the satisfaction of winning. And being right. Never mind that now, what do you think of my idea?"

Kit turned to Laura.

Laura smiled. "It does sound like a good idea. We could be together whenever we're not working. Even have breakfast together. Then I could drop you off at the library when I drive around checking on the orchards in the mornings."

Kit smiled back at her. "I guess that could work. Won't it be weird being my landlady and my—"

"Lady?" Aimee chirped, clearly pleased with her wordplay.

"Girlfriend?" Kit finished.

Laura stared into space. "You know what, I think we're adult enough to handle that. You've managed to live with your boss and I've managed to live and work with Aunt Sybil despite the Dylan affair."

"True. Okay. Let me think about it."

George ran past with his knitted monstrosity shouting, "Squirrel bored now."

Aimee donned a serious expression. "Ladies. The squirrel is bored. We better go see the cottage before the squirrel files a complaint with its maker and Ethel comes to scold us by telling us we need fattening up and thick jumpers."

Kit grabbed her arm and adopted an old-fashioned, posh accent. "By Jove, we must make haste."

Aimee nodded. "To yonder cottage! Doth lead the way, brave, ginger squirrel."

She pointed out the direction, and George, squirrel held aloft, ran across the gravel path and straight into the meadow leading to the workman's cottages. The three women followed at a more comfortable pace.

"Does he know that we're going to the spring fete with the kitten races after this?" Kit whispered.

Aimee shook her head. "I didn't dare to tell him. He'd be whinging about wanting to see kittens from the second I mentioned it to when he clapped eyes on the first fur ball entering the maze. How is the maze, by the way? Did Rajesh and the others get it finished?"

"Yep," Kit said. "A mini version of the Swiss Alps in papier-mâché, decorated in watercolour. I haven't seen it yet, so I have no idea how that's supposed to work as a maze."

Laura waved her hand dismissively. "Oh, it doesn't much matter. There'll be three or four kittens of different ages and they'll all end up playing with their tails, having a nap, or running towards the smell of the tuna and mayo sandwiches."

Aimee clapped her hands. "Come on, let's hurry to see the cottage and then get down to the square. I can't wait to see kittens sleeping in the Swiss Alps."

Laughing, they all picked up the pace.

❧

Finally, Kit and Aimee got a chance to fulfil their ambition of seeing a Greengage kitten race. Sat on folding chairs on Greengage Square, they feasted on Gage Farm cider and jam-drenched, crust-less triangles pretending to be sandwiches.

There was a buzz of excitement in the air. When Laura had suggested they move the kitten races forward to June instead of July, the whole committee had agreed immediately. Then someone suggested that they could invent guinea pig races to have in July instead. To which dear old Marjorie had replied that they could race the guinea pigs and kittens against each other in August. Apparently, Laura had stopped the meeting there, before things escalated further. Kit had no idea how Laura was going to handle the next meeting.

Today, however, it was all about the kittens. And the sandwiches. And the extremely boozy cider.

Maybe I should've stuck to juice? No, it was South Gage Farm juice. I've got to support the home team.

She finished her Gage Farm apple cider, stifled a hiccup, and placed her cup under her chair.

On Kit's right side sat Laura and on her left was Aimee, who had George on her lap to restrain him when the kittens came out.

Kit edged closer to Laura, trying to get her attention but finding her busy talking to Rajesh who was next to her.

Kit looked past them, scanning the rest of the crowd. She spotted smiling faces, many of which she recognised. She nodded to the ones who waved at her, while adjusting her faded T-shirt and wishing she'd made more of an effort.

"Looks like someone's been accepted by the locals," Laura whispered. "Next they'll be nominating you for the events committee. Or ask you to run for councillor."

Kit turned so she could brush Laura's nose with her own. After a couple of Eskimo kisses, she said, "We'll see. I don't care as long as they accept that I'm dating the island's favourite daughter and that I'm only trying to make her happy."

Laura placed a quick kiss on her lips. "I think that's obvious."

"Honestly," Aimee groaned. "You're thirty, not fourteen. Stop snogging in public."

Rajesh leaned forward and looked past Laura and Kit to address Aimee. "Imagine what it's like watching a movie with them. The kissing ruins the musical numbers.

Anyway, I heard you and the little nipper are leaving Greengage soon?"

"Yep, we move into a two-bedroom flat in Southampton this weekend. And on Monday I start my new part-time job as a receptionist for an estate agent."

He whistled. "Not bad. Obviously, it would be better if the job and flat were on Greengage, but you can't have it all."

Aimee looked like she was about to say something about Greengage, so Kit kicked her shin. Aimee closed her mouth and joined the crowd in watching the papier-mâché course in front of them.

Steve Hallard, Charlie Baxter, Leslie Stevenson – Dylan's burly mum – and a bloke Kit didn't recognise slowly and carefully walked to the maze with pet carriers.

The crowd went wild. The loudest whoops came from George, who had recently been informed that not only would there be shortbread after he finished his sandwich, but that kittens were also arriving.

The cat carriers were put down by the entrance to the maze. Kit wasn't sure, but she thought she could hear mewling from them.

Rajesh rubbed his hands in glee. "I have two quid on the little black one. He's young but feisty."

Then whispers started. It sounded like wind blowing through trees. Kit scanned the crowd again and saw people murmuring to each other, some behind their hands, all while looking at the people by the pet carriers.

How can something like this be so tense?

The whispers turned into gasps. Kit followed the audience's gaze. Leslie Stevenson was pushing Charlie Baxter. As she was well-built, with as much muscle as height, the shoves made the elderly Charlie stumble backwards. He was holding up his hands in surrender, but his face looked like that of an angry pug.

"What's happening?" Aimee asked.

Laura was the one who replied. "Greengage. That's what's happening." She stood up. "I'll have to intervene." She marched over to the maze, back ramrod straight.

Kit's stomach knotted as she watched her beloved put herself between Leslie and Charlie.

Rajesh shook his head. "Daft girl."

"What do you mean?" Kit asked.

He pointed to the combatants. "Well, what's going to bother an enraged Stevenson more than anything else? A Howard telling her to calm down."

Kit realised he was right just as they all heard Leslie shout, "Get your fancy ginger bum out of my way, Howard!"

Before she knew it, Kit was on her feet and heading to the miniature Swiss Alps, shouting, "Whoa! Mrs Stevenson. Wait. Laura was just on her way over to talk to Mr Baxter. Meanwhile, why don't we have a chat? I'm very curious to hear what he's done to you."

That stopped Leslie, who looked like a rhino who had sat on something sharp, in her tracks. She brushed matted, honey-blonde hair from her face. "What he's done to me? You mean that someone finally understands that this isn't my fault?"

Nailed it. Now keep her calm.

"I'm sure it's not. I don't really get the situation, though. Could you come over here and tell me? Maybe we can find a solution?"

As they walked a little to the side, she heard Laura speak with Charlie.

Leslie was squinting at Kit. "I'm not sure I should trust

you considering that you... well, you know... bob for apples with the Howard girl."

Kit bit her tongue. She couldn't afford to laugh at the euphemism. "No matter what I do with Laura, I'm talking to you because I want to know from your point of view what's happening here. Was it something about the kittens?"

Mrs Stevenson drew herself up to her full height, giving Kit reversed vertigo as she looked up at her. "In a manner of speaking. There's been a rumour of that we Stevensons..." She stopped to purse her lips. "That we *cheat* during competitions taking place at island festivities."

Kit pushed her glasses up. "Ah, I see. So, did Charlie Baxter hint that you might've cheated with your bets on the kittens? Maybe given some of the others catnip or something?"

"No. He didn't say that." Leslie crossed her arms.

"Okay. What did he say then?"

Leslie gazed at the car park on the other side of the square and Kit wondered if she was about to stomp off to her car and leave. Which would save the day, of course, but Kit wasn't going to point that out. She knew better than to poke a hairy, blonde she-bear.

"To give you some context, Alfie Smith," she nodded towards the kitten-carrying man Kit hadn't been able to identify, "is the one who's been saying that we cheat. He was grumbling something along those lines as we walked out."

"Aha." Kit combed her fingers through her hair, avoiding pulling it out in frustration. "Then why were you pissed off with Charlie?"

"I was offended by Charlie Baxter due to his words in my defence."

"Uh. Not sure I follow. How can him defending you be a problem?"

Leslie sniffed. "He said that the Stevensons weren't smart enough to cheat. That," the words seemed to pain her, "that it would take thirty Stevensons to outsmart one kitten."

Kit coughed to cover up her smirk. "Ah. Gotcha."

"Then," Leslie squirmed, "he added that even then, his money was on the kitten."

Kit's fake cough certainly sounded like a chuckle this time. Luckily, Leslie was too busy staring daggers at Charlie, who was holding his hands out in apology, to notice.

While she did that, Kit mulled the situation over. By the time Leslie had finished throwing icy and dramatic glares towards the moustachioed man who had wronged her, Kit had a suggestion.

"How about a new tradition? Why don't we let you Stevensons judge all the competitions? That way, not only will you never be accused of cheating, you'll also have the honour of the most important job at the festivities. You'll be able to prove your intelligence through your excellent judging too."

Leslie took a painfully long time to think that over. The spring sun beamed down, burning Kit's neck as she waited.

"But then we can't compete and win," Leslie eventually pointed out.

"True, but you'll always be winners because you'll have the most prestigious and important job. What's a few pounds to such a rich family anyway?"

Leslie's uncertain face turned smug, and Kit knew she'd hit the right note.

"You may have a point there. I'll have to discuss it with my husband and my sister-in-law." She pointed to two other blonde giants seated on the far side of the crowd.

"Great! Why not go do that now? The guy who's judging the race, he's Greengage's mayor, right?"

"Yes. Bruno Bruce."

"What? He's called that?" Kit shook her head. "Never mind. He looks pretty worried about the commotion. I'm sure he'd give up his prestigious position to the Stevensons right away if he knew it would appease you."

If it would shut you up, more likely.

Leslie smiled in a way which made Kit's head hurt. "You're not as stupid as you look, Londoner. Despite that haircut and those glasses. I'll go discuss it with my family and come back to you with an answer."

She didn't wait for a reply but stormed off towards the other light-haired bears.

Kit took a deep breath and paced over to Laura and Charlie. The latter stopped covering his mouth to say, "Dearie me. I've caused another spot of bother, haven't I?"

"I'm afraid you have," Kit said. "You were totally right in that the Stevensons are too dumb to cheat even themselves, but still, you shouldn't have said that. Especially not after Leslie was already wounded by Alfie Smith accused them of cheating."

"And upset over Dylan leaving for Provence," Laura said.

Charlie stroked his moustache. "I'm most dreadfully sorry, don't you know?"

"It'll be okay." Kit rubbed the stinging back of her

neck. "I went ahead and improvised a solution. Sorry about not checking with anyone, but I had to say something before Leslie used her big hands to crack someone's head like a walnut."

Laura beamed. "Don't worry about that. I knew you'd come up with a plan! What is it?"

Kit relayed her solution.

Charlie only gave her a thumbs up and snuck back to his cat carrier. Probably bolting before Leslie Stevenson returned.

Laura tapped a finger against her lip and said, "Hm, that ought to work. The mayor hates judging competitions anyway. Aunt Sybil is leaving Greengage, meaning she can't complain about the Stevensons being given prominent positions. No one can say that the Stevensons cheat if they only judge and don't compete or bet. Yes, it's ideal."

Kit gave her a pat on the lower back. "Great. You let the mayor and the committee know. Mrs Stevenson went to discuss it with the other Viking lookalikes over there. I'm convinced they'll say yes. You should've seen her eyes light up when she understood what I was suggesting."

"Clever *and* cute. I'll have to keep you around," Laura said and stood on her tiptoes so that Kit's hand now rested on her arse before adding, "Leslie complained about my 'ginger bum' being in the wrong location. What do you think?"

"I think it's in the perfect place now," Kit whispered and gave it a squeeze. "Besides, you're auburn, not ginger."

"Right on both accounts, dearest," Laura purred.

They were facing the crowd so no one could see where her hand was. It made Kit a heady mix between coy and excited. Some of that could have been due to the cider, of course.

Laura went to talk to the mayor and the committee while Kit remained to keep an eye on things. She felt surprisingly comfortable in front of all the Greengagers, who smiled at her over their crust-less sandwiches. One or two even toasted her with their cups.

There was a sensation growing in her that she couldn't identify. She stayed smiling back at them, willing to swear they were looking at her with approval. Behind Aimee and George, she saw Rajesh, Mabel, Ethel, Marjorie, Steve Hallard, and so many other people Kit had quickly gotten to know and care about.

Then the penny dropped. The sensation she experienced was feeling at home.

❧

Fifteen minutes later, all was calm again. In the umpire chair was Leslie Stevenson and by the starting line were the pet carriers with the mewling athletes.

In the thrilling tension of the race about to start, Laura broke the quiet by saying, "I guess we've found your role in Greengage society, dearest. You're the one who comes up with the plots and solutions. Sorting out rifts, strange situations, and arguments."

Rajesh belly-laughed. "Oh, Katherine, you're going to be blooming busy."

From behind them was a dainty cough. They all turned and saw an old lady waving at them.

Laura whispered into Kit's ear. "That's one of the ladies Rajesh dates, Widow Caine."

Mrs Caine scooted her chair forward, put her hand on Kit's, and said, "I heard what Little Laura Howard said about you sorting out strange situations."

"Yes?" Kit said, ignoring that Laura had deflated at hearing her nickname.

Mrs Caine lowered her voice. "Would you call it strange if an old woman's books were meddled with?"

Kit adjusted her glasses. "Meddled with?"

"Yes, one day last week, they were all moved around. I keep my bookshelves exceptionally tidy, so I know they'd been tampered with. I hadn't even had any guests! Then, a few days later, the books were moved about again. And this time, one of them had vanished."

Kit leaned in, always happy when the subject was books. "I'd certainly call that strange."

"Mysterious, even," Aimee butted in, George squirming in her arms.

"Splendid. My name is Alice Caine, and I need your help, Ms Sorel. I will gladly pay you for your assistance. In pounds or in biscuits, whichever you prefer."

"Um." Kit chewed the inside of her cheek. "This isn't usually the sort of thing I help with, but if I can assist in any way, I'll gladly do it for free. Although, I do love a Garibaldi."

Alice Caine smiled in a way which took ten years, or approximately thirty percent of her many wrinkles, off her face. "Splendid. We'll speak more later, young lady. I think the race is about to start."

Kit, Laura, Rajesh, and Aimee turned back around to face the maze.

The carriers opened, and the world seemed a little brighter as one kitten sat down to wash, another ran off towards the crowd to be scooped up by a little girl, the third one did a wee against a small mountain, and the final one stayed in the carrier, probably asleep.

Kit leaned back in her chair as the crowd stopped

shouting about the competition and their bets and instead began laughing at the kittens doing everything other than race.

Kit took Laura's hand and smiled to herself as she realised three things.

One. She was sure now, she'd found her home on Greengage.

Two. A plot failing wasn't necessarily a bad thing. Not on Greengage at least. Here, it could even bring you love.

Three. If she asked Rajesh, he would probably lend her Phyllis to sniff around Widow Caine's shelves to see if anyone really had been messing about with the books.

Laura squeezed her hand just as George exclaimed, "Kittens boring. Phyllis more fun. Want Phyllis, Mummy!"

To which Aimee griped, "This island and all its animals. Kittens, dogs, beetles. Not to mention all the bonkers situations and people. Who the hell would want to live with all of that?"

Kit brought Laura's hand to her mouth and nuzzled it happily, not even having to give the obvious reply – Kit Sorel certainly would.

ABOUT THE AUTHOR

Having spent far too much time hopping from subject to subject at university, back in her native country of Sweden, Emma finally emerged with a degree in Library and Information Science.

She now lives with her wife and two cats in England. There is no point in saying which city, as they move about once a year. She spends her free time writing, reading, daydreaming, working out, and watching whichever television show has the most lesbian subtext at the time.
Her tastes in most things usually lean towards the quirky and she loves genres like urban fantasy, magic realism, and steampunk.

Emma is also a hopeless sap for any small chubby creature with tiny legs, and can often be found making heart-eyes at things like guinea pigs, wombats, marmots, and human toddlers.

Connect with Emma
www.emmasternerradley.com

Reviews are essential for authors, especially in small genres like lesbian fiction. Regardless of quality, books without reviews quickly fall down the charts and into obscurity.

That's why authors need ARC Reviewers. These are people who are willing to provide an honest review in exchange for an early, free copy of a book.

If you would like to be an ARC Reviewer for me, please click the link below:

http://tiny.cc/emmaarc

LIFE PUSHES YOU ALONG

Zoe's on autopilot. Rebecca is stagnating. When change comes knocking, will they open the door?

Twenty-something Zoe Achidi feels safe in her unchallenging life in a London bookshop. Bored, but safe.

Her only excitement comes from pining over frequent customer, Rebecca Clare, unobtainable as this beautiful businesswoman in her forties seems.

One day, Zoe's brother and her best friend bring Zoe and Rebecca together.

While they connect, and it turns out Rebecca is also bored with her life, their meetings remain all business. When things take a turn for the worse, life pushes along.

But will Zoe and Rebecca end up being thrust in the same direction?

If you're looking for an age-gap romance that will inspire you to shake up your life, then look no further.

Take the leap with Life Pushes You Along by Emma Sterner-Radley

LIFE PUSHES YOU ALONG | PREVIEW

by Emma Sterner-Radley

CHAPTER ONE

Z oe watched as one of her favourite customers
observed her with what seemed to be desperation.
She felt her heart twinge with sympathy.

"So, do you have it?" he asked.

She knew she was going to disappoint him.

"I'm not sure, Mr. Evans. A book with a bird on the
cover that was based somewhere with a big forest... that
doesn't ring a bell, I'm afraid."

The bookshop's unpleasantly sharp fluorescent lights
showed every crease on his wrinkled face as it took on an
embarrassed look.

Zoe quickly added, "I know the feeling though.
There's lots of books I have been looking for and I can't
remember anything but the cover, or a piece of the plot, or
half of the author's name. It's a pain."

He nodded. "Yes. Yes, my dear, it certainly is."

"Do you remember anything else about the book?
Who was the main character?"

He looked up at the ceiling for a moment. "I suppose she was quite a bit like you, actually."

Zoe felt her brow furrowing. She didn't want to be rude but that didn't narrow it down much. Did he, perhaps, mean that the main character was someone who worked with customers, someone who dressed like her, or someone who was in their late twenties? She hoped he wasn't alluding to the fact that she wasn't white because she wasn't sure if a conversation with this elderly gentleman would stay politically correct if they got onto that subject. She liked Mr. Evans and wanted to continue liking him.

"I see. Um, how was she like me?"

"Young and likable," he answered simply.

Zoe was relieved. It was still just as impossible to find the book he was looking for, though.

"I'm afraid that doesn't give me much to go on. Tell you what, I'll keep an eye out for a book with a forest setting and a bird on the cover. We have your contact details on file, so I can call you if we get it in?"

His face lit up. "That would be splendid! Thank you ever so much for your help."

She smiled at him, happy to be able to help. Mr. Evans put his trilby hat back on, and she couldn't help but smile at his posh, old-fashioned sense of style which perfectly matched his way of speaking.

"Goodbye. I hope to hear from you but if I do not, I shall come in to purchase another book instead."

"You do that, Mr. Evans. Goodbye."

Just as he was leaving the bookshop, he turned around and shouted, "Oh, by the way, it might have been something other than a bird, now that I think about it. I think it was something that flew. So, maybe t'was a bat, a moth, or perhaps a ferret? Anyway, cheerio."

The door closed behind him and Zoe stared into space, puzzled.

Had he meant to say 'ferret'? How the hell was that categorized as something that flew?

Zoe's manager, and the owner of the bookshop, Darren, walked in with a small box under one arm.

He held out the box to her. "We've got a book delivery. Who was that?" He inclined his head towards the door.

"Oh, it was Mr. Evans."

Darren's bushy eyebrows met at the bridge of his nose. "Who?"

"Mr. Evans. You know, the retired bank manager who likes books about nature and sea journeys. Comes in here every week?"

Darren still looked like he was trying to do complicated arithmetic.

Zoe managed not to sigh. "The old guy with the big mole on his right cheek?"

"Oh, that crazy, posh old badger. Right. Anyway, here's the new batch. Put them on the system and then shelve them, will you?"

She gave a curt nod and took the box from him. There was no reason why he couldn't do this himself–well there was one reason and that was simply that he was lazy. He'd stand at the counter and watch her put the books out, and as soon as she was done he'd slink back into the breakroom, leaving her to man the counter as always, while he drank his bodyweight in sweet tea. *No wonder he always needs to use the loo*, she thought as she unpacked the books.

She put them on the system and looked at the packing slip to check the details as she did so.

Her job wasn't the dream that most other book-nerds conjured up when she told them what she did. Yes, she worked in an independent bookshop. However, it was a lacklustre bookshop, where she was overworked, her boss didn't care much about the running of the place, and the clientele was dwindling.

As Zoe began to shelve the books, she looked around at the cheap birch bookcases, faded beige walls, and harsh fluorescent lights and thought about how she had ended up here.

She had been in dire straits when she applied for this job. She had been out on the street since her parents kicked her out. She didn't think she was focused enough for further education, she was down to her last twenty pounds and totally unqualified for any job.

Out of desperation, she had applied for this position and when Darren had asked her, in the interview, why he should hire her and not the other two applicants, who both had degrees and experience, she had broken down in tears. He had grumbled about not being able to stand seeing people cry and after a long chat about her situation, he had agreed to give her the job on a trial basis. She had never known how to thank him for that, and so she merely put up with him as a way of showing her gratitude.

She had just turned eighteen back then and she had stayed in the job for the following eight years out of loyalty, habit, and a feeling that there was no other job out there for her.

She sighed as she placed another book on the shelf. What was she qualified to do? Other bookshops were run a lot more professionally than Darren's Book Nook. Her quick foray into wanted-ads told her that they would demand that she "showed initiative" and "managed her own workload." She was sure she wasn't ready for that. She figured that a trained monkey could do the job she was doing right now and so that was what she would stick with, no matter how much it bored her.

The little bell above the door rang out. Before Zoe had time to turn to see who their new customer was, she heard Darren's sharp intake of breath. She knew immediately who must be at the door. Rebecca Clare.

Their favourite customer was shaking drops of water from her elegant brown coat and looked unfairly beautiful despite her red hair being wet and her glasses covered in little raindrops. Zoe stole as many glances as she dared while Rebecca rid herself of the worst of the rain. She admired the fancy high-heeled shoes, the black stockings, and what she could see of the knee-length black dress under her coat. And that was saying nothing about her face; those stunning eyes and the heart-shaped lips were truly mesmerizing. Especially this close up. Rebecca was near enough for Zoe to be able to reach out and brush her cheek. Not that she was daydreaming about that, of course.

Zoe knew she shouldn't be staring. Not only because it was rude, and borderline objectifying, but because Rebecca was way out of her league. And far too old for her. Zoe didn't know how old Rebecca was but she was certainly older than her own twenty-six years. Oh, and to make Rebecca even more of an impossible choice, she was Darren's huge crush too.

Just as Zoe was dragging her gaze away, she saw Rebecca quickly remove her drenched glasses. The water that had rested on them shot out in Zoe's direction, some hitting the side of her face.

Rebecca looked mortified. "Oh, I'm so sorry. Are you all right, there?"

"Yeah, sure! I'm, uh, waterproof," Zoe replied. She hoped her tone was light and jokey but worried that she sounded as terrified as she always felt when this woman spoke to her.

They had never had any long conversations, she realised. Zoe, and by extension, Darren, only knew Rebecca's name because she had ordered books and they always took contact information to be able to call or e-mail the customer when their book arrived.

Rebecca Clare, RebeccaClare@acacia-recruitment.com, Zoe repeated in her head, stopping herself before she reeled off the memorized phone number too.

The contact information, which showed that she must work in recruitment considering the company's name, and Rebecca's fondness for crime-fiction was all Zoe knew about this woman. Well, that and the fact that she had the sort of presence that you couldn't miss. Despite Rebecca's feminine looks and apparel, there was almost a masculine air to her behaviour. Zoe realised that what she saw as masculine could probably be boiled down to confidence, calm, directness, and a sense of power. Rebecca was polite and friendly but in a way that spoke of a person who you couldn't take for granted.

Either way, Rebecca Clare demanded all the attention of her onlookers without having to fight for it. And that, combined with her obvious beauty, took Zoe's breath away. Just as it was doing right now as she stood with droplets of water running down her cheek and Rebecca smiling politely at her.

Zoe wiped away the water from her face with her sweater sleeve and watched Rebecca dry her glasses on a tissue she had taken out of her pocket. Then she put the glasses back on. Zoe struggled to find something to say. Something normal. Something witty.

She heard Darren clear his throat and come rushing over.

"Mrs. Clare, isn't it? Come to pick up your latest bloodcurdling chiller?" He grinned at Rebecca. Zoe realised that he probably thought it was a charming smirk. It wasn't.

"It's *Ms.* Clare," Rebecca replied casually. "And yes, please. I got an email a few days ago and haven't had time to pop in until today."

"Terrible weather for it, though. You should have waited until tomorrow," Darren said, his strange smile still fixed in place.

Zoe saw Rebecca raise an eyebrow for a brief moment.

"Well, it's meant to rain all week, so planning to only go out when it's dry seems futile. We're Londoners, right? We're experts at dealing with rain."

Darren laughed, far too loudly and for far too long. Zoe wondered if Rebecca was suffering from second-hand embarrassment as much as she was right now. Deciding to rescue the other woman, Zoe put the books down and went behind the counter to pick up the book Rebecca had ordered and put it through the till.

When she was done, she handed Rebecca the thick tome. "Here's your book. I've never heard of this author. Is she any good?"

"Very good. Or, at least, her last three books have been. Here's hoping her latest doesn't disappoint." Rebecca looked down at the book and gave the front cover a quick pat. Then she looked back up at Zoe, with a smile.

Zoe felt herself freeze. She was meant to be telling Rebecca the total for the book, and asking if she wanted a bag but all she could do was stare. The charming smile was bad enough but Zoe had just ignored her own advice – never look this woman in the eye.

Rebecca Clare's eyes were a common blue-green colour, but what made them so dangerous was that they always seemed to glimmer. As if Rebecca was constantly happy. Or constantly flirting. It was insanely distracting and Zoe had to force herself to ignore those gorgeous eyes and just say the total sum. She barely remembered to offer a bag for the book.

When Rebecca had paid and thanked her, she turned on her high heels and click-clacked back out into the rain and out of Zoe's line of vision. Zoe sighed deeply and stopped herself when she realised that Darren could probably hear her.

It turned out that she didn't need to worry about that. Darren was busy staring after Rebecca, looking like an abandoned puppy. Zoe looked around at the shop which suddenly looked ten times duller and knew how he felt.

Published by Heartsome Publishing
Staffordshire
United Kingdom
www.heartsomebooks.com

Also available in paperback.
ISBN: 9781912684113

First Heartsome edition: July 2018

33403006R00176

Printed in Poland
by Amazon Fulfillment
Poland Sp. z o.o., Wrocław